PENGU

THE TA

Guy Bellamy was born in B. ... his life in Surrey. After Na ... vice in Germany with the Royal Air Force, he went into journalism and has worked on newspapers in Cornwall, Bournemouth, Brighton and Fleet Street. He has written several short stories for *Punch* and his previous novels include *I Have a Complaint to Make*, *The Sinner's Congregation*, *The Nudists* (Penguin 1987), *The Secret Lemonade Drinker* (Penguin 1988) and *In the Midday Sun* (Penguin 1989). He is married and has a young daughter.

Rave reviews for *The Nudists*:

'Whip-crack wit and street-smart prose . . . funny, caustic and gloriously readable' – *Evening Standard*

and *The Secret Lemonade Drinker*:

'An expertly engineered sexual comedy' – *Observer*

'Sparkling . . . It cracks open a thousand jokes, some old, some new and some blue. As hideously addictive as drink' – *Sunday Times*

and *In the Midday Sun*:

'The blue skies blacken very funnily indeed' – *Mail on Sunday*

GUY BELLAMY

# THE TAX EXILE

PENGUIN BOOKS

PENGUIN BOOKS

Published by the Penguin Group
27 Wrights Lane, London W8 5TZ, England
Viking Penguin Inc., 40 West 23rd Street, New York, New York 10010, USA
Penguin Books Australia Ltd, Ringwood, Victoria, Australia
Penguin Books Canada Ltd, 2801 John Street, Markham, Ontario, Canada L3R 1B4
Penguin Books (NZ) Ltd, 182–190 Wairau Road, Auckland 10, New Zealand

Penguin Books Ltd, Registered Offices: Harmondsworth, Middlesex, England

First published by Viking 1989
Published in Penguin Books 1990
3 5 7 9 10 8 6 4



Made and printed in Great Britain by
Richard Clay Ltd, Bungay, Suffolk

For Gordon Williams

# PART ONE

Wealth is not without its advantages, and the case to the contrary, although it has often been made, has never proved widely persuasive.

J. K. Galbraith
*The Affluent Society*

I must have in a long life ground through between a hundred and fifty thousand and two hundred thousand hours of perfectly useless work.

Leonard Woolf
*The Journey not the Arrival Matters*

# ONE

WHEN lying on the bed becomes an Olympic event I shall be photographed at Heathrow with a gold medal round my neck, he thought as he watched a spider's cautious journey across the stippled ceiling. He reached over and turned on the transistor radio at the side of his bed, hoping that today had perhaps been cancelled, but the barrage of information that poured into the room told him that the world, oblivious to every signal, had decided remorselessly to press on. The day's first challenge, getting from the horizontal to the vertical, was ignored for some time. Most mornings, by the time he had got up, washed, shaved and dressed, he was so tired that he was ready to go straight back to bed again, and he lay there now wondering what meagre rewards lay in store for the expense of so much energy. He looked at the poster he had recently taped to the magnolia wall at the foot of his bed. IS THERE LIFE BEFORE DEATH? it asked.

The radio told him that it was Saturday, a fact which in other circumstances would have been cause for celebration. For most people who worked, Saturday was a day off, a holiday, a fleeting opportunity for enjoyment, but he wasn't working and Saturday had the same flavour for him as the rest of the week. At any given moment only a very tiny proportion of the world's population was actually working and it was not a minority that he was attracted to. The financial problems that accompanied indolence were a nightmare that he had learned to live with.

He kicked off his duvet as a sort of interim measure but the loss of body heat, a loss that was by no means staunched by the cold linoleum which greeted his feet, persuaded him to get up. He made his way to the tiny bathroom and had to stoop against the low slanting ceiling, the underside of the building's roof.

Dressed in old jeans and a white shirt, he went back through the bedroom to the third room, which was an uneasy combination of living room and kitchen. This ridiculously small flat, perched precariously over a pet shop on the outskirts of the town, had been his home for twelve years. It was let to him cheaply by the pet-shop owner, who, fazed not a whit by the recurring joblessness of his lonely tenant, exhibited a saintly patience when the rent failed to appear and an inordinate gratitude when it did. The problem of finding another occupant who would relish such cramped accommodation – never mind the occasional odours that emanated from the pet shop – was one that he had already encountered and he was grateful to have someone who showed no disposition to move.

The postman brought a bill as usual, this time from his credit-card company; confronted by evidence they could hardly miss, they felt they had discerned the need for a higher credit limit. His debt was already surging towards his present limit of £1,200; they would raise it to £1,500. A minimum payment of £60 would keep the credit-card company happy, an amount which would come out of a bank overdraft recently negotiated over several pints of lager with the new, enthusiastic assistant manager at the bank who, unusually in his calling, seemed anxious to be liked. Staying solvent was merely a question of shuffling debts.

He made tea, boiled an egg and squinted through the

window at what looked remarkably like sunshine, rare enough round here in July, let alone March. The morning newspaper that should have been lying on his mat was nowhere to be seen, a little mystery that he imagined would be explained by an unpaid bill. He went out.

The town that he walked into had changed quite a lot in ten years. Its central point, a wide Georgian street that led down to the town from a deserted castle, was untouched and untouchable by the planners' whims, as was the narrow shopping street it met in a T-junction at the bottom. The old shops with their crooked roofs and bow windows were here until hell froze over and when repairs were essential they emerged exactly as they had a century before. But in other nooks and alleys the developers had nibbled away, building shopping yards and mews houses in corners that had been neglected, amid predictable cries from the stentorian guardians of the town's history, who had only to see a new brick to talk of philistine vandalism.

Little old ladies with little old dogs threaded their way through the people who crowded Saturday's streets. Men who yesterday wore pin-striped suits appeared, today, somewhat self-consciously, in bright short-sleeved shirts and old slacks and headed for the do-it-yourself store with a list of their requirements. Work yesterday, work today – a car to be washed, a lawn to be mowed, a tap to be fixed. Whey-faced youngsters, freed from some constriction, pushed boisterously past him on the way to a music shop. The things that young people had triumphantly got rid of when he was young – braces, haircream, viciously short haircuts – were now not only back but actually fashionable. But fashion was what helped insecure people to feel that they belonged and he wasn't going to criticize them. He didn't belong either.

The bars were still shut and he loitered for a while in W. H. Smith, keeping one eye on his watch. He gravitated morbidly towards a medical dictionary and discovered that he was the luckless victim of acedia, asthenia and atrabiliousness – and that was just the As. A book on 'making the most of your leisure hours' turned out to be about gardening and not, as he had supposed, drinking lager.

But a check with his watch told him that lager-drinking time had arrived while he was reading and he slipped out of the shop with hope in his heart. At the centre of the town a sixteenth-century coaching inn had become an ivy-covered three-star hotel, but its timber-framed walls still carried coachmen's whips and post horns to remind today's customers that here was history and that this establishment, unlike so many of its rivals, had not been thrown up overnight. A dozen stone steps led to the Cellar Bar beneath the hotel where customers sat at an oak counter on stools that were made from old beer barrels and covered in red padded leather. Here the town's successes – bankers, solicitors, accountants, estate agents – sipped halves of bitter or gin and tonics while discussing what passed for excitement in their lives; but when he came down the steps the person who stood out in this rigidly bourgeois assembly was Dermot Ryan.

Dermot Ryan was wearing sandals, a very old pair of corduroy trousers and a khaki shirt. His prematurely grey hair was combed forward in a fringe which rested on a battered face that looked as if it had already endured several lifetimes. At one time he had been an antique dealer, a grandiose title for a man who dealt almost entirely in junk, and he had had a small shop on the edge of the town above which the words TRADER RYAN had been painted in elaborate yellow letters. His congested and untidy premises had contained life-size china nudes, stuffed dogs, antler hat-stands, military uniforms from the Boer War, human skeletons, old records and older paintings, stamps, badges and books, and furniture that was poised uneasily between the antique and the decrepit. But the shop had long gone, replaced by a barn-like supermarket, and today Trader Ryan lived by his wits. He was still a snapper-up of unconsidered trifles and once a week had a market stall which, without the overheads, did better than the shop. But his life was a quest for money-making ideas, which occurred to him with extraordinary regularity despite the fact that few were ever pursued. However, some were successful and although a normal person's reaction to a financial shortage was to economize, to spend less, Trader Ryan's was to earn more, to go out and get it. He had never said 'I can't afford it' in his forty-six years.

'Cardboard Fred!' he said now as the new arrival appeared through the crowd. The nickname stemmed from his surname, Carton, but seemed to be particularly suitable for a man who lacked steel in his soul and who not so much crumbled under pressure as avoided it altogether. 'I'll buy you a drink because I know you like that sort of thing.' He procured the attention of a hollow-eyed barmaid who was gazing hungrily at a youth with dandruff.

'I have a new money-making idea,' he announced when, after much fussy adjustment of the taps, a pint of lager had been produced. 'A gender-determination test. Non-invasive. Done in the privacy of your own bathroom.'

His listener, quite accustomed now to a new money-making idea every week, gazed round the bar in search of familiar faces. In what he took to be his middle years – he was thirty-five – Cardboard Fred, a tall, lean man with a pale, thoughtful face, had shaken off the somewhat morose disposition that had accompanied him like fog in his twenties when the world posed problems – professional, social, economic – which often appeared insuperable. Today his perspective had shifted: although the problems were still insuperable, they were no longer important. He knew now that life wasn't serious at all and it was only those people who always seemed faintly ludicrous who believed that it was. This discovery cleared his mind of the worries that had haunted him in his twenties. Life began by accident and could end at any moment: it was fatuous to greet the brief interval between with anything other than a smile.

He smiled at Trader Ryan. 'And what,' he asked, 'is a gender-determination test? Most people know what sex they are already, don't they? They use a thing called a mirror.'

'As it happens I'm talking about unborn babies. You send me twenty pounds and I send you a test tube and a packet of powder. Add urine and the colour tells you whether it's a girl or a boy. If only 10 per cent of the county's pregnant women take it up, I'm going to make £140,000 a year.'

Fred smiled again. The amount had removed the subject from serious conversation. 'How you get such big ideas into your tiny mind is a miracle of accommodation. Does it work?'

'Well, there are no absolutes in medicine. This stuff is a spin-off from a research programme they've been doing in Japan on hormones and enzymes, a tangential benefit which could benefit me. I think I can get the British franchise but even if I can't, what the hell? I can make powder. I must get half right if I tell them all that they're going to have a girl, and if the other half demand their money back, I'm still making £70,000 a year.'

'What happened to the inflatable crash helmet?'

The previous week's idea had been an inflatable crash helmet so that motor-cyclists would not have to carry 'those bloody great bone domes' around with them. The helmets, made of rubber and plastic, could also be used as a bag and would be inflated before each ride from the wheels without affecting the tyre pressure. The idea before that had been an aerosol spray to de-ice the freezer compartment in refrigerators.

'I've put the inflatable crash helmet on hold,' said Trader Ryan. 'It would need considerable investment. That's the story of this septic isle, Fred. Ideas galore and no investment capital. People would rather make a fast buck in the money market than invest in British brains. Talking about money, how are your finances?'

'I owe you 400 quid.'

'I didn't mean that,' said Trader Ryan, somewhat chagrined. 'You can borrow some more if you need it.'

Fred's mind brooded over other debts: to the bank, the credit-card company, his landlord, a television repair bill, the payment on a camera he had bought with some fanciful idea of earning money. He had learned to live with debts but money owed to a friend embarrassed him.

'Perhaps I'll get a job,' he said. 'I've heard that's what people do.'

'Work for yourself, Fred. It's the only way to make money. Start a business, build it up and sell it. That's where most of today's millionaires come from. What you want is a commodity with a big mark-up, like second-hand cars, and small premises with a low rent.'

'Fred's Used Car Kiosk?'

'Better not. It could be the first business in history to be closed down because of its initials. What happened to your last job? It was so long ago that I've forgotten.'

'I was a clerk in a builder's office. I worked my way up to ordering the milk.'

Trader Ryan finished his beer and waved for more. 'Everybody is good at something, but you seem to be the exception to that rule,' he said.

Fred produced some money for the drinks. 'I always thought that life was too short to worry about work. Think how seriously we'd take it if we all lived to be 200. But people keel over at fifty these days. It hardly seems worth starting. I'm thirty-five already.'

Trader Ryan looked at his friend. 'You've got the brains of a rocking horse, Fred. Do you know that? Perhaps I should take you into business with me. We could be the greatest partnership since Tom Spencer teamed up with Michael Marks, although I must admit I doubt it.'

Fred reached across the bar for a fistful of peanuts. Free food. 'But life passes so quickly,' he said. 'Do you realize that the Kennedy assassination is now nearer the Second World War than it is to today? It seems like the week before last to me. I know what my final words will be if I'm given the time: "Was that it?"' He stuffed the peanuts into his mouth and reached for more.

The Saturday lunchtime crowd who now filled the bar depressed him with the cheerfulness that they brought to the weekend, as if they knew something that he didn't. Their determination to separate this piece of the week from the rest of it was proclaimed by their dress: bank managers in jeans, solicitors in garish open-neck shirts, high-flying civil servants looking like hippies at Stonehenge; they gave a strange impression of not having dressed themselves but having been 'got ready' by playful partners who, with the week's work behind them, hoped to produce a quite different personality in their conventional consorts.

'You know what your problem is?' said Trader Ryan. 'The second stage of your rocket has failed to ignite. You're plummeting when you should be soaring.'

'Plummeting implies height,' Fred said. 'I don't think the first stage of my rocket achieved much of that. I've been sitting on the launching pad for years. Mission Control is pretty embarrassed, actually.'

'What's needed, in the technical language of the space agency, is a boot up the arse. You've spent ten years wondering what to do.'

It was true. He had a decade of indecision behind him. He had been handicapped in his forlorn quest for a vocation by his subversive conviction that work wasn't a natural instinct but an acquired habit and – apart from bees and ants, who weren't over-endowed with grey matter – most creatures on this earth had never acquired it. There had been dozens of abortive starts in jobs that required very little training because he was too old to train or too old to accept the tiny salaries that went with learning on the job. Now there was a world out there that was a complete mystery to him, of main boards and financial targets, of tax-free emoluments and non-contributory pensions.

He turned round and saw a girl whose beauty made his heart jump. Her round face appeared to owe nothing to cosmetics and yet her dark lashes and red lips would have been at home on the cover of a magazine. Her black hair was tied in a pony tail and she was wearing white jeans and a mauve shirt.

'She's lovely,' he said.

Trader Ryan followed his gaze through the crowd. 'It's not what they are, it's what they become, Fred,' he said. 'Who is she?'

'I've never seen her before.'

'Nor have I, but she's with a turgid public-school windbag.'

Fred hadn't noticed that she was with anyone, but he turned his attention now to a man in his early twenties who was standing next to her. He had a sun-tanned face with staring eyes and a lot of black curly hair. The sleeves of his grey linen jacket were, in the current fashion, pushed up.

'Jeremy Tyrrell,' said Trader Ryan. 'His daddy is so rich he goes to Switzerland to buy his handkerchiefs.'

'That sounds rich,' Fred admitted. 'And what does Jeremy do?'

'He works for Daddy when he works at all. To him work is what interrupts the holidays, brief periods of activity between baggage-laden trips to airports. He caught me in here once. He'd just had four foreign holidays in six months. You can imagine how impressed I was.'

Fred tore his eyes away from the girl. If she didn't notice his admiring gaze, Jeremy Tyrrell would.

'Actually I've got a powerful desire to bonk a woman on crutches,' Trader Ryan announced. 'I wonder why that is?'

Fred picked up his lager and wondered whether he could risk another look at the girl. 'Your sexual tastes have always been a mystery to me,' he said. 'Not one I want to investigate, either.'

The bar was so full now it was difficult to move. 'Where

did my youth go?' shouted a man who didn't look a day over twenty-five. Girls laughed loyally at the wisecracks of their escorts, some of them alerted to the appearance of humour by the raucous cackle of the wag himself. Make a woman laugh and she's yours for life, Fred had once read. How many jokes did you need?

He put his drink down and turned to see Jeremy Tyrrell and the girl approaching. Tyrrell led the way through the crowd until he was alongside Trader Ryan. Trader, being one of the town's characters, was often approached by people who thought that his unpredictable company would bring a dash of colour into their mundane lives, but most of them retreated quite quickly, their curiosity cooled, on finding that, socially, he was a bit of a handful.

'Hallo, Trader,' said Jeremy Tyrrell. 'How's the lovely Lena?' He had a resonant voice that seemed to come from his chest.

'Hallo,' said Trader. He was talking to the girl. 'Who the devil are you?'

'This is Kate Seymour,' Jeremy Tyrrell said. 'Trader Ryan.'

'And this is Cardboard Fred,' said Trader Ryan to the girl.

'Cardboard Fred?' she said. 'What sort of name is that?'

'I think it's called a nickname,' said Fred. 'I haven't seen you around here before.' Her voice, he decided, was quiet and seductive.

'My father has come to work in Arton,' she told him. Arton was one of several affluent villages, filled with large detached houses and huge gardens, that lay in rural splendour beyond the boundaries of the town. He wondered what on earth her father could find there to do for a living, but he couldn't ask; inquiring about people's parents was an unpleasant way of trying to categorize them.

'I discovered her in a supermarket,' said Jeremy Tyrrell. 'Shopping, of course, not working.'

Trader Ryan remembered something. 'How do you know my wife?' he asked. 'Did you meet her in a supermarket?'

'As a matter of fact, I did,' said Jeremy Tyrrell. 'Women go to supermarkets – that's where you find them.'

'What do you do – ambush them in the aisles?'

'He offers to get things off the top shelf,' said Kate Seymour with a smile. 'At least, that's how he snared me.'

Fred listened to this conversation with some irritation. He had plunged in and out of supermarkets for years and never met anyone. His were flying visits: it had never occurred to him to loiter and lure.

'I obviously go to the wrong supermarkets,' he said.

Kate Seymour gave him a cool, appraising look at this admission, and then consulted a watch with a white strap that was slightly too big for her dainty wrist. 'I must be off,' she said.

When she had gone, accompanied reluctantly by Jeremy Tyrrell, who evidently had his eye on a couple more drinks, Fred found that he didn't want to stay any longer either. The beautiful girls who had wandered in and out of his life could be counted on the fingers of one hand but this was definitely one of them. He found that even after such a brief appearance her departure left an unwelcome gap.

He walked out of the town towards his flat wondering what excitement British television had planned for him that afternoon. The financial considerations that governed sport on television probably meant that instead of the cataclysmic clash between Nottingham and Liverpool it would be Denver versus Dallas at American football, or croquet or hang-gliding.

He was approaching the steps to his flat when Mr Patten, the pet-shop owner and, more significantly, his landlord, came out of the shop looking grim.

'I'm afraid I have some bad news for you, Fred,' he said. One hand clasped the other in front of him as if the news was unwelcome to him too.

He's going to throw me out, Fred thought. He's tired of waiting for his rent.

'There's been a phone call,' said Mr Patten. 'It's your mother. I'm afraid she's died.'

'Oh no,' said Fred. 'Really?'

'I'm afraid so.'

Fred paused and then turned without speaking. He began to walk away from the flat and when he eventually returned to it he had walked for more than ten miles.

# TWO

IN the customary drizzle of a spring morning he came to Dover, a town that always filled him with unease. Its forts, barracks, redoubts and castles suggested a violent blood-stained history, and where land met sea there was the commercial smell of docks, piers and ferry terminals instead of the palm-fringed sand which he felt was a more suitable conjunction.

British Rail had hurried him 100 miles east on the production of his credit card and he had sat on the empty Sunday morning train thinking about his mother. She had been a cheerful, energetic woman who took all things in her stride, even an errant son who had managed to inherit neither of these virtues. The long years of widowhood had been filled intelligently with bridge parties, theatre visits and charitable activities, which provided a social life that Fred had come to envy. When he made his regular visits to Dover to see how she was he discovered that her life was more satisfying than his – the reverse of most family situations. Her death was unexpected.

The grey brick bungalow near St Margaret's Bay looked as spruce as ever. The flowers of early spring made tidy patterns in the front garden and the lawn had already been cut. He let himself in and was engulfed immediately by a huge wave of depression. The bits and pieces of his mother's life lay all around him and he would have to go through them all: her handbag, her writing desk, her cupboards and drawers, her letters and her clothes. At some stage – worst of all – he would have to start throwing things away.

He sat in one of the two green armchairs and looked around the large drawing-room. A photograph of his five-year-old self looked back from the top of the writing desk in the corner. Beyond it was a smaller picture of the three of them, taken at Brighton when he was ten. Even then his father looked harassed beyond endurance. He was going across the room to have a closer look at this picture when there was a knock on the front door. A little old lady with hair so smart that it was surely a wig stepped past him into the room, tripping slightly. She turned to stare accusingly at the step she had just descended.

'I always forget it,' she said. 'You must be Fred. I saw you arrive. I'm Mrs Stroud.'

Fred shut the door behind her and showed her to a chair.

'Hallo, Mrs Stroud,' he said. He had no idea who she was.

'I am the person who rang you,' she said, sitting down. 'Your mother gave me a number to ring if anything ever happened to her. It was a pet shop,' she added as if she would like this explained to her.

'What happened to her, Mrs Stroud? I thought her health was excellent.'

'It was, Fred. I can tell you that. I was her closest friend. She got up yesterday morning and I saw her briefly after breakfast. She was fine. But she dropped dead during the morning. The doctor thinks it was a heart attack. I came round for a coffee and there she was on the floor.'

'Who was the doctor?'

'I've written it all down for you here.' Mrs Stroud

produced a sheet of paper from the pocket of her blue cardigan. 'Her doctor, her solicitor and the name and address of the undertakers. She wanted to be cremated, by the way.'

'I know.' He took the paper and put it unread in his back pocket. 'She wasn't lonely, was she?' he asked.

'Lonely? Never. She had a lot of friends and a busy life. But living alone is not much fun, Fred. My husband was killed in a gliding accident in New Zealand twenty years ago and your mother and I were two widows together. I don't know what I'll do without her. But I was coughing up blood myself one evening last week and thought I was going to die.'

'What did you do?'

'What can you do? I said goodbye to everybody and went to bed.'

The large Victorian families, with cousins, uncles and grandparents bobbing round the edges, had been swept away, Fred thought. People didn't seem to have the emotional capacity to cope with lots of relatives any more. They had grown selfish and the family was a shrinking unit. Single-person households had doubled in ten years.

'I hope you're not going to be lonely,' he said. He seemed to be transferring his concern for his mother to Mrs Stroud.

'The problem is that when you get to my age you only want to meet the people you already know and quite often you don't even want to see them,' she replied, getting up. 'I must leave you now. I suppose you have a lot to do.'

She headed for the door and paused to talk to a pot plant. 'Plants respond to a voice, cucumbers to a flute,' she said. 'Your mother loved her plants. She was a wonderful gardener.'

Fred opened the door for her.

'I'm next door,' she said. 'That way. You will let me know when the funeral is – and, Fred, you must go and see her. You'll feel better if you do.'

The prospect daunted him and he pushed it from his mind. Instead he set off on a slow, sad tour of the bungalow to see what there was that he had to do. It was as spotless as usual, with everything in its place. It was also surprisingly large. The front door opened on to the sitting-room he was in; it led into a small hall in the centre of the building that led into one bedroom at the side and another in the corner which shared the back view with a kitchen and a bathroom. Up the other side was a large dining-room which shared the front view with the room he was in. At the back of the bungalow was a small garden and beyond that a neglected two-acre field.

His mother had slept in the back bedroom and on the table beside her bed were a pair of spectacles, a novel by Anita Brookner and a small photograph album which was full of family photographs, nearly all of them black and white. The poignancy of this scene unsettled him and he went into the other bedroom and dumped the half-empty holdall he had brought with him. The bed was already made in anticipation of his next visit. He wandered across to the dining-room where a beautiful mahogany table and six matching chairs stood in the centre of the room. It must have been a long time since six sat down to dinner here, but perhaps it wasn't. Perhaps the bridge parties produced a momentum of their own and filled the room with hungry guests and gay reminiscences about the Charleston and tram rides and life in the air-raid shelters with powdered eggs and snoek. Against the inner wall was a large bookcase which, apart from Dickens, the Brontës,

Mrs Gaskell and Jane Austen, also displayed a surprising number of books about Oscar Wilde.

He went back into the sitting-room and sat down. What was he supposed to do with all this stuff? Sell it? Keep it? Burn it? There were things that he would like to keep but there was no room in his flat. At the same time he could hardly bear to part with them. The emptiness of this house oppressed him. He was quite used to his own company, but the bungalow needed the presence of his mother. It seemed to him that nobody – relatives, politicians, stars in any creative field – was appreciated much until they were dead. He didn't yet know how much he would miss her, but on the train that morning he had read, in a newspaper left lying in the carriage, that when your last parent died it forced you to confront your own mortality.

He went over to the writing desk and looked at the photograph: Brighton, 1962. He remembered the day because there had been so few trips with his parents. He could even remember the headline in the papers they were selling on the seafront: Marilyn Monroe found dead. His father must have been about forty-four then but he looked much older. Life for him had meant continuous hard work, which had brought him little happiness and an early death. Fred sometimes wondered whether his psychotropic aversion to the paid slavery which many men regarded as a normal existence wasn't formed during painful years observing his father's circumscribed life.

The pictures on the walls were mostly original watercolours of this crowded corner of England, the work, most probably, of friends or unknown local artists who had exhibited at polite wine and cheese parties and, to their surprise and delight, found a buyer. He didn't want the pictures but it didn't seem right to discard them. The books worried him too. They had been cherished by his mother, read and re-read, and to get rid of them now would require a callousness he didn't have.

He sat in the Victorian farmhouse chair that his mother had always used at the writing desk and opened the lid. It was the desk of a methodical woman. Writing pad, envelopes, a book of stamps, an address book and an engagement book were piled neatly in one corner. In the middle were pens, fountain and ballpoint, pencils, a pocket calculator, some scissors, a roll of Sellotape and a Staedtler rubber. The other corner seemed to be the business department – a cheque book, a dozen bills paper-clipped together and each date-marked with 'paid', a recent bank statement, a television licence and, in a cloudy plastic envelope, an insurance policy.

For a moment he wanted to shut the desk, feeling like an intruder who was violating somebody's privacy; he had to remind himself that he was doing his duty. He picked up the bank statement that had evidently been placed there most recently. His mother, he discovered, had a high-interest cheque account in which the credit balance the previous week had been £25,351, the residue, he imagined, of an insurance policy taken out by his father, who had been obsessed with insurance. He was surprised at how much was left, although he had never known how much she received in the first place. 'I will be comfortable,' she had told him when he had tried to raise the subject. In the fourteen years since his father's death she would have lived largely on his company's widows' pension money but he had never known what that was either. He had a distant relationship with money and his knowledge of finance did not encourage his mother to confide in him.

He took up next the plastic envelope containing the insurance policy, imagining that it had to do with thefts from the home or fire or storm damage. But he saw immediately that it was a policy on his mother's life. The idea that his mother should have insured her life had never occurred to him, but now that he thought about it the reason was obvious: his father had spent his life in insurance and they would each have had the very best policies to benefit the survivor.

This one, typed on stiff yellow paper, was the size of a tabloid newspaper when he opened it out. It was over thirty years old. His eyes ran down the page bouncing off strange phrases and legalistic jargon, clauses and sub-clauses. At the bottom he came to the 'minimum death benefit'.

'Provided this policy is in full force on the sum assured becoming payable as the result of death, the amount payable, including any reversionary bonus attaching to the policy, shall in no case be less than £50,000.'

He returned the document to its envelope and walked out to the back garden wondering whose this money was. The rain had stopped. On a small lawn surrounded by flower beds there was a teak garden seat where his mother used to embroider cushion covers for some local charity. He sat down and remembered how she used to enjoy evenings out here, occasionally awarding herself a sherry if her work on the garden had pleased her. He had sat here with her often, nervously skirting the dreaded subject of his lack of progress in the world.

'There's no point in working in an office if it will make you unhappy,' she used to say to him. 'I'm sure you'll find your *métier* one day.'

This hope, which had sounded encouragingly plausible

in his twenties, had been aired less often recently. Too many days had elapsed in which he had found nothing – or not anything that his mother would describe as his *métier*. Painter and decorator, market research assistant, night stockist in a supermarket, petrol pump attendant, switchboard man at a radio cab firm, kitchen porter in an hotel, kennel assistant, window cleaner, barman, double-glazing salesman – the jobs had come and gone leaving him temporarily solvent but suicidally depressed. Any fool could go to work, he decided. Surviving without it was a much more subtle manoeuvre, although this was not a doctrine he expounded in Dover. His failure to find a career hung over their conversations like a cloud and, like determined holidaymakers carrying their towels to the beach, they ignored the cloud.

Sitting in the garden now the recollection filled him with shame. Who knew what dreams a mother harboured for her son? Who knew what wild hopes were nurtured during those long years that began in pain and then developed into a series of exhausting demands – time, patience, work, expense – to produce what? A delinquent, a junkie, a hooligan, an adult son who broke your heart? Being a mother was a long gamble on which you staked your happiness, and there were too many losers.

The following morning he went to see her.

The undertakers, or funeral directors as they called themselves, had a modern one-storey building in one of the town's quieter streets. He had consulted Mrs Stroud's note and then rung them and his mother's solicitor to announce his impending arrival. Across the road a poster declared THE WAGES OF SIN ARE DEATH, as if the virtuous never encountered the depressing firm which stood opposite.

In a small airless office he discussed details of the funeral with a middle-aged lady who seemed to be wearing a type of uniform. Then she showed him into a small room in the chapel of rest. His mother's typed name was on the door.

She lay, apparently asleep, on her back in a pine coffin.

'Did she do her hair like that?' the lady asked.

Fred had the impression of a last-minute shifting of bodies: his visit was unexpected.

She left him then and he waited there a while, consumed by a feeling of waste and of effort unrewarded. He wanted her to speak. He wanted to speak to her, to say thank you, but the room held only an awful emptiness. After a few minutes he walked out of it, feeling strange. Once a man has seen his mother lying in her coffin the world is never quite the same again.

Half an hour later he climbed three flights of stairs to a tiny, cramped office over a furniture store where Mr Pringle, a solicitor, earned his living. If each brown folder piled up on a shelf beside his desk contained the details of one client, he was a busy man.

'Sit down, Mr Carton,' he said. 'I was so sorry to hear about your mother. She's been a client of mine since I don't know when.'

He was a short, energetic man who gave the impression of a jack-in-the-box. He had a round, beaming face with big, round spectacles.

'Have you notified the bank?' he asked.

'Not yet. I'm a little out of my depth.'

'Leave it to me,' said Mr Pringle. 'I understand they hold the deeds. Now your mother made a will about five years ago and deposited it with me.'

He produced it immediately from one of his brown folders. 'I can tell you that she left everything to you. Here we are.' He handed an envelope to Fred, who pulled out his mother's will.

'I give and bequeath unto Frederick Carton all I possess,' he read. The words before his name were printed on the form.

'You're the sole executor and the sole beneficiary,' said Mr Pringle. 'Leave it to me to get probate.'

'Good God,' said Fred. 'There seems to be a lot of money about.'

'Well, it's yours,' said Mr Pringle.

'She had a sister and nieces in Australia and she was a great believer in charities. I thought most of it . . .'

'Have you any idea how much it is? If there are any insurance policies I'll need the documents.'

'There's a life policy for £50,000,' Fred told him. 'And she had about £25,000 in the bank. Then there's the bungalow. I don't know what that's worth or whether there's still a mortgage.'

'Ninety thousand,' said Mr Pringle as if his property valuations had never been questioned. 'It's worth £90,000 at the moment, although by next month it could be more. And the mortgage was paid off by insurance on your father's death. Over £160,000, I make it, and then there's the field.'

The very amount made Fred feel numb. He had once saved just over £1,000, the only time his bank account had reached four figures, a magical bench-mark it had seen very briefly.

'It seems so sad that someone should benefit from another's death,' he said. 'You don't feel right.'

'I can understand that you're in no mood to celebrate,'

said Mr Pringle. 'But the insurance is only paid at death, and she needed the house and the money while she was still alive.'

A brisk way with death. Fred could see why solicitor was just another job for which he was temperamentally unsuited.

Mr Pringle leaned over the desk towards him.

'The field, Mr Carton,' he said. 'Do you know about the field?'

Fred stared back at Mr Pringle's round face.

'I know nothing about a field, Mr Pringle,' he said.

'It's the field at the back of your mother's bungalow. Two acres, I believe, or slightly over. She bought it when your father died in case anybody built there and spoilt her view. I think it's in order to tell you what she said to me once. "Fred is hopeless at finding himself a career. The field will keep him in his old age." It was a surprise present for you, I gathered.'

Fred struggled to absorb this new information. He had craved many things in his life and secretly imagined owning them, but a field was not on his list of coveted possessions.

'What did she imagine I would do with it?' he asked. 'Grow potatoes?'

Mr Pringle's eyes glinted behind their round spectacles.

'Grow houses, Mr Carton,' he said. 'That land is ripe for planning permission, as your mother well knew. The Channel Tunnel is putting a lot of pressure on land around here. Sell the field to a developer and you're a rich man.'

Fred stared evenly at Mr Pringle's glasses.

'How rich?' he asked.

Mr Pringle pushed his folder to one side and produced a new, empty one.

'Look, Mr Carton, would you like me to handle this for you in a professional capacity?' he asked. His hand hovered above the folder, anxious to inscribe the name of a new client on the brown cover.

Fred nodded slowly. 'I think you'd better,' he said.

Reassured that his efforts would be rewarded, Mr Pringle produced a new large pad and a pocket calculator.

'The land that your mother bought for a couple of thousand twelve years ago will be worth a million and a half with planning permission,' he said. 'Let's work it out.' He began to punch his pocket calculator and cover the first page of his pad with figures. 'It's a little over two acres and at eighteen homes an acre they'll build forty, which they'll sell for around £100,000. That's £4 million. Yes, they'll pay a million and a half. It will cost them around £30,000 to build each house – that's, let's see, £1.2 million. Profit: £1.3 million. That's about how they cost it.'

Fred listened to these figures with mounting bewilderment.

'Why did whoever it was sell the land to my mother so cheaply?' was his first question. 'It doesn't make sense.'

'He was eighty and he wanted to retire to Cornwall. He knew that there would be no planning permission for some years and he was too old to wait. Also, he was a great friend of your mother. Next question?'

Now that he was dealing with a paying client Mr Pringle had assumed a veneer of super-efficiency.

'Isn't there something called death duties that will take most of this away?'

Mr Pringle picked up his calculator again. 'I'll work it out for you,' he said. 'There is something we call inheritance tax these days, but for that the land will be worth

£3,000. After all, that is what it's worth at the moment. The tax starts at £110,000 and is 40 per cent, so on the £165,000 you'll pay £22,000. Of course there is capital gains tax of 40 per cent on the land sale – say £600,000, but that will leave you with £900,000, which, together with your mother's will, gives you just over a million. You'll be a millionaire, tax paid.'

Mr Pringle's dark eyebrows pushed high, leaving his spectacles behind: he looked like a man who had plucked a large rabbit from a very small hat, but his audience was a disappointment.

Yesterday evening Fred had sat in his mother's bungalow wondering how he could pay for her funeral. Nothing had stayed ahead of inflation like the cost of a funeral and undertakers did not carry labels in their windows welcoming the use of credit cards.

Today the world had turned once and he was discussing £600,000 tax bills. The transformation in his situation was too colossal for him to digest. He sat and looked at Mr Pringle as if he were indeed a conjuror and would presently set about entertaining his visitor with a spot of levitation or a deck of cards. There was nothing left that could surprise him this morning.

Mr Pringle looked at him thoughtfully. 'I suppose this is all something of a shock?'

'Quite a shock, Mr Pringle,' said Fred, wishing that he could reach a drink. 'I've never had any money, you see. I saw some in a bank once. My present concern is paying for the funeral.'

He was wondering why his mother had never spent her money on some fun. She couldn't sell the field because she didn't want a housing estate at the bottom of her garden, but she had enough money in the bank to pay for the sea cruise she had always wanted. But she had hung on to it, not knowing how much she was going to need, not knowing how long she was going to live. It filled him with a sadness that showed on his face and quite distracted the busy solicitor.

'I'll advance you £1,000 and deduct it later on,' he said, producing a cheque book. 'The money in your mother's bank account will be transferred to yours quite quickly. Let me take down a few details about you, Mr Carton. Address, bank, phone number – that sort of thing. And then how about lunch? There's a rather good restaurant just down the street.'

'Do they take credit cards?'

Mr Pringle held up both hands. 'It's on me, Mr Carton. Once you get money you find that you no longer need it.'

# THREE

ON a stool in the crowded Cellar Bar Dermot Ryan compiled a list of the options that seemed to him to be available.

1 Emigration
2 Divorce
3 Suicide
4 Suicide (faked)
5 Murder
6 Submission

The prospect of none of these restored the feelings of enjoyment and anticipation that he usually brought to his daily routine, and some of them he found deeply distasteful. He picked up his drink and looked round at the other people in the bar. The drink was a new lager, a heavy, sleep-inducing product of Australia that seemed to take you from alertness to somnolence without any intervening period of unbridled jollity. The mid-week customers were mostly the walking wounded, the unemployed or unemployable, all of whom he knew by name and none of whom he encouraged to share his company. Life was difficult enough without embarking on one of the conversational quagmires that lay around him here. On a stool at the corner of the bar was a man in his late twenties called George, who today was wearing a bright red hat that he evidently hoped might add a shimmer of interest to a personality which had hitherto encouraged eyelids to droop and jaws to sag. A roll-up cigarette was stuck to his upper lip and although it never went out, it never seemed to grow shorter either. His companion was one of the town's trouble-makers who moved from bar to bar as he was banned from each; he was now in the process of getting himself banned from this one by refusing to pay the full amount for his drink. If intolerance of authority is the first sign of a creative mind, this yobbo is going to write the sequel to *Ulysses*, thought Dermot Ryan returning to his list.

'My wife won't talk to me,' he told the barmaid when she came his way. The barmaid was too young to have heard this before and too inexperienced to know that if she stayed in the job long enough she would hear it many times again. 'Why's that?' she asked.

'I forget. I'm not sure I ever knew. But the silence is deafening and she has moved into the next room. What sort of marriage is that?'

The barmaid slid away to respond to the demands of other customers. The staff turnover was so fast here that he didn't even know her name. She was attractive, though, with bright eyes that looked as though they had seen things. If he could forgive her for yawning without covering her mouth, which he probably couldn't, romance loomed. When his glass was empty he called her back.

'Buy her a present,' she suggested as she filled his glass with the narcotic fluid.

'I bought her a saucepan for her birthday and for my birthday she hit me with it. I should have bought her a scold's bridle.'

'I meant jewellery.'

The idea horrified him. Expensive presents, humbly offered, were an admission of guilt. They were liniment on a wound but the wound was still there when the liniment had gone and, by that time, the money had gone too.

'I do buy jewellery occasionally,' he said. 'And then I sell it at a profit.'

'What about your children? Are they talking to you?'

'We don't have any children. We had an ectopic pregnancy a few years ago but twenty years of marriage have produced no contribution at all to the population explosion.' He sipped his new pint and thought about it. 'In a zoo they tell whether the animals are happy or not by whether they're breeding, don't they?'

But she had gone again, summoned this time by a recently unfrocked traffic warden who had been unduly selective with his tickets.

Lena Ryan was forty, a dangerous age for a woman. It was an age when reality had crept up on dreams. Wild possibilities, romantic and professional, the thought of which had sustained them during the hopeful years, began to fade and die, and the dwindling future took on a bare look and became a depressingly barren landscape. The future grew shorter and tempers grew shorter with it.

Her husband was aware of this and he knew that the possibilities remained alive longer for a man. But being aware of it didn't make it any easier to live with, now that the little indiscretions and occasional infidelities that were once greeted with a sigh were met by a wall of silence, hostility and violence.

He ran through his list again and felt a hand on his shoulder.

'Cardboard Fred,' he said, turning on his stool. 'Where the hell have you been?'

'Touring the town. Looking for you. The Rose and Crown and Golden Star are dead.'

'It sounds like a Tom Stoppard play I saw once. Blokes tossing coins. I meant where have you been for the last two weeks?'

Fred Carton somehow looked different. He wore new cavalry twill trousers, new brown shoes, a new yellow sweater. He had a new haircut. He didn't seem his normal indecisive self.

'I've been to Dover,' he said, sitting on the next stool. 'My mother died.'

Trader Ryan studied his friend thoughtfully. 'I'm sorry to hear that,' he said.

'I was fairly sorry myself,' Fred told him. He waved a hand at the vanishing barmaid. 'I found that the death of a loved one is quite hard to take if you're an atheist.'

'Of course. That's why man invented religion. To cope with death.'

Fred pondered this as he ordered a pint. He could see how it happened. He delved into his back trouser pocket to get his wallet. He paid for their drinks and then peeled off eight £50 pound notes, which he placed on the bar.

'I owe you £400,' he said. 'At least, I used to.'

Trader Ryan trousered the money without thinking about it.

'My wife isn't talking to me,' he said, 'or sleeping with me. The breakdown of communication which is such a feature of modern marriage has, in our case, produced a silence so exquisite that you could almost orchestrate it.'

'Not a word need be spoken in your language of hate. What happened?'

'A girl rang her up to ask her why I hadn't been in touch. The malignant little cow did it deliberately. I got home howling pissed and Lena threw the microwave at me.'

'It's not exactly Mills & Boon,' Fred said, picking up his pint. 'Who was the girl?'

'Someone I met at an antiques fair in Brighton. We went out a couple of times but I had to give her the elbow. She said something rather strange to me and I did a runner. "I know it's not very fashionable at the moment," she said, "but I'm into masochism." Well, I could see myself ending up in a flat in Chelsea, caked in sweat and frenziedly lashing her buttocks with a cane when the pubs were open.'

'Not your scene at all, I should imagine.'

'Too right, as it happens. The sad thing was that if I was giving marks out of ten, I'd have given her fifteen.'

'I always thought Lena was remarkably tolerant about your little escapades.'

'Not any more. She's been reading some book by that woman who looks like an undertrained quarter-back. *Go For His Gonads* it's called, or perhaps I dreamt that bit. The gist of it is that men have been an unpleasant irrelevance for some time, but poor abused women have been too brainwashed to notice.' He scratched the side of his head as he considered the implications of this venomous theory. 'Men are callous, grubby and selfish. I didn't know that, did you?'

Fred shook his head. 'Nobody told me.'

'They've done research,' said Trader Ryan darkly, 'and it's put the tin hat on my marriage. It's all come as a blinding revelation to my old woman, who had spent all these years thinking I was all right.'

He finished his drink and called the barmaid for more. She took their glasses without speaking.

Trader Ryan looked at Fred and shook his head. 'The game's up. Sluggish arteries, stained lungs, no wife.

There's nothing for it but to sit here among this bunch of hand-jobs and wait for death. Not that I give a damn about death, it's dying I don't fancy much. I'm banking on a bit of thermo-nuclear vaporization. Everybody's scared of it but it's much better than the death that's waiting for them.'

He put his hand in his pocket to pay for the drinks and pulled out £400.

'Where did this come from?' he asked.

'I gave it to you just now.'

'You couldn't have done. You never have money. You're like Prince Charles.'

Fred pulled a wallet from the back pocket of his new trousers and opened it to reveal many more £50 notes, all of them new and only recently folded. It made him feel guilty and he shut the wallet and returned it to his pocket.

'I could be seriously rich in a minute,' he said. 'I've inherited some land from my mother.'

Trader Ryan's eyebrows dropped until his eyes almost disappeared. 'I never knew your mother owned any land,' he said.

'Nor did I. It's only a couple of acres but with permission to build houses it could be worth –'

'A million.'

'Something like that.'

Trader Ryan drank some lager and took Fred's arm.

'You're obviously the person to hear about my new money-making idea,' he said. 'All I need is capital. The options market. I'm getting quite sophisticated, aren't I?'

'What is it?'

'It's called the traded options market. You don't buy the share, you buy an option to buy the share. If it goes up, you can take up the option and buy it at the old cheap price and sell it immediately at the new expensive price. Or you can sell the option back at a profit without ever actually owning the share. What do you think?'

'I think it's a privilege to sit here garnering the fruit of your intellect. Kindly burble on.'

'The advantage is that it costs only a fraction of the actual share price. All I need is capital. Remember me when you're rich.'

Fred looked round the bar and wondered how many other people in here had ideas that they couldn't afford, schemes that would stay permanently grounded through lack of funds.

'What are you going to do about Lena?' he asked.

Trader Ryan shrugged. 'It's over. Separate bedrooms, separate lives. I think it's now just a question of whether I kill her or she kills me.'

'It's a strange thing to happen,' said Fred, 'when you've been married so long.'

'Strange things are happening to women, Fred. Some bugger's put ideas in their heads. They've got aspirations, they make demands. It turns out they've got rights. Bring back the past, that's what I say. I get nostalgic for last week. In the old days it was sex that kept us going. Do you remember those teenage years of passion and exploration? I was at my sexual peak then.'

Fred tried to remember this. There was certainly a lot of sex about but wasn't that simply because all their female contemporaries were single?

'Come back, Mavis Higgins,' said Trader Ryan staring into his beer. 'She really got me going. She couldn't keep her hands off me. I remember once, on a bus, I ejaculated over a woman's *Daily Mail*. She was pretty surprised because she was reading it at the time.'

'What did you do? Lend her your *Express*?'

'We got off the bus very quickly.'

'You and the woman?'

'No, me and Mavis Higgins.'

A wry smile flickered briefly across his careworn face at the distant memory of golden days of trouble-free relationships and instant sexual gratification.

'Let me get the picture,' said Fred. 'Where was this woman sitting with the newspaper?'

'On the seat in front, of course. Otherwise she'd have seen what we were up to.'

He shrugged as if the story wasn't worth telling – there had been too many embarrassments in his life. 'Anyway, there it was. Splat! Another abandoned crossword.'

He said it as though an abandoned crossword somehow summed up his life.

On Friday mornings, with a whiff of leisure in the air, Trader Ryan became a huckster in the market place, setting up his stall at the end of the wide Georgian street that brought visitors down into the town from other, less elegant neighbourhoods. He wore old jeans and, regardless of the weather, a thick khaki sweater and naval cap tugged jauntily down on one side.

The stall, a long gate-leg table, defied classification and consequently attracted a curious crowd who could never be sure what they were going to find. Today a cursory glance revealed a model galleon, a pile of records, a row of paperback books, a sword, a pair of candlesticks, a brass tray, six clocks, medals, coins and postcards bearing mysterious stamps so that even the vendor was never sure whether the public was buying the card or the stamp.

Buried among the dross were strange items that Trader Ryan had collected over the years and which were used as bait to start the conversation that ended, if only out of politeness, with the sale of one item or another. These included a hokey-pokey glass used once by ice-cream sellers, a top-hat brush, a ceramic model of Snow White with a cavity behind her skirt for toothbrushes, and a folding button hook which had been used to fasten the buttons on boots.

Cardboard Fred, on his way to an appointment with the morning newspaper and a cup of coffee, reached the stall before the commerce was in full flow.

'I've had a wonderful idea,' he said, picking up a strange glass lid which had a glass ring as a handle. 'What the hell is this?'

Trader Ryan rubbed his hands together in the manner of a man anticipating a sale.

'That, sir? That's a ceiling protector. They used to suspend them from the ceiling above a gas lamp to protect it from carbon stains from the lamp. To you, a fiver. What's the wonderful idea?'

'I'm going to get married.'

'Why don't you take your money out of the bank and burn it, and then have your balls cut off? It will achieve the same effect but be less painful in the long run.'

Fred replaced the ceiling protector gently on the stall. 'I realize that this is hardly the moment to look to you for a ringing endorsement of the joys of matrimony, Trader.'

'It never was, kid. You lose your spare time and your spare money, which are the only two things you had in the first place. Your food bill doubles, your phone bill trebles, and toilet rolls don't last five minutes. What gave you the idea, anyway? You on drugs?'

Fred picked up a book. 'I'm just reorganizing my life in the light of my new financial situation. It is a truth universally acknowledged that a single man in possession of a good fortune must be in want of a wife. It says so in this book here.'

'Don't think I haven't read it. I've been trying to sell it for twelve months. But Jane Austen has been dead for 150 years and wives were different then. They were more like au pair girls.'

'And today they're more like sergeant majors?'

'That's it. The hand on your arm as you walk down the street is the hand of restraint, not affection. Don't do it, Fred. It's like jumping in the river because you're thirsty.'

He was distracted by a woman who had picked up the pair of candlesticks. She examined them from every angle and then held them at arm's length, squinting slightly.

'Eighteenth century,' he told her.

'They were made in 1920,' said the woman. 'But I'll have them anyway.'

Fred replaced the book and picked up a small brass pig with its head on a hinge. Opening it he saw that it was used as a match holder in the days before the safety match. The match was struck on the ridged surface of the pig's stomach.

Trader Ryan was taking money and giving change from his pocket. There were no tills here to tempt today's larcenous youths, and no tell-tale till roll for the taxman.

'What is it you are looking for, anyway?' he asked when his eagle-eyed customer had departed with her candlesticks. 'A teenage virgin, I'll bet. It would be easier these days to find a bi-lingual dustman.'

Fred put the pig down and moved along the stall,

curious at the diversity of the stock. 'Perhaps a more experienced lady would fill the bill,' he said.

'You'd be pliable putty in her scheming little dandy-pats, Fred. Don't do it. Live in sin. Give it a trial run for a couple of decades. Why put your head in a noose?'

'Commitment, Dermot. It's what my life has always lacked.'

Trader Ryan began to rearrange a small corner of his stall, to cover the gap left by the candlesticks. 'In my experience with women the best moment is the first moment. Things start to deteriorate after that. It's a thought you should remember. You sound as if you're about to rush into something.'

Fred was now examining a pile of records, old seventy-eights with barely remembered names on the labels. He had no intention of rushing into anything but he was not affected by Trader's dyspeptic chat. It was no use discussing the awesome majesty of the ocean with a man who was drowning. There were other witnesses who could tell him that marriage was the driving force in their lives, the greatest single source of happiness, the event which made sense of everything else.

'It's coffee time for the jobless,' he said. 'Have a busy day.'

Walking down the street to the coffee bar, he reflected that it wasn't only commitment that was lacking from his life; a bit of sexual activity would be a welcome addition to his far from crowded programme. Sometimes he wondered whether he would ever achieve it. A magazine had reported recently that men aged fifty-five had intercourse 1.5 times a week.

He was looking forward to that.

*

Lena Ryan was sitting in the coffee bar reading *Homes and Gardens*. She liked to torture herself with these surreptitious peeks at the exquisite lifestyles of more fortunate people, to gauge how far she had fallen short of the targets she had set herself as a girl. At forty her dark hair was greying prematurely and her once beautiful face looked tired. She sipped her coffee and turned the pages of her magazine, discovering a world of elegant conservatories, stylish kitchens and sensual bathrooms.

'Good morning, Fred,' she said when he joined her at the table. 'Are you between jobs again?'

He put his coffee down and edged himself into a seat that was designed for a smaller race.

'I've just been talking to your husband,' he told her. It was surprising how little he had seen her over the years. Her husband's excursions to the pub were not something that she chose to share. She was much discussed and seldom seen, but Fred found Trader Ryan so unusual that he always imagined there had to be something remarkable about his wife, too.

'I'm glad somebody's talking to him,' she said. 'He could get lonely.'

She was wearing a green ankle-length dress that looked vaguely oriental. Whatever their problems, the Ryans shared an unconventional taste in clothes.

'I gathered you were having a difference of opinion,' Fred said, stirring his coffee.

'Is that what he told you?' Lena Ryan asked, looking up at him. 'His perception of the truth is what you might call blurred. There's no difference of opinion. No opinions are being expressed. There is just a beautiful silence. It's taken me twenty years to realize that I'm closeted with an idiot.'

Fred had no doubt that Lena Ryan's grounds for

complaint were almost endless, but he couldn't join in this condemnation of his friend.

'Well, he's certainly eccentric,' he said eventually. 'I always thought that was part of his charm.'

'Eccentric?' she said. 'We went to my sister's wedding a few months ago and what do you think he bought them as a wedding present? Two gerbils.'

'Original.'

'Embarrassing is the word you are looking for, Fred. He's been embarrassing me all my life. Even his job's an embarrassment now. A stall in the street! At least the shop had a sort of respectability.'

Lena Ryan gazed down at the table between them, shaking her head. Her conversation surprised him, and he wondered what belated social ambitions were suddenly nagging her at forty.

'He's always been good at earning money,' he suggested, 'whatever method he chooses.'

'And very bad at spending it. He's so mean he washes his toothpicks. But it's his promiscuity I can't take any more. There's a girl somewhere. I don't know who she is but she's welcome to him. At my age I need more than a mechanical donkey.' She finished her coffee and pushed the cup to one side of the table. 'I think I'll have my hair streaked and get myself a toy boy. I mean it.' She allowed herself a smile, the first of the morning.

'You look better when you're cheerful,' he told her. 'It's amazing how few cheerful people you see around.'

'The last one I saw had a nervous breakdown,' said Lena Ryan. 'It's not natural to be cheerful, I've concluded. It's a strain. I must say you look more relaxed yourself this morning, Fred. Your financial problems usually give you a slightly haunted look.'

'Financial problems?' said Fred. 'I don't have financial problems.'

And when Lena Ryan had gone, on a quest for summer shoes, he turned first to the financial pages in his newspaper.

# FOUR

THE news arrived on a wet morning in early May when rolling clouds and a brisk wind carried with them the assurance that another dud summer was in the pipeline. Soon thousands would face the choice between being stranded in a rain-swept hotel in Britain and being stranded in a strike-bound airport abroad. Such dismal options were of no interest to Cardboard Fred, who never took a holiday. He was exploring the interior of a boiled egg with a slightly burnt finger of toast when the post hit the mat.

The large white envelope, postmark Dover, arrived in the company of a gas bill, an electricity bill, another credit-card bill and an invitation to subscribe to a new money magazine whose promotion office had correctly guessed that here was one man in need of financial advice. The invitation, no doubt kindly meant, was dispatched to the bin, and he tore open the envelope from Dover.

Cedric Pringle's letter carried a hint of impatience that his client was stubbornly soldiering on without that pre-requisite of modern living, the telephone. 'I have tried to contact you,' he wrote, 'but directory inquiries can find no trace of your number. There are several developments here which we should urgently discuss. Planning permission has now been granted for the land for forty homes, and two developers are anxious to buy it. The top offer is £1,500,000, and I have also received an offer of £95,000 for your mother's bungalow. Could you please get in touch as soon as possible?'

Fred abandoned the egg and ran downstairs with the letter. There was a telephone kiosk about 300 yards away. He could, in an emergency, have used Mr Patten's phone in the pet shop but his instinct told him that this was going to be a conversation that did not need an audience.

The telephone system was being no more aggravating than usual and after about ten minutes he heard Mr Pringle's voice.

'It's Fred Carton,' he told him. 'I could come over this afternoon.'

'Oh, that's excellent,' said Mr Pringle. 'What time could you be here?'

'Four o'clock?' Fred imagined that if he left now not even British Rail could take more than six hours to carry him 100 miles.

'I would like you to meet my brother,' Mr Pringle said now. 'In a professional capacity. He's an accountant and I think you're going to need one.'

'I am?'

'You certainly are. I've already discussed you with him and he has a suggestion or two. May I bring him in?'

'Please do.'

The line went dead suddenly and a brief silence was followed by a flurry of urgent beeping. It didn't seem necessary to get the call re-connected, even if such an ambitious project were possible.

Instead Fred returned to his flat and collected his yellow waterproof jacket, which seemed an appropriate garment for the onset of the English summer. He had forgotten it in the rush to the phone and now his damp shirt needed changing too.

Hector Pringle, in contrast to his bouncy brother, was a cadaverous soul, weighed down by balance sheets and margins. The two men were sitting side by side at Cedric Pringle's desk when Fred, predictably late, rushed in breathless from his ascent of the three flights of stairs. They were surrounded by a sea of paper – letters, land documents, planning applications, the deeds of the bungalow and the land behind it, draft replies awaiting Fred's approval.

He imagined that this was what going to work was like.

'My recommendation,' said Cedric Pringle when he had introduced his brother, 'is that you accept this offer of £1,500,000 for the land. I'm not saying we couldn't get more if we wait but, with inflation, you can always get more if you wait. It's a fair price, it's the right price at the moment and I believe it's the figure I anticipated when we spoke before.'

'It is,' said Fred. 'I'm quite happy with it.'

'The offer of £95,000 is slightly more than I expected for the bungalow, though of course a few weeks have passed and prices are going up all the time. It may be that you would like to hang on to the bungalow as an investment. As you own no other home in Britain you could always sell it later and pay no tax. You hardly need the money now.'

Fred was considering this line of action when Hector Pringle raised a hand.

'Something I want to say may have a bearing on that,' he said in a tired voice. Fred could only imagine the unremitting tedium of an accountant's life, and wondered whether Hector Pringle secretly nursed dreams of a more exciting existence, like an acrobat's in a circus, or membership of the SAS.

'What we have to discuss, Mr Carton, assuming you want to use me as your accountant, is what you intend to do with the money.'

Hector Pringle's gaunt appearance was now so firmly implanted in Fred's mind as being what an accountant should look like that he had no doubt that if he was going to hire an accountant, he wanted one who looked like this.

'I would be grateful if you would act for me,' he said. 'But I have no plans for the money at all.'

'That's good,' said Hector Pringle. 'We can start from scratch then. After inheritance tax you will have about £150,000 from the bungalow, the life policy and the money your mother left you in the bank. After capital gains tax on the land sale you will have £900,000. Say a million all together. Give that to an investment manager and you'll get 12 per cent – £120,000 a year – without touching your capital.' Unlike his brother, Hector Pringle did not seem to need a pocket calculator.

He stopped talking suddenly and stared across the desk at Fred.

'Have you ever thought of going to live abroad?'

Fred stared back. The question seemed to have no connection with what they had been discussing.

'Abroad?' he said. 'No.'

'There would be serious financial advantages, Mr Carton. For instance, the tax on that £120,000 would be £48,000 if you stay here. In Monte Carlo you could rent a flat for £1,000 a month and save yourself £36,000 a year. It's warmer in Monte Carlo.'

'You haven't got any ties, have you?' Cedric Pringle asked. 'It really is something you ought to consider.'

Fred tried to consider it, but the jump from bankrupt to tax exile in three months was too big a leap even for his teeming imagination.

'As long as you haven't got any property here,' Hector

Pringle said. 'That's why I think you should sell the bungalow.'

'But do I want to live abroad?' Fred asked. 'I went there once and the grub's awful.'

'Where was that?'

'I once managed seven days in Ibiza.'

'Nobody's talking about Ibiza here, Mr Carton. Monaco is French. I go to the Dordogne for my holiday every year and I can tell you that France is an oasis of civilization. Certainly I've never heard anybody say that the grub's awful.'

Fred felt that he should promise to go abroad, to please these two gentlemen who were trying to help him. At the same time he was beginning to feel an ambivalence that he could not have envisaged a few hours earlier towards this unexpected windfall. Already he could see how money edged people into courses of action they wouldn't gladly have chosen, how they allowed themselves to be pushed and then controlled by the wealth that was supposed to liberate them. He had spent his life avoiding such nudges from whatever direction. Was his easy-going existence about to be destroyed by a developer's cheque?

His failure to respond to the idea of abroad moved Cedric Pringle on to fresh ground. 'There's another thing,' he said, spreading his hands on his paper-covered desk. 'Have you made a will?'

This was the last question that Fred expected to be asked. Eventually, finding no answer, he shook his head.

'We're talking about a lot of money. You have no next of kin so far as I can see and if you die intestate the government will snaffle the lot. You ought to make a will now, even if you only leave it to the cats' home.'

'Now?' said Fred.

'I would be failing in my duty to you if I didn't recommend that you get it done as soon as possible. We can draft it here now. A loose tile could fall on your head as you left our office.'

Fred felt his darkest fears confirmed. What was simple had become complicated; stress was replacing leisure.

'If your roof is in such a bad state of repair I'd better think about it,' he said. But who could he leave his money to? His first thought was Trader Ryan and then he remembered, as he often did, the beautiful Kate Seymour. To leave a small fortune to a girl he had met only once was the sort of romantic gesture the world needed. He looked at the blank sheet of paper that Cedric Pringle had placed in front of him for a list of those who would benefit from his death and wrote 'Kate Seymour, Arton' at the top. Then he thought of Trader Ryan and his endless fund of money-making ideas that perished at birth through lack of capital and wrote 'Dermot Ryan' as well. He added the Ryans' address and then wrote 'Half each' underneath.

Cedric Pringle called in his secretary from another room and handed her the sheet of paper. 'We'll just turn these scribbles into an impressive legal document,' he said.

Hector Pringle, who had sat impatiently on the sidelines while this was going on, suddenly sat upright.

'You must get out of the country at once,' he said.

Fred, picturing the delight of Kate Seymour on hearing of this bequest from a shy millionaire who had only seen her once, was tugged back to the solicitor's office with a jolt.

'I must?' he repeated. 'It's beginning to sound like expulsion.'

'I've just realized something,' Hector Pringle said. 'If you establish residence in some tax-free shelter before we sell the land you won't have to pay the capital gains tax either.' Confronted by an expression of evident disinterest, he felt obliged to spell it out. 'For living in Monte Carlo for a year you would effectively be paid £600,000. That's what the saving would be, Mr Carton, if we delay the land deal until you've moved abroad.'

Fred groped for an answer but there seemed to be something unanswerable in what Hector Pringle had said. To be paid more than half a million pounds to live in Monte Carlo for a year was just the sort of job that he had been looking for all his life. He could see now that he was going to be plucked from his cosy flat and dumped in a foreign land for twelve months. It was not a prospect that he relished.

'I believe that you are allowed in the UK for ninety days during that time,' said Cedric Pringle. 'You can always fly home for a couple of weeks if you feel like it.'

'The important thing is to get a resident's card,' said Hector Pringle. 'It's got to be official to satisfy the taxman.'

'In a year's time you can come home and buy yourself a mansion,' his brother suggested. 'A year really isn't very long and it's got to be worth it for £600,000.'

The two brothers looked across the desk at their client as if they would be glad if he joined this conversation. It seemed to be a long time since he had said anything.

'Well, Mr Carton?' said Hector Pringle eventually. 'What are you going to do?'

Fred looked back at them and nodded slowly. They had given him the best advice that they could. It didn't seem right to disappoint them.

'I'm going to get myself to Monte Carlo as quickly as possible,' he said, hoping that the idea would grow on him. He had only the vaguest idea where it was.

Three days later when the non-appearance of Trader Ryan had become the subject of curiosity, Fred took the long walk to his home on a run-down estate outside the town. The house was a drab white semi-detached which looked as if it had been built by some charitable institution for the deserving poor of an earlier generation. It was separated from a pot-holed road by a totally neglected front garden where tumbleweed, dandelions and thistles blissfully thrived, safe from the threat of human depredation.

Lena Ryan opened a front door that needed paint. She was wearing a short flowery dress which revealed shapely legs that Fred had never seen, and her hair had been cut and streaked. He gaped at the transformation – as Trader Ryan grew older, his wife was getting younger.

'Good morning, Fred,' she said. 'You're an early bird.'

Fred looked at his watch and realized that it was still only eight o'clock. 'Early to bed, early to rise, makes a man healthy, wealthy and boring,' he said. 'So I suppose your spouse isn't vertical yet?'

'I've no idea,' she said with a shrug. 'You'll find him round the back.' She gave him a smile which seemed to contain both suffering and forbearance, and gently shut the door.

Mystified, Fred walked round the side of the house. If the front garden was neglected, the back garden was more like a nature reserve, with waist-high grass sharing the cramped space with a profusion of brightly coloured weeds. If an animal more accustomed to the domesticity of the zoo had come trotting through the undergrowth Fred would scarcely have been surprised. He gazed round at this urban jungle and suddenly saw, almost hidden in the middle of it, a low khaki tent. He fought his way through the grass, opened a flap and peered in.

Trader Ryan lay on his back in a green sleeping bag, his hands behind his head. His eyes, focused on the tent's roof, moved fractionally to identify his intruder.

'I expect you're wondering,' he said, 'why I've got a piece of toilet paper stuck up my nose?'

Fred ducked under the flap and found sitting room on a corner of the groundsheet which formed the tent's floor. A half-empty bottle of Old Crow lay beside the sleeping bag.

'What's going on?' he asked. 'You haven't been at the whacky baccy, have you?'

Trader Ryan, preoccupied now with removing a piece of blood-stained toilet paper from his left nostril, grinned at the idea.

'She hit me on the nose with a bottle and it wouldn't stop bleeding. I must have fallen asleep with the paper still in.'

'What on earth was the bottle?'

'Crosse & Blackwell low-calorie dressing, I believe it was. It was difficult to read the label.'

He seemed to have a hangover. There were haphazard patches of colour around his nostrils and mouth, but the rest of his face was white. He lifted himself on his elbows and looked round the tent.

'She picked up the bread knife last night,' he said.

'Is that why you're living in a tent?'

'Too right. Microwave ovens bouncing off your head are one thing. Bread knives are something else. I'm too young for a vasectomy, particularly without an anaesthetic.' He picked up yesterday's *Financial Times*, which lay on the groundsheet beside him. 'According to this organ there were nearly five thousand suicides in Britain last year and two thirds of them were men. It didn't come as any surprise to me.'

'What are you going to do?'

The size of the question drove Trader Ryan back to the recumbent position in which Fred had found him. He lay on his back, both hands covering his face.

'That is the question,' he said finally. 'I'm dead if I stay, and I'm dead if I go.'

'I can see how you're dead if you stay,' said Fred. 'Why are you dead if you go?'

'Dead financially. I have a mortgage on this old, cold house. Being self-employed I wasn't able to prove much of an income to the building society and I had to borrow from the bank at a horrendous rate of interest. If I move out, I'd have to find rent for a flat as well. Business isn't that perky just now.'

'Perhaps she'll move out,' said Fred. 'She looks poised for flight.'

Trader Ryan nodded. 'She does, doesn't she? She's shed ten years in two weeks. Another two months and people will think she's my daughter. Fly, baby, fly! The farther the better. Her emotional parabolas are no longer my concern, unless I finish up on the wrong end of a bread knife.'

The triangular prism of a bar of Toblerone chocolate, either last night's uneaten supper or this morning's breakfast, was visible in a corner of the tent and he reached for it now, removed the paper and began to eat.

'I suppose I ought to get up,' he said, 'but then again, I say to myself, "Why bother?"'

'I can remember when "get up in the morning" was the only rule I had,' Fred told him. 'And today has definitely started. I heard it on the radio. Get up. Being horizontal isn't natural unless you're a British heavyweight boxer.'

'I'm not a boxer but I'm getting a little punch-drunk as it happens. I know that you duck a swing and block a hook but I never learned about bottles of salad dressing.' He rubbed his nose gingerly. 'The trouble with today is that it's the tomorrow I worried about yesterday. You haven't got a suit of armour with you, I suppose?'

He eased himself out of his sleeping bag. Fred was surprised to discover that he was fully dressed. He even had his shoes on.

'Do you always sleep in your shoes?' he asked.

'Only when I might have to run like hell in the middle of the night. What brings you here, anyway, Fred? I can't remember the last time you visited me at home.'

'I bring you good news and, all things considered, it looks as if you could use it.'

Trader Ryan, doing up two buttons on his blue denim shirt, which was all that getting dressed involved this morning, looked up.

'What's that, Fred?' he asked.

'There's been a deal on the land. I'm rich beyond the dreams of average.'

The news, which seemed to be of monumental significance to Fred, didn't appear to move Trader Ryan one way or the other. He folded up his sleeping bag until it made a cushion and then sat on it.

'How much did you get?'

'Over a million.'

Trader Ryan found his bar of chocolate and took another bite.

'I've been worrying about it,' he said. 'You're our token pauper. I'm not sure money will suit you. What are you going to do with it and, more important, what's it going to do to you? Apart from giving you crazy notions about finding a wife.'

'I'm going to invest it, Trader. And then, rather than face a tax bill of £600,000 I'm going to leg it to Heathrow. I'm going to be a tax exile.'

'Tax exile?' Trader repeated, examining the phrase. 'I always thought exile was one of the saddest words in the language.'

'Not half as bloody sad as tax,' said Fred. 'But put the two together and what have you got? A happy man quaffing champagne under a sunshade while topless ladies frolic in the pool beside him. At least, I hope that's what you've got.'

Trader Ryan shook his head. 'You've probably got some homesick johnny incarcerated in his lonely apartment with a television he can't understand, a newspaper he can't read and a radio tuned to the BBC World Service which he can't hear properly. He hates the locals, dislikes the beer and pines for the English climate.'

Fred could see that it was difficult to mobilize enthusiasm for anything, let alone his exotic scenario, if you lived in a tent.

He said, 'I think it would be helpful to my equanimity if you cheered up.' He pulled a large brown envelope from inside his shirt and threw it on the groundsheet.

'On top of all my other problems, you're going to sod off and I'll have no one intelligent to drink with,' Trader Ryan said wanly. 'I had a feeling this money was going to be bad news.' He finished the chocolate and screwed the wrapper in his fist.

Fred paused briefly at the imputation that he was deserting a friend in need for reasons that were essentially selfish and frivolous, if not falsely based. Perhaps, in a minute, Trader Ryan, whose hard-earned income managed mysteriously every year to fall just short of the taxman's net, would deliver an astringent homily on the shortage of patriotism round here, along with a tearful reference to the unbuilt hospitals which would – pigs may fly – spring up like mushrooms if the government could only gets its hand deeper into the workers' pockets.

His attention was taken, however, by the envelope on the floor.

'What's that?' he asked.

'It's for you,' Fred told him. 'I've always seen you as a man with business acumen but no business, a man with the robust instincts of a millionaire but no capital to fund them. Well, there's your chance.'

Trader Ryan opened the envelope and pulled out four plastic packets, each bearing the name of a bank on the side. He opened one and emptied a fistful of £50 notes on to the groundsheet.

'How much is here?'

'Ten thousand, I hope. I didn't count it. I want you to invest in one of your money-making ideas. You're not allowed to buy alcohol with it or get a flat. Those are the conditions, OK? You've got to test one of your ideas that never got anywhere because you didn't have the capital. If you make a lot of money you can pay me back. If not, not.'

Trader Ryan looked at the money and then he looked at Fred.

'That's jolly sporting of you.'

'It's a test. Dermot Ryan, sham or shaman? What will you do with it?'

'Oh, it's the options market. I've got it all here.' He waved his copy of the *Financial Times* as if it contained every secret a man could need. His disgruntlement was already a thing of the past as he opened the paper to the relevant page and pointed at a column of tiny figures.

'Trader, you do what you like with it,' Fred told him, moving now from the discomfort which the tent had imposed. 'I always had a weakness for the inflatable crash helmet myself.'

'That may come later. I would need a bit more than ten grand. But with the options market I can increase this stake tenfold and then look at the possibilities.' He gathered up the notes and returned them to the plastic bag, and then hoisted himself up on his knees. 'I'd better go to the bank, a new bank. If Lena gets her hands on this, there'll be a sports car outside.'

They both crawled out of the tent and looked at the house. The blue sky was almost cloudless.

'I wonder if it's safe to go in and shave,' Trader Ryan muttered.

'Who will be holding the razor?' Fred asked.

But then they heard the front door slam and, looking round the side, saw Lena Ryan leave and set off down the road.

'I wonder where she's going?' Trader said. 'She hasn't even got a shopping basket like a proper wife.'

He watched his wife – his new wife – floating towards the town in her pretty new dress and her pretty new hairstyle and fancied that there was even something new about the way that she walked. She seemed to be gliding, as if she would leave no footprints.

Her husband watched her until she disappeared round a corner. 'What's going on, Fred?' he asked. 'My wife's turned into a teenager, you've turned into a millionaire and my nose hurts.'

'That's the colourful pageant of life.'

'Life? It's only temporary, thank God. Well, I must go in and put some scent on my pulse points. Shall I see you in the Cellar at lunchtime? You're going to miss all that.'

'I'd better be there then. But first I've got to sort out what I'm going to pack.'

'Where did you say you were going?'

'Monaco. Monte Carlo to be precise.'

'Racing drivers, tennis stars, shady entrepreneurs involved in off-shore deals. Is that your style?'

Fred shrugged. 'How do I know until I get there?'

# PART TWO

I have never liked working. To me a job is an invasion of privacy.

Danny McGoorty

There is no duty we so much underrate as the duty of being happy.

Robert Louis Stevenson
'An Apology for Idlers'

# FIVE

THE Air France Lockheed Tristar took off at 160 miles an hour and flew south at six miles a minute. Fred, installed uneasily in a plane for only the third time in his life, studied the safety instructions in the seat pocket in front of him, and peered nervously at the billowing clouds which began to thin out once they had crossed the channel.

After 650 miles the plane began to lose height over the Mediterranean but the captain's comments accompanying this alarming development were impossible to hear. Fred watched the approaching sea tensely from his window seat but when a collision between aircraft and water had apparently become inevitable land appeared miraculously beneath the aircraft's wheels and they were on the runway at Nice.

He had hoped to arrive in the brightest sunshine but the delays which were now an intrinsic part of international air travel meant that it was already dark. He stood in the brightly lit airport waiting for his cases, trying to feel like a new man. The humiliation of not being able to buy a friend a drink, the embarrassment of long overdue rent, the shame of grovelling for a job, the frustration of not being able to travel – all this was behind him. Suddenly – uncharacteristically – he had made a quantum leap, a jump into the unknown, his stasis unlocked by money. When his luggage arrived he went out to look for a taxi.

He woke up the following morning in a small bedroom in an hotel at the back of Monte Carlo. He had been dropped there by a taxi driver who knew the place too well to waste time traipsing round the larger hotels, which were usually filled with delegates to one of the huge international conferences that were a feature of Monaco's commercial life.

The cliff-top journey from Nice, which he had been told was a visual treat, had, in the dark, been a mystery tour of darkened rocks and distant beads of lights. Jigging through the crowded streets of Monaco, the taxi driver had offered him the Hôtel Olympia, an old five-storey building in a narrow backstreet. For 200 francs a night Fred had a new home. His room on the third floor had a tiny bathroom attached, a recent conversion that had no room for a bath, only a shower. In the bedroom there was a large built-in wardrobe and a television set high up on one wall with a remote control beside the small double bed. Below the television was an Electrolux fridge, the minibar, which contained beer, fruit juices, Evian water and a small bottle of Bricout champagne.

Fred unpacked, hung up his clothes – a dozen shirts, three pairs of trousers, a suit he had bought and worn only once, at his mother's funeral – and took a shower. Wrestling with strange semi-circular knobs that had to be turned in opposite directions, he felt a great sense of exhilaration at the step he had taken.

He went down to the bar where the only beer came in bottles and two old people sat in armchairs watching television. The gloomy atmosphere was quite at odds with what he had expected to find and after one drink he went back upstairs.

In bed he read a book about Monaco. A sovereign and

independent state for seven centuries, it was the smallest country in the world after the Vatican, with 30,000 people crammed into less than a square mile. Only one in six was a native Monegasque, most were French, and the avaricious eighties had brought in many of the rest in search of tax-free sunshine. The port separated Monaco Ville, the capital of the principality, from the town of Monte Carlo; where rich men's yachts waited today for the occasional appearance of their globe-trotting owners, Caesar's fleet had once waited in vain for Pompey.

The guide book said that Monaco 'laughs with the murmur of sea foam and champagne and bubbles with an infectious feminine gaiety' but all Fred could hear when he awoke next morning was the creaking of cranes and the clanking of scaffolding as more and more buildings were erected in less and less space. The windows of his room, he saw now, opened on to a small balcony overlooking the dusty rue du Marché, the venue of the municipal market where, while he had slept, dozens of stalls had been set up, each apparently selling the same selection of fruit and vegetables.

He found his way downstairs by a succession of button light switches which illuminated the next part of his journey only briefly. The lift seemed to be out of action. In a room on the ground floor which was also the bar two couples sat at tables eating what passed for breakfast in this part of the world: a croissant and coffee. Fred sat at an empty table and was immediately given the same by an elderly man in shirt sleeves who said nothing beyond '*Bonjour*.' Listening to the stilted conversation at the other tables, Fred realized that he would soon be wishing that he had been more attentive at school; but the interminable French lessons had been of such mind-bending boredom that he had taken refuge in the infinitely more relevant *Wizard*, folded discreetly in his lap. At Heathrow he had bought a Berlitz book, *French for Travellers*, to provide him with a few rudimentary words and phrases, but he was determined that language would not be one of his problems. It was his subversive belief that the greatest single legacy of Britain's much-criticized colonial past was that it had taught the rest of the world to speak English.

What *would* be his problems? Homesickness? For what? Boredom? In Monte Carlo? Loneliness? But he had always lived alone – it had once seemed to him to be the best chance of contentment. You did what you pleased without having to defer to someone else's wishes; you went out or stayed in, got drunk or fell asleep, exactly when you wished. Other people's needs or moods were not able to disrupt your independent progress through days designed to please only you. He had never understood why so many people disliked the idea of living on their own.

With the spirit of a pioneer he decided to spend his first day as a tax exile on foot. He picked up a map at the reception desk and went out into the sun for his first look at Monaco. He was in a drab street of old brown residential buildings, their windows balconied and shuttered. He walked along it for some way until he came to dozens of steps that seemed to lead down to the centre of Monte Carlo. The view from here was of flat roofs covered by television aerials and satellite dishes, with the sea beyond and below. He could see already that the town was built on different levels with each parallel street higher than the next. Monte Carlo was concrete clinging to a rock.

He went down 117 steps and found himself in the main street, the boulevard des Moulins, where the same expensive shops that jostled for space in the main streets of larger cities were packed in here between bars and estate agents: Gucci, with costly suitcases you wouldn't care to entrust to any airline, Rodier, Lacoste, and countless *parfumeries*, armed with the magic of Chanel, Nina Ricci and Christian Dior, whose cosmeticians had struggled in obscure laboratories to produce a smell to defeat the sticky environment.

From the shiny red pavement on one side of the street he looked up at twenty-storey apartment blocks with orange sun blinds pulled down over their balconies, and he saw between them other higher buildings erected on a higher level and beyond them the curve of the Alpes Maritimes, which contained the bulging principality on a tiny fragment of coast; on the other side of the street he looked down through man-made canyons at other tower blocks on lower levels. From here, he could look straight into the bedroom of an apartment which turned out to be on the fifteenth floor of a building not fifty yards away.

At one point in this crowded street there was a lift which took you down to sea level. He walked on, reflecting that in most towns you travelled by bus or taxi: in Monte Carlo you travelled by lift. Even the old ladies, he now noticed, had muscular legs, their limbs developed by a vertiginous existence in which even a shopping expedition threatened to pop the ears.

He left the street and cut through some colourful gardens in the direction of the sea. There were exotic trees and ponds amid the sea of flowers. PELOUSE INTERDITE said the notice on the grass.

Wherever he looked towering cranes were swinging overhead. The buildings were going up so quickly that half the postcards were already out of date. The land had run out long ago in this baroque fortress, and the expansion was skyward and seaward. Vast amounts of land had been reclaimed from the sea, apparently by throwing things into it.

He came to an attractive square with the famous ornate casino at the bottom and the Hôtel de Paris looking across more gardens at the Café de Paris on the other side. Here crowds sat under square white sunshades on the terrace having their morning coffee. Churchill, Caruso and the Prince of Wales had dallied here, according to Fred's book. He decided to add his name to the list. The waiters and waitresses all wore black waistcoats, black ties and white aprons, and all the male customers, apart from Fred, had their names on plastic envelopes flapping from their shirts, delegates, evidently, to a business conference. The women were all elegantly dressed in flowery hats, beautifully cut dresses and expensive shoes, with plenty of conspicuous gold jewellery. He was surprised that his coffee only cost 11 francs. When he got up to continue his exploration he discovered that in the hotel opposite a plate of soup could cost 140 francs.

He walked on down towards the sea wondering how he would find the energy to walk all the way back up again. Yamaha scooters zoomed endlessly through the narrow streets, the owners tired of steps and hills. The cars were not at all the luxury limousines that Fred had expected, but small, spotless vehicles more suited to the busy streets. Driving in this congested region was a matter of endless negotiation as motorists conducted signalled discussions with each other about who should now occupy a suddenly empty piece of road. They eased their cars into the flow and then out again, dealing placidly with horrendous junctions that consigned them, usually via a tunnel, to

Italy or France. A wrong turn here and it could be an hour before your loved ones saw you again.

A theatrical impression of Monaco as a stage, with the mountains as backdrop and the unseen audience watching from the sea, was enhanced by the view from the port: the tiny concrete country rose in layers before him until it met the immovable, cloud-topped mountains behind it. The port was a harbour crammed with yachts.

What Monte Carlo lacked, he now realized, was a seafront. How could a town be built on the sea and not have a seafront? There was, according to his map, a small artificial beach at the other end but that hardly seemed adequate. He walked into the tunnel through which he had seen Grand Prix cars hurtle on television and discovered men sitting on the wall fishing for mullet in the clearest sea water he had ever seen. Instead of a seafront there was a tunnel. Below, dozens of people sunbathed on huge blocks of concrete that had been dumped in the sea to protect the harbour wall. Had they become rich so that they could sunbathe on cement, with the smell of boat oil in their nostrils? Le Calypso snack bar had been built near the concrete slabs to cater for these lizards, but this wasn't the picture that Fred had imagined when the Pringle brothers had pressed him to head for the sun. Where were the miles of golden sand, and the golden girls to go with them?

Vague feelings of unease began to stir as he headed back towards the town, sweating now in the clammy heat. The picture of the tax exile as painted by Trader Ryan was beginning to look nearer the truth than his own optimistic vision of sun and fun. He decided that his best route through this mood was via a bar and as he walked up the hill he began to look for one. They were not as plentiful as he had expected and for some time he couldn't find one at all. But then, in a corner jammed with parked cars, he discovered Flashman's English Pub, attached like a wart to the foot of the sandy, 23-storey Banco di Roma tower block. The bar's name, in yellow letters on a deep green awning, seemed like an invitation and he hurried in and climbed on a stool at the counter. A notice on the wall read: 'Plat du Jour – roast pork, 44 francs'.

A tall French girl wearing a diaphanous blouse stood behind the bar shovelling ice cubes into an ice bucket shaped like a top hat. She broke off to serve Fred with a pint of Holsten. The taste, so much nicer than the stuff served up in real English pubs, did much to assuage his growing misgivings.

The bar itself was like any bar at home except that the conversation among the men round the counter seemed to be exclusively about business.

An American wearing a casual open-neck shirt, but who had a very business-like steel brief-case, was saying, 'The market's really weird right now. The yen went crazy last week. With the election coming up, nobody knows what to do.'

He was talking to a fat German who sat on a stool facing him, not speaking very much.

Fred glanced at a postcard that was pinned to the wall beside him: 'Girl needed to live on 22-metre yacht in Cap d'Ail harbour, to do house cleaning during weekdays and cooking when owners come on board at weekends.' This sounded a much more interesting job than a girl might be offered at home, although he could see that there may well be other duties expected of the applicant which had been discreetly omitted.

The American said, 'As they always say on Wall Street,

somebody makes money, somebody loses money.' He had sheaves of paper on the counter in front of him, suggesting that he and the German were involved in a deal. 'I'll get Harvey to call you,' he said. 'He's a man of great integrity and I'll talk to him first. The numbers I have for you in Germany – are they OK?'

When the barmaid answered the phone Fred noticed that there was not only an ordinary phone that she put to one ear but an earpiece that was placed over the other so that she was listening to the caller with both ears. Presumably, in another half century or so, this brilliant idea would reach Britain.

The German climbed off his stool and left the American to shuffle through his papers. Fred, who had not spoken to anybody for more than a day, felt the need for conversation.

'You're obviously not a tax exile,' he said.

'Tax exile?' the American said. 'I work my butt off. Wanna see my schedule?'

He pushed a piece of paper along the counter towards Fred. It consisted of seven columns, each headed by a day of the week and filled with a list of duties and appointments.

'What's that word there?' Fred asked.

The American glanced at the sheet.

'Lavatory,' he said.

'You're not going to the lavatory until seven o'clock next Thursday?'

'Not for any time, no.'

Fred pushed the paper back. He realized, not for the first time, that the human race was something he would never understand. He also realized that there were going to be some people round here who worked very hard indeed: there was so much money in this little country that the rewards for a workaholic must be enormous.

Walking back to his hotel he stopped at the tourist office to pick up a more detailed map of his new home. If he couldn't learn the language, he could learn the streets. Back in a room that had been newly cleaned, he unfolded the map on a bed that had been newly made. It was a new experience for him, this feeling of servants trailing in his wake. Living alone he had – intermittently – cleaned up his own mess. The idea came to him that he could stay in this hotel for a year and never have to make his own bed. It was a small room but already after twenty-four hours it was beginning to feel like home.

But when he studied the map on his bed he received a shock. At first he was amused to discover that this cramped state was so brimful that neither the Monte Carlo Country Club, where the world's best tennis players gathered every year, nor the Monte Carlo Beach Hotel, which was clearly proud of its address, were actually in Monte Carlo, but were stranded beyond the borders in France. And the Monte Carlo Golf Club, for which there would never be room in Monte Carlo, played their games at altitude, in the French mountains to the north.

His mood changed abruptly when he discovered to his horror that he wasn't in Monte Carlo either. Squeezed out at the edges, the Hôtel Olympia was on the wrong side of the road which divided Monaco from France. It was actually in Beausoleil, and it was only when Fred stepped out of the hotel and crossed the narrow, dusty boulevard du Général Leclerc that he had entered the principality.

He wasn't a tax exile at all!

*

The thought that a tax bill for more than half a million pounds would be the penalty for his poor geography galvanized Fred into action that evening. He climbed down the 117 steps to the boulevard des Moulins and headed east. The hotel manager, whose English, it emerged, was a great improvement on Fred's French, had assured him that in this direction lay an English bar called, somewhat unpromisingly, the King's Head. The boulevard des Moulins became the boulevard d'Italie but he walked on past shops, restaurants and sudden, soaring apartment blocks until he crossed a bridge at the border and was in the French village of Roquebrune.

Monaco, whose frenzied drive towards municipal cleanliness was constantly thwarted by its incontinent dogs, nevertheless managed to sparkle beside its litter-strewn neighbour. The dirty brown buildings and dirty streets seemed, with Italy only a few miles down the road, more Italian than French.

The King's Head was a small pink building that, like Fred's hotel, was in France only by a matter of inches: Monaco was just over the road. It attracted its clientele from the mixed crew of *émigrés* who had chosen to work in Monte Carlo. Not having to make a distinction between pay and 'take-home pay' seemed to have cheered them up. It was a bar filled with laughter, bright conversation and the output of Radio Riviera ('good music from San Remo to St Tropez').

Fred ordered a pint of Pelforth Pale and found it so pleasant that he was soon ordering another. By the time he was on his third he felt obliged, contrary to his normal bar practice, to introduce himself to his host. His name was Roy Day and he came from Bristol. He had bought this bar after working for others in Monte Carlo. Roy, who was short and stocky with short fair hair, spent his off-duty hours keeping fit. He played rugby for Monte Carlo and one night a week hired girls to run the bar while he went down to Nice to train.

He was full of valuable advice. 'What you've got to get is a *carte de séjour*,' he said. 'It's like a plastic credit card with your photo on. That's your resident's permit and you won't be a tax exile until you get one.'

Delighted to find himself understood in this Gallic paradise, Fred bought himself another drink. It was something which the climate positively encouraged.

'How do I get one?' he asked.

'First you need an address and a bank statement that you can show the police,' said Roy, who was obviously accustomed to dispensing advice on this subject. 'Then they'll interview you and check that you haven't got a criminal record. They'll check you politically, too. You're not an anarchist, are you?'

'Only mentally.'

'Of course, nobody actually lives here. Monaco's a village. Once they've got a tax-free address they all sod off up the coast to Antibes or St Tropez. You look at some of the apartment blocks at night. There's one across the road where you can live for £1,000 a month. The lights are never on. They're all away.'

'Does it matter?'

'You're supposed to live in Monaco for six months and one day or they take your permit away. The ones who live up the coast come back and get a parking ticket or make a scene in a restaurant to let the authorities know that they're here.'

He moved up the bar to serve a young man clutching a scooter helmet. He turned out, despite his unlikely garb, to be an English lawyer employed by a sinister Saudi conglomerate. In the course of a drink he managed to pass on information too: it was illegal to bounce a cheque in Monaco or drive a dirty car, but seat belts were not compulsory.

Fred looked round the bar. There were many pictures of British sports teams on the wall and one picture of the Queen. In a corner near the counter four French boys were playing darts.

Another young Englishman came in, who was the captain on a rich man's yacht. He had been on what he called 'the milk run', to St Tropez and back.

'They think they'll fall off the world if they go as far as Marseille,' he said. 'Do you know what they all want now? An English captain, a Swedish steward, a German engineer and a French chef.'

Fred pondered this. Most of it seemed to make sense.

'Why do they want a Swedish steward?' he asked.

'The Swedes are good at languages, aren't they?' said the man. 'I suppose they have to be.'

Fred could see a social life developing here. He ordered another pint of Pelforth Pale. Roy said it came from northern France despite sounding so English. Fred took it eagerly. It had never occurred to him during the long years in Britain that the rest of the world was drinking better beer than he was. If only somebody had told him, he would have tried to get here earlier.

Another man came in carrying a scooter helmet. It seemed to Fred that if Trader Ryan's inflatable helmet ever went into production, Monaco's unexpected swarm of scooterists would provide an excellent market.

'I made £13,000 this morning,' he announced. 'Who wants a drink?'

'Roger,' said Roy, 'this is Fred. You can do some business with him.'

Roger was in his thirties and nearly bald. Fred wondered whether the scooter helmet was more to keep his head warm than protect his skull. He shook hands with Fred and paid for a pint for him.

'What can I do for you, sir?' he asked.

'I've no idea,' said Fred. 'What do you do for most people?'

Roy produced what was apparently a standard order for Roger, a rum and coke. 'He works for an estate agent,' he said. 'He'll find you an apartment.'

'Are you looking for an apartment?' asked Roger.

'Urgently,' said Fred.

'To rent or to buy?'

'To rent for one year.'

'What a shame,' said Roger. 'I work on commission. The pay is poor but the commission is wonderful. This morning I sold an apartment to Bjorn Borg and made 13,000 quid.'

'I thought Borg already lived here,' said Fred.

'He was buying it for somebody else.'

Fred was sweating and he was relieved to see that Roger was, too. The humidity was gruesome and not helped at all by a single fan in the bar's ceiling. He could see how with this climate Monaco, on the same parallel as New York and Vladivostok, had, according to something he had read, nevertheless managed to grow Mexican cacti and African euphorbias more than ten metres high. And he ascribed another bizarre physical fact to the weather: although in England three or four pints would have him heading for the toilet, here he could drink five or six pints without even thinking about asking where it was.

Humidity, perspiration and dehydration had produced an undemanding bladder.

'Roy says there are apartments across the road for a thousand a month,' he told Roger. 'That's about my mark.'

It occurred to him that he could afford very much more than a thousand a month if the Pringle brothers were to be relied upon, but spending money was not a talent that he had had much opportunity to develop.

'Park Saint Roman?' Roger said. 'Do you want to have a look? I think I've got the keys with me.'

They put down their drinks and went out of the bar. The skyscraper, separated from them by the bridge, dominated their view from the door. Fred counted twenty-eight storeys but the hill was so steep there could be another ten on the other side if the foundations were lower there.

'I sold an English millionaire two apartments here and he knocked them into one,' said Roger as they walked over the bridge. 'He had a carpet specially made in England to fit the whole place. He didn't want any joins. Of course when the carpet finally arrived they couldn't get it into the lift.'

'What did he do?'

'He hired a helicopter to lower the carpet through his tenth floor balcony. I've still got photographs of it somewhere.'

They walked into the reception area of the block and Roger waved to a security man who was studying a screen.

'Nobody can get in without his approval,' he said. 'There are charges of 1,500 francs a year for security, gardening and the pool.'

The lift seemed to have taken them up four or five floors but when they came out they were already on the roof, gazing across at Italy.

'That moved quickly,' Fred murmured. The view was extraordinary and he felt dizzy. He looked down at the Mediterranean and the twinkling coastline of Monaco, and thought of film footage he had seen of skyscraper fires with the flames creeping upward and the highest inhabitant waiting to fry last.

He was relieved when Roger took him down again to the sixth floor, where they ambled along green-walled corridors until Roger produced his keys and showed him into a one-bedroom flat. It had a large living room with white walls, a small kitchen, a bedroom and a bathroom. From the balcony he could look down at the apartments' private garden where there was a swimming pool.

'Ten thousand francs a month,' said Roger.

'I'll have it,' said Fred.

'Are you a tax exile?'

Fred nodded.

'Well, pay your electricity bill and phone bill on time. It's always a good test for the authorities of whether you actually live here.'

They got back into the lift and this time they plunged five floors below ground level to emerge in an enormous garage, packed with expensive and highly polished cars. As they walked about they broke a beam which turned on lights and cameras.

'We're now being watched by the security man on the screen in reception,' Roger announced. 'The garage is five floors with a spiral ramp. Do you have a car?'

'No,' said Fred.

Roger insisted on showing him the garden and the pool

before they returned to their beer. There was a pool-side bar, sauna and showers, and a special 'dog park' for the residents' pampered pets.

Afterwards in the sudorific hubbub of the King's Head he tried to imagine his life as an expatriate hermit in a sixth-floor cell, its loneliness and its compensations. The loneliness didn't worry him, but the compensations posed challenges that his sudden arrival in a sunny and exotic landscape couldn't hide. There was a beach but he couldn't swim; there were places to go but he couldn't drive. He had spent his entire life accomplishing very little. The years had flitted by and he had never learned to ski or ride a horse. He couldn't play a musical instrument or speak a foreign language. He couldn't even dance.

Suddenly, with all the opportunities that now presented themselves, the feeling of time having been wasted was almost unbearable.

# SIX

HE had been in Monaco for nearly a week when he saw Lena Ryan on the beach.

It had been a week of sitting in offices, filling in forms, signing contracts, and lending Monaco's amiable bureaucracy his passport and his bank statement while they checked his promise that he was neither a bankrupt nor a revolutionary. He found that he had to make lists, and then rearrange the order of the items. The land in Britain couldn't be sold until he had a *carte de séjour*, which legitimized his tax immunity, and he couldn't get that until he had an apartment, which would only become available when he produced a year's rent.

Lloyds Bank ('your partner in the Principality of Monaco since 1924') had big, gloomy offices at 11 boulevard des Moulins. Fred sat waiting on a brown leather chair at a table that was covered with copies of *La Tribune*, a financial paper that he decided to ignore. The dull green carpet had been laid in squares, and on the wooden walls were colour pictures of Prince Rainier and Queen Elizabeth, side by side.

Fred had spent some of his most embarrassing moments in banks and he found it faintly peeving that now that he could finally tell them, with the pent-up fury of the years, what he thought of their miserly behaviour, the staff were all talking in another language, and even non-abusive communication was going to be difficult. In the event they produced a young bilingual Frenchman with a

Chaplin moustache who assured him in nearly flawless English that, following his instructions in England, £50,000 had been transferred to an account for him here, becoming, during the journey, more than half a million francs. A passport and a few signatures would produce a *carnet de chèques* which would enable him to draw on it.

With his resentment dissipated by their cool efficiency, Fred walked out into the street whistling Bach's *Sleepers, Wake!* – a tune the bank had used along with a black horse to burnish its image in television commercials in Britain.

The lift to the beach one hot afternoon dropped him at the end of a spotless tunnel. It looked as if a hundred cleaners slaved here at least twice a day. He walked along it beneath two other parallel streets, one at a lower level than the other and both at a lower level than the street he had left, to emerge on the avenue Princess Grace, a shady, tree-lined boulevard that ran along the foot of this tilting town where it joined the sea. The Larvotto beach, which was only a short walk away, seemed at first to be the golden sand he had been hoping for, but it had actually been created from pebbles so fine that it was hard to tell the difference.

He spread out his towel and removed jeans and shirt to reveal a new pair of black and white striped swimming trunks; their début was greeted by wild indifference from the other sunbathers, many of whom, unlike most of Europe's beach users, read hardback books, breaking off only occasionally to dab themselves with protective cream.

It was a long time since Fred had been to the sea and he could never have imagined that his next visit would be to here. He sat for a while, looking round him. At the back of the beach, below the level of the road, was a row of shops and restaurants. Among them, mysteriously, was a police office. Blue litter bins were everywhere and at the centre of the beach was a select area where you could pay for sunbeds and parasols. Lying on the pebbles Fred wondered whether this wasn't an extravagance he should consider, but he couldn't quite see the logic in coming all this way to find the sun and then paying a lot of money to lie in the shade.

Eventually he fell asleep. He dreamed that he had murdered someone and not been found out so that his life was spent in constant fear of discovery. He awoke disorientated, sat up and saw Lena Ryan. At first he thought she was part of the dream.

She was lying on one of the sunbeds, beneath a red and white sunshade with a drink on a small table beside her. She was wearing a white bikini which, as she hoisted herself up for a drink, looked as brief as a bikini could.

My God, thought Fred. Trader's living in a tent and his wife is in Monte Carlo!

She was with a man who was lying on the next sunbed, but she obscured his view of him. They were talking and laughing and her laughter carried across the beach.

Fred lay and watched them for a while as he disentangled the reality from the dream, but curiosity got him to his feet. They were so preoccupied with their conversation that Fred had reached their sunbeds before they noticed him.

The man was Jeremy Tyrrell, whom Fred had last seen with his arm round Kate Seymour. Today he had one muscular arm draped over Lena Ryan's thighs.

'Fred,' he said. '*Comment ça va?*'

'This is a bit of a coincidence, isn't it?' said Fred, perching on the end of Lena Ryan's sunbed.

Lena Ryan, who now looked like a wise and sexy 25-year-old, shook her head. 'It isn't a coincidence at all, Fred. Dermot told me that you were going to Monte Carlo and I thought, how wonderful, I've always wanted to go there. Two days later Jeremy asked me where I would like to go so I naturally said Monte Carlo.'

'I fancied Angkor Wat or Albania myself,' said Jeremy Tyrrell, 'but this place has its points.'

Fred looked at the pair of them trying to adjust to this new situation. They looked like a couple on honeymoon. Where was Trader? Where was Kate Seymour?

'How long are you here for?' he asked.

'Indefinitely,' said Jeremy Tyrrell promptly. 'We're not tied by time at all.'

Lena Ryan put her top teeth over her bottom lip in an aren't-I-naughty? expression. Jeremy Tyrrell got hold of her thigh.

'Can I borrow your leg for half an hour?' he asked.

'What for?'

'I want to sort of slobber over it.'

Lena Ryan looked as if this was the nicest thing that anybody had ever said to her. Fred was reminded of a mating display by birds in a zoo but then he thought that the animal more properly brought to mind by this scene was a stallion.

'How's Trader?' he asked. 'Is he still in the tent?'

'Do you have to bring him up?' asked Lena Ryan. 'I've no idea how he is but I imagine that he has moved back into the house. What are *you* doing? Have you got an apartment?'

Fred told her what his situation was while Jeremy Tyrrell stroked her leg. He could tell by the dreamy way she said 'Yes' that she had not absorbed the information.

'I think I'm going to love it here,' she said. 'I love Frenchmen, particularly in restaurants. Englishmen shovel it in but a Frenchman makes it a sensual occasion. When an Englishman belches you feel insulted but a Frenchman somehow makes it seem a compliment.' She sat up and took another sip of her drink, which looked like gin. 'Of course my knowledge of France comes from television.'

Jeremy Tyrrell went to pour himself a drink from a Vodka bottle he had half buried in the sand but it was empty.

'I'm going to the bar for a bottle,' he said. He jumped off the sunbed and walked energetically up the beach. His body was already brown from other foreign trips and he had the strong muscular legs of a professional sportsman beneath smart black shorts.

'How old is he, for God's sake?' Fred asked.

Lena Ryan smiled. 'Twenty-four.'

'You found the toy boy you wanted, then.'

'What does any woman want, Fred? A man with a nice face, big willy and lots of money.'

Fred smiled now. 'Is it really as simple as that?' he said. 'Does Dermot know that you're with him?'

She shook her head. 'I left a goodbye note telling him that he'd be hearing from my solicitor. Not that I've actually got one.'

'And how long do you think this is going to last?'

For a moment Lena Ryan's new-found happiness lost some of its potency. 'Who can tell, Fred? He's quite besotted at the moment. He hadn't met a woman before, only girls. "Boring words falling out of beautiful faces" was how he described them.' She smiled an unfathomable smile and sat up. 'I should have done it years ago,' she said. 'When I think of the years I have wasted I could cry.'

Despite feeling sorry for Trader Ryan, who had at odd moments over the years led Fred to believe that he was incurably fond of his wife, Fred couldn't help admiring the way that Lena Ryan had turned up on a Monte Carlo beach at the age of forty with a handsome young lover who seemed to have unlimited financial resources. At the same time he had the darkest misgivings about her prospects. What would happen to her when Jeremy Tyrrell moved on?

She looked round to see where he was, as if she already knew that one day he would be gone. He appeared clutching a bottle.

'*Une vodka*,' he said. '*La mer est très calme*. How's your French, Fred?'

'I'm still memorizing *parlez-vous anglais?*'

'Where do you go here?' he asked. 'Where do you drink?'

'There's a nice English bar called the King's Head on the border in Roquebrune.'

'The King's Head?' said Lena Ryan. 'I haven't come to Monte Carlo to drink in a place called the King's Head.'

'It would be nice to drink in a place where you can understand the conversation, though,' said Jeremy Tyrrell. 'My O-level French is a bit stretched.'

He had, Fred now saw, brought a glass from the bar for him and he poured a third vodka. His manner, which had once seemed to suggest self-satisfaction in odious quantities, had perhaps been tempered by the company of an older woman.

The world was full of Jeremy Tyrrells now – they were the wave of the future. They found life simple and had never faced the problems which once tormented Fred. Girls? Easy. Money? No problem. Career? They were spoilt for choice. Their conversation was strident and buoyed up by a raw confidence that had never seen a doubt. They talked of Charterhouse and speedboats and Lotus cars and referred proudly to their architect-designed houses as if other people's houses had been designed by butchers. Fred did not clamour for their company: there was no greater social danger than an intelligent bore.

But today the man seemed reasonable. Fred took the vodka and asked, 'What happened to Kate Seymour?'

Jeremy Tyrrell pushed his lips together and raised his eyebrows. 'I can't answer that,' he said when the facial activity had finished. 'We left England in rather a hurry.'

'You can say that again,' said Lena Ryan. 'At lunchtime I didn't even have a passport and that evening we were having dinner in the Beach Plaza Hotel just there.' She pointed to a big hotel along the beach. 'It's Trusthouse Forte. Makes you feel quite at home.'

Fred didn't want to discuss this, although he was interested to know that they were staying in a luxury hotel with three swimming pools while he was surviving in a tiny back-street establishment that didn't even have a restaurant.

'What does she do?' he asked.

'Kate? She's a freelance artist – posters, advertisements, that sort of thing. A very talented girl.'

'And beautiful,' said Fred. How an eligible young man like Jeremy Tyrrell could have abandoned the delicious Kate Seymour to decamp even with the new, redesigned Mrs Ryan was a mystery to him, although he had to concede that the latter, with her long, shapely legs, her suddenly sexy eyes and her streaked hair was now the sort of woman who attracted glances. She was also, presumably, the sort of woman who could teach young Jeremy a few things in the bedroom that he wouldn't pick up in the back of his car from an admiring teenager; what he would pick up there these days was more likely to require a painful jab in the buttocks from a doctor's syringe.

'She is beautiful,' he said in his most declarative public-school manner. 'However, she is somewhat mixed up. Her father is a vicar, which is a bit of an impediment in this day and age. The message she gets at home doesn't quite mesh with the message she gets when she goes out. He's in the ice age and she's in the space age.'

'What he's trying to tell you is that she wouldn't sleep with him,' said Lena Ryan. 'She doesn't know what she missed.'

This compliment seemed to disconcert Jeremy Tyrrell, who buried his face in his vodka glass.

'I never kiss and tell,' he said.

'I never seem to kiss,' said Fred.

'And you don't mind telling us,' said Lena Ryan.

Fred drank his vodka and wondered what Kate Seymour was doing back in Britain. He liked what he had heard about her, her artistic ambitions, her self-employed independence, her refusal to succumb to Jeremy Tyrrell's well-bred lust. Cleric as dad was a bit of a downer, but it could have been worse. Some vicars were lively old souls.

Jeremy Tyrrell stood up and ran his hand through his thick black hair.

'I think it's time for a spot of *nage*,' he said. 'Are you coming, Popsy?'

'If that means swimming, I am,' said Lena Ryan. 'Coming in, Fred?'

'Not now. I'm going to investigate the Miami Plage Restaurant. This humidity seems to have stopped me eating.'

Jeremy Tyrrell bowed, very politely. '*A tout à l'heure*,' he said. He put his arm round Lena Ryan and they ran like children towards the water.

A week later Fred woke up in his new apartment and wondered how on earth he was going to fill the year.

It stretched before him now, not exactly like a prison sentence but certainly a challenge of time and survival. He was tempted to draw himself a chart, so that he could tick off the days like a reluctant soldier, but felt that this would be the wrong approach to a year in the sun.

He got out of the new double bed that he had bought in a mood of sexual optimism two days earlier, along with a table, two chairs, a sofa, a television, a cooker and a fridge. A few more shopping expeditions would be necessary before the flat looked like home, although his flat at home had never been exactly crowded with the accoutrements with which people filled their houses.

He went into the bathroom and considered his day. Perhaps, like Philip Larkin, he could read the Bible in instalments each morning as he shaved. When he had dressed he went out on to his balcony and looked down six floors to the swimming pool. Already an elderly couple were sitting in comfortable chairs on the grass. The man was reading a German newspaper; the woman seemed to be writing a letter. Learning to swim, Fred decided, would be a useful early entry on a list of things to do this year. With a swimming pool and little else for recreation it was difficult to see how he could fail.

He made himself some tea and scrambled two eggs, bought during a last minute dash round the Genty supermarket in Roquebrune the previous evening. The first significant omission in his new life hit him now: there was no newspaper to read with his breakfast. He found instead an American paper he had bought yesterday and flicked through its pages as he ate. In the classified columns people were looking for partners.

> Young woman sought who can teach me the difference between synecdoche and metonymy in sensual terms.

Fred wanted a wife but he had never considered this approach. He tried another.

> Tall burly man, forty-one, wants bright, sensuous woman to share his yurt. Must like tennis and yak butter.

It was reading things like this over the years that had contributed to his fatal feeling of estrangement from the rest of the human race; in his younger and more confident years he had no trouble in dismissing it as pretentious guff, but he grew less confident as he grew older – the years had certainly provided no cause for confidence – and now the people who wrote advertisements like this seemed to have taken over the world's reins and it was he who had been left on the sidelines.

His own advertisement for a wife would be a much more straightforward appeal. Since women had publicly sought sex he had rather gone off it – they had taken the thrill out of it. But the right woman would correct that, or so he hoped. His advertisement would steer well clear of synecdoche and metonymy and contain no decrees about yak butter. It would simply describe a girl like Kate Seymour and offer her the earth.

He finished his breakfast, washed up, and wondered what to do. The previous evening, his first in the flat, he had stayed in as a sort of test. The temptation to head for the nearest bar, which from here was the King's Head, was almost overwhelming, but he wanted to adjust to his new home and satisfy himself that he could endure the loneliness without rushing, at every odd moment, to the nearest beer tap. Monte Carlo television was a disappointment. On what was evidently a chat show the guests held their own microphones to their mouths, which rather detracted from the necessary informality of such occasions. In a burst of extravagance he had bought three books: *Richard Burton, My Brother*; *My Husband Rock Hudson*; and *John Lennon, My Brother*. He found that he couldn't read any of them but reflected that if he had any relatives he could have become a writer himself.

But today there were things to be done and he suddenly remembered one of them. He had to let Cedric Pringle know that he was now officially a tax exile, even if it was only by about thirty yards. He had tapped his way through thirteen digits four times before he heard the solicitor's voice.

'Mr Carton, how are you?' he said, as if this was the bright moment in a grey day. 'Also, where are you?'

'I'm in Monte Carlo, Mr Pringle,' Fred told him. 'I have an apartment and a *carte de séjour*, so you can now go ahead with the land sale.'

'That's good news. They are getting a bit impatient. I'll get on to them now. Can you put all your details in the post to me today?'

'Details?'

'Address, phone number, bank address, account number and anything else that might be useful.'

When this chore was behind him Fred decided to use another sheet of paper to brighten Trader Ryan's day.

'Have you mislaid your wife?' he wrote. 'I have found her among the sun-tanned rich, exposing her shapely limbs on a Monte Carlo beach. And there's more. She is Not Alone. Am I telling you more than you want to know? Her appreciative escort is Jeremy Tyrrell. The man you once called "a turgid public-school wind-bag" is now Mrs Ryan's tumescent toy boy. I await your instructions.'

# SEVEN

THE problem was to create an agreeable life in alien territory. His solution was to impose a daily pattern of events on his lonely existence so that appointments appeared at the same time each day providing him with something to look forward to. It was, he thought ruefully, just the sort of standardized routine that he had always avoided by not going to work in England.

At noon he called in at the Bar Tabac on boulevard des Moulins, which sold everything from spaghetti to cigarettes. He sat at one of the small, round marble tables, each bearing a vase with three flowers in it, and drank a coffee. From here he could watch the Yamaha scooters roaring along the street outside, some of them in great danger from the huge air-conditioned coaches which swung in from the east packed with Italian tourists. Friendly but scruffy waiters flirted with elegantly dressed girls who all had long finger nails, jewellery and expensive hair-dos.

There was an elegance about the place that he was only now noticing, some of it imposed from above. From his table in the Bar Tabac he could read a notice on the pavement that said, 'It is forbidden to walk around bare-chested, wearing only a swimming costume or barefoot. Failure to comply with these regulations could result in prosecution.' The notice was in French, Italian, German and English. Fred had now learned that the drivers of dirty cars were stopped in the street and told to get them cleaned, and that at one time back-packing tourists had been intercepted at the station and shown the way back to France. This last restriction had now been relaxed, perhaps with the realization that these enterprising youngsters would sooner or later include among their number a future president of the United States. But every morning the police dropped last night's alcohol victims on the border like rubbish that was more suitable for France.

Monaco was a benevolent dictatorship ruled by a mysterious council of government under the authority of a 65-year-old Prince who had been educated and abused at an English public school and got his own back by marrying a beautiful American film star. Fred felt that he now knew all there was to know about the place except how long he could stand it. He lacked the props and comforts that he had relied on in England: the television, the library, the Cellar Bar, the possibility of a friendly face in the street, even, occasionally, a party.

When the English newspapers arrived on the news-stand outside he rushed out to buy one as if it were a letter from home and then read it over his coffee. Today the main story on the back page was about an England footballer who, after a clash of personalities with his manager – a hard enough thing to imagine in the monosyllabic world of football – had been transferred the previous year to Monaco and played in the French first division. His problem now was that his three-year £1 million contract was endangered by his wife's homesickness. She craved, apparently, for the organized gloom of British department stores, Australian soap operas on television and damp chats with friends on pavements. The footballer seemed prepared to forgo the millionaire status his boots had provided in the interests of domestic peace.

Fred was vastly cheered by this story. He was not going

to be ranked with the footballer's wife who preferred poverty in the rain to affluence in the sun; the tale stiffened his resolve.

He decided that it was time he saw the palace where the man in charge lived. He went out, crossed the road and got on one of the many single-deck buses that the residents of this hilly neighbourhood relied upon. As it carried him down the avenue d'Ostende towards the port, he thought: travelling by bus? The metamorphosis into rich young man hadn't even begun to happen. Once a peasant, always a peasant.

The bus swept round the harbour and climbed the steep hill up the peninsula rock on the top of which Monaco Ville, the old town that was the capital of the Principality, perched. It was here that Prince Rainier's palace, built on the site of a thirteenth-century fortress, attracted tourists from all over the world; there were hundreds of them milling about now. Palace guards in white uniforms patrolled the front but the marauding throng who beat a path to the royal threshold were armed only with cameras and wherever Fred walked he seemed to encroach on some tourist's viewfinder. Soon he was pressed into service himself to snap kissing honeymoon couples who hadn't brought their photographer with them, and doughty Japanese ladies, evidently travelling alone, who smiled inscrutably with the palace as their background. Without its red and white striped sentry boxes out front, the sprawling palace could have been taken for a luxury hotel in the Scottish Highlands.

The old town was cooler than Monte Carlo, its narrow streets amply shadowed by fine old buildings that were elegant, clean and full of history. Fred walked past shops that all seemed to be selling souvenirs – plates, ashtrays, sun-hats, shirts – and then found the spotless white nineteenth-century cathedral, where thirty-two years earlier David Niven, Ava Gardner, the Aga Khan and King Farouk had attended the royal wedding, and where, only six years ago, a later raft of celebrities, including Nancy Reagan and Princess Diana, had attended the royal funeral. Pictures of the woman who was once Grace Kelly were to be seen everywhere, even in bars, as if the Monegasques were reluctant to let her go.

From the edge of the rock nearby Fred looked down on a new town built round a new port on land reclaimed from the sea. New twelve-storey buildings, the colour of sand, already had trees on their roofs and underground car parks, and he gazed in wonderment at what men could achieve if there was money behind them.

Later, when he was waiting at the bus stop, he remembered that he had money behind him, too. He crossed the road and got in a taxi.

One evening, propelled by a thirst which the humidity had magnified to epic proportions, he made a fast descent in the lift and went in search of a pint of Pelforth Pale. Crossing the bridge into France, he looked up at Mont Agel on his left, a towering mini-mountain three quarters of a mile high. It was while driving down its hairpin bends in her Rover 3500 that Princess Grace had careered off the road to land upside down in a vegetable garden.

In the King's Head Jeremy Tyrrell, wearing a garish shirt, was telling a couple of customers about the time that he had snow blindness in the Bernese Oberland. Lena Ryan, incredibly, now looked even younger in a green T-shirt and very short red skirt that revealed most of her newly brown legs. If this trend continued for much longer, Jeremy Tyrrell would be wheeling her around in a pram.

'The very man,' he said, when Fred came in. 'We were hoping to find you here.'

Fred ordered a pint from a German girl behind the bar. 'Where's Roy?' he asked.

'Training for a fun run,' she told him. She had a big nose and small eyes, the opposite of what he was looking for.

'We have a problem,' said Lena Ryan. There were no stools at the bar but she had fetched two small ones from the tables in the room and put one on top of the other to make a bar stool. 'We thought you could help.'

Fred drank an inch or two of his pint, liquid his body wanted urgently. Some residents in the apartment block, he had noticed, even had fans on the ceilings of their balconies.

'You know me,' he said. 'Helpful Harry.' He could see that he was about to enjoy a new experience: somebody was going to ask *him* to lend money. They could hardly imagine what pleasure he was going to get from being on the other side of this familiar negotiation.

'You've lost your travellers' cheques,' he said. 'How much do you want to borrow?'

'Borrow?' said Jeremy Tyrrell. 'That *will* be the day. No, it's Kate Seymour.'

'Kate Seymour?' said Fred.

'She's coming out,' said Lena Ryan.

'Coming out?'

'You don't have to repeat everything, Fred. You look as if somebody has hit you over the back of the head with a cricket bat.'

'Sorry. Kate Seymour is coming to Monaco? Have I got it right?'

'That's it.'

'Why?'

'I think she's after his body.'

'There seem to be some gaps in this story,' said Fred. The lawyer came into the bar clutching the statutory scooter helmet. He waved to Fred, who waved back, delighted that people who lived here were beginning to acknowledge him.

Jeremy Tyrrell took Fred's empty glass from his hand, looking slightly stunned at the speed at which its contents had vanished. When he returned it, newly filled, he said, 'She rang my parents to see where I was and my mother gave her the name of the hotel.'

'Didn't your mother tell her that you were here with Lena?'

'That wasn't a piece of information that was in her possession.'

'I see,' said Fred.

'So Kate says, "I'll fly down for the weekend to see him" and my mother says, "That would be nice, dear. Give him our love." She rang me this evening to give me the good news. By that time Kate had rung again to say that she was booked on the Air France flight that comes in on Friday evening.'

'And his mother says, "I'm sure Jeremy will meet you at the airport,"' said Lena Ryan, looking vexed.

'Now you see the problem,' said Jeremy Tyrrell.

Having Kate Seymour fly down to meet you in the south of France didn't sound like much of a problem to Fred, but he nodded sympathetically and drank his beer.

'Tell me, Jeremy, old boy, what's your secret? Is it money, is it your looks, is it your wonderful accent?'

'It's that he actually likes women,' said Lena Ryan. 'Not many men do.'

Fred frowned. 'Is that true?'

'Oh, they like creature comforts, they like having an attractive servant around. They thoroughly approve of sex. But they don't actually enjoy a woman's company. They'd much rather talk to a man. Well, Jeremy wouldn't, and women can always tell.'

The hiss of the Italian coffee machine, suddenly called into service, prevented Fred consulting Jeremy Tyrrell about the truth of this, but he could understand that after years of marriage to Dermot, Lena Ryan would find an attractive male a bit of a novelty.

'We were rather hoping,' said Jeremy Tyrrell, looking embarrassed, 'that you could help us out.'

Jeremy Tyrrell looking embarrassed was a difficult thing to imagine, thought Fred, like Ronald Reagan ironing shirts or the Queen throwing a javelin. But for a moment his confidence had deserted him.

'How could I do that?' he asked.

'Meet her,' he replied immediately. 'Go to Nice and meet her off the plane.'

'It wouldn't be any good,' said Fred. 'She knows what you look like.'

Jeremy Tyrrell started to explain and then saw that Fred was joking.

'Will you do it? Meet her and explain the position?'

'Isn't that your job?' Fred asked. He didn't want to be too persuasive: going to Nice to meet Kate Seymour was the best assignment he had ever been offered.

'I haven't invited her down,' he said. 'I'm not responssible for her coming here. But if she gets to the hotel and meets Lena, she's going to be pretty upset.'

'I'm not going to be all that thrilled,' said Lena Ryan. 'Intercept her, deflect her, seduce her. Just keep her away from the Beach Plaza.'

Fred was beginning to like the sound of this mission, but he wasn't going to show it. 'Why don't you ring her?' he asked.

'There's no phone in her studio. She can't stand interruptions when she's working. It's too late to reach her with a letter and fax machines aren't her style.'

'And how do you think she's going to react, expecting Jeremy and finding me?'

'That will depend on how charming you are, Fred,' said Lena Ryan. 'You could take her mind off things.'

'Take her to the Art Centre to see the Nelson Rockefeller collection,' said Jeremy Tyrrell. 'She'll like that. Take her to the national museum to look at the dolls. Take her to Cannes.'

'Take her to bed,' said Lena Ryan. 'She's not ugly, is she?'

'No,' said Fred. 'She's not ugly.'

The venture, despite its attractions, could be a disaster, he thought. Kate Seymour could resent his intervention and take a dislike to him that she might not otherwise have had. On the other hand, stranded alone on the Côte d'Azur, she might see him as her knight in shining jeans.

'I'll meet her,' he said. 'What do I tell her?'

'Tell her I'm here with a lady. Explain that I'm unable to meet her.'

'Will she burst into tears?'

'Not Kate,' said Jeremy Tyrrell. 'I'm very grateful to you, Fred. Let me buy you another drink. Popsy and I are off to the open-air cinema at the Monte Carlo Sporting Club. Do you fancy coming?'

'I'll have the drink instead,' said Fred. 'I prefer novels to films. You don't get that awful background music.'

An hour later he left the bar and headed for his apartment. It was an hour in which he had imagined every possible sequel to the arrival of Kate Seymour, from hysteria at the airport to their own decorous wedding in Antibes.

He walked into the apartment block's reception area and was beckoned by the security man at the desk.

'*Il y a un ami anglais qui vous attend là-bas pour vous voir*.' he said.

Fred struggled to translate this with the small amount of French that he was now dutifully absorbing from his Berlitz book each morning, but the guard was already pointing to a seat across the hall where what looked like a genuine French *clochard* was sprawled, asleep. Fred walked towards him, and realized that it was Trader Ryan, who opened one eye and looked up at him.

'I thought you'd turn up sooner or later,' Fred said.

'*Je suis le mauvais* penny,' said Trader Ryan.

By the time they had reached Fred's apartment he had woken up. He darted from one room to the next, weighing up the accommodation.

'Bit spartan for a millionaire, isn't it?' he said. 'Why don't you get some pictures on the wall?'

'I haven't been here five minutes,' Fred protested. 'And I don't want to overload the place. I'm only here for a year. But I've got a blanket – you can sleep on the sofa.'

Trader Ryan sat on the sofa as if to test it. 'Any coffee?' he asked.

He followed Fred into the kitchen while he made it. 'I hope you don't mind me busting in on you? Your letter was a bit of a shock. I was certain that Lena had gone to stay with her mother.'

'It's good to see you,' Fred told him. 'But what are you going to do now that you're here?'

'I'm going to talk to my wife.'

'I saw her this evening. She seems remarkably fond of her toy boy.'

'The malignant little turd. He's looking for a kick up the terminal part of his large intestine. It could be a cement boots job.'

Fred carried the coffee into the living-room and they sat down at the table.

'Actually I'm protecting my position,' said Trader Ryan. 'It will look good if it's going to come to court. "He flew to the south of France in a desperate attempt to save his marriage, but found his wife in bed with a man sixteen years her junior." You'll need an umbrella to keep the tears off.'

Fred drank his coffee and looked at Trader Ryan. He seemed a lot healthier than when he was living in a tent.

'I take it you've moved back into the house,' he said. 'How's life on your own?'

'Apart from ending up with an odd sock every time I go to the launderette it's all right. I didn't mind sleeping in the tent actually. Did you know that thirty-five million Chinese still live in caves?'

Fred shook his head very solemnly. 'No, I didn't know that, Dermot,' he said. He was wondering what sort of reception Trader Ryan would get from his wife. She could hardly start throwing microwave ovens about in the Beach Plaza Hotel, but his sudden appearance would surely count among history's more unwelcome arrivals, somewhere just below the Black Death.

'What's it like here anyway?' he asked. 'How are you settling down?'

'It's going fine.'

'Beautiful women, cantilevered sexpots, topless table tennis on the beach? I'm a bit partial to the alfresco bonk myself. I'm so mired in domesticity that I've missed out on these things.'

The following morning he had cheered up. The bright sunshine poured on to the balcony and flooded the room, and from the balcony he could see a pure blue sky and a blue sea. He folded up the blanket, went into the bathroom to wash and then banged on Fred's bedroom door.

'*Petit déjeuner, monsieur, s'il vous plaît.*'

Fred came out.

'Your French is good,' he said. 'Let's hear some more.'

'*Beaujolais Nouveau. Un rapide saut.*'

'What does that mean?'

'A quick jump. *Blau travail.* Blow job. Do you think it means the same in France?'

'I expect you'll find out. Have you just farted?'

Trader Ryan looked hurt. 'Of course I've just farted. You don't think I smell like this all the time, do you? I spend the first ten minutes of every day picking my nose and farting. I thought everybody did.'

'I can see that sharing a flat with you is going to be a wonderful experience. What do you want to eat?'

'Tea and toast,' said Trader Ryan, wandering out again on to the balcony. The suitcase he had brought with him lay open on the floor, revealing a selection of brightly coloured summer shirts, a pair of jeans, some swimming trunks, a few books and a pair of espadrilles.

'I said toasted, not cremated,' he said when Fred produced breakfast. 'What's the tea? Darjeeling from the Himalayan hills? Oh no, tea bags.' He sat down and started to eat. 'Judging by the ladies round the pool below there are money-making possibilities here.'

Fred took the top off his egg. 'Like what?' he asked.

'A couple of juggernauts packed with depilatory cream for hirsute continental ladies looks like an earner to me.'

'Talking about money-making possibilities, what has happened to the ten grand?'

Trader stopped eating. 'I'm glad you asked me that. It's all invested in traded options. I went to see a man I know.'

'A man?'

'An expert in London. Once he'd got over the initial shock of discovering that I'd got ten grand he was quite helpful.'

This news was a relief to Fred who had, in his darker moments, imagined the money leaking away on ephemeral pleasures, most recently an air ticket to Nice. 'What have you invested in?' he asked.

'A Racal company,' said Trader Ryan. 'I chose them because their boss Ernie Harrison lives down the road. The shares were £2.40 and going up so I got an option to buy 200,000 shares at £2.60 between now and September at a cost of 5p each. Total: £10,000.'

'I hope you know what you're doing.'

'I may have to become a tax exile myself.'

There was a piercing shriek from the wall, which turned out to be the telephone. For a moment Fred wondered what it was. He had not received any phone calls and the noise sounded like a fire alarm.

'Mr Carton?' said a distant voice. 'It's Cedric Pringle. I

thought you'd like to know that the million and a half has arrived.'

'Oh, good,' said Fred, as if this was the sort of amount of money that reached him every day.

'I'll get £500,000 credited to your account in Monaco, and my brother will set about investing the rest.' Fred nodded, a useless gesture on the phone, but Mr Pringle was still talking. 'I believe that he will have to invest abroad. Apparently there is a danger that you could still be taxed on income arising from this country, so we won't risk that.'

'I should hope not,' said Fred.

'How's Monte Carlo?'

'Very sunny.'

He put the phone down and said, 'I'm now officially rich. Houses are about to grow in Kent.'

'Why don't you take me out and show me this place?' said Trader Ryan. 'You can afford to buy me lunch.'

'Put your walking shoes on,' said Fred.

As they went down in the lift Trader Ryan had an idea. 'Do you think I might meet a svelte, lissom mademoiselle who goes like 50,000 rattlesnakes?'

'There are women here,' Fred told him.

Trader Ryan seemed encouraged by this news.

'What I'd really like is a woman who would show some enthusiasm about my willy. My willy has had all the apathy it can take.'

'What does it want – a round of applause?'

'It wants to be made to feel important.'

'Well,' said Fred, 'perhaps it isn't important.'

'You try telling *it* that.'

# EIGHT

THE casino was a marble palace that was curiously at odds with its ritzy reputation. Where they had expected to find men in dinner jackets sipping champagne while they played *chemin de fer*, they found tourists in shorts eating hamburgers and playing fruit machines. What had once been the fashionable gaming centre of Europe now seemed to be a *fin de siècle* amusement arcade.

They had reached the casino after a tour of Monaco that had left Trader Ryan breathless for more. He had taken to its curving hills, its *belle époque* architecture and its carefully created compactness that had produced a tiny land of fun between the mountains and the sea. They had walked down the avenue des Spélugues, looking at the night-clubs that would open much, much later, and strolled through the gardens opposite them eating a *croque monsieur*.

'I've always regarded eating in restaurants as the height of extravagance,' said Fred. 'Why pay £50 for a meal you can do yourself for a fiver?'

'It's a strange thing to hear from a millionaire and a dismal one if the bloke is your host,' said Trader Ryan.

'I keep forgetting. I'll buy you dinner tonight. What do you want to do this afternoon? There's a golf course up in the hills.'

'I can't hit a cow's arse with a banjo,' said Trader Ryan. 'Let's go to the casino. To be in Monte Carlo and not visit the casino would be like going to Agra and not seeing the Taj Mahal.'

They had to show their passports and pay 50 francs before they were allowed past the fruit machines and into the *salon de roulette*.

The gambling rooms were sumptuously decorated with golden pillars and chandeliers; painted, unclad nymphs floated around on the ornate ceiling smoking cigarillos.

They chose the cheapest table, where the minimum stake was 20 francs, and sat down. Fred put piles of chips on to even bets and won and lost, but Trader Ryan, less cautious, was going for the numbers which, if they won, paid thirty-five times the stake money.

When a woman opposite him won on twenty-two, a black number that was right in front of him, he watched the croupier push the pile of winnings towards her with his rake and decided that he liked the number, too. He put his 20-franc chip on twenty-two and winked at Fred.

'*Rien ne va plus*,' said the croupier and the only sound was the little white ball spinning in the wheel. It slowed and dropped into twenty-two.

'I think I've got a new money-making idea,' said Trader Ryan, as the rake pushed 700 francs in his direction. He decided to play with the casino's money and sprinkled 200 francs over the table on numbers and *chevals*.

He sat back to see what fate had in store but realized that there was a hiatus in the proceedings. The wheel was not being spun.

'Of course it was mine,' the woman opposite said. 'I always repeat a winning bet.' She was speaking English, but she was not English. Trader Ryan thought for some reason that she was Dutch. She was about fifty, expensively dressed and obviously known to the croupier.

'You may well have had that intention, madame, but

you did not give any such indication.' The croupier, a small, vulpine man, spoke a strangely stilted English.

'I saw there was a chip on twenty-two and assumed it was mine,' said the woman angrily.

'It was with the monsieur over there whom I have paid,' said the croupier.

'But that was a mistake,' said the woman. 'It was my chip.'

Trader Ryan didn't like the sound of this, and neither did Fred. He wasn't yet sure who was at fault but he was beginning to think that to take Trader Ryan into a casino was not the best idea he'd had.

The croupier hesitated, but now turned to Trader Ryan. 'Monsieur, I am sorry but there has been a mistake. I paid you incorrectly. It is for madame.'

'It is most certainly not madame's chip,' said Trader Ryan. For a moment Fred thought that he might try to turn the table over. Instead, he broke into French: '*C'est à moi!*'

The woman tried some French herself on hearing this. '*Donnez-le-moi!*'

The croupier now stood up and came over to Trader Ryan. He was accompanied by the man whose job it was to supervise the table.

'Give me the chips,' he said.

Trader Ryan gathered up the chips and put them in his pocket. Fred put his hand on his shoulder and said, 'For God's sake don't hit him. You could disappear for months.'

Two other men now appeared beside the two who wanted the chips. The new arrivals were somewhat larger than their colleagues. They helped Trader Ryan to his feet and frog marched him to the cash desk.

'Give us the chips,' said one of them.

'Piss off,' said Trader Ryan. 'I demand to see the inspector.' He turned to Fred. 'Do they have an inspector in these places?'

'I believe they do,' said Fred. 'Stick to your guns, kid.'

'What I really want is to hit him.'

'Hitting him is a very bad idea.' Seeing the frustration which this produced, he added reassuringly, 'You can always hit him outside later.'

A conversation among the casino officials while this was going on now produced an invitation into the inspector's office. They were led into a small room where a man who did not seem over-worked sat at a grey metal desk. The inspector demanded to see his passport.

'Monsieur Ryan, you have been cheating at the casino and you are banned for life,' he announced. 'First, hand back your chips. Then you leave the premises.'

Trader Ryan tried to remember some French phrases he had been studying for his visit. '*Je voudrais me faire raser*,' he said. He realized too late that he had asked for a shave.

'You will be fined ten times the amount you won,' said the inspector, ignoring this incomprehensible stab at his own language. 'I shall call the police.'

'*Pas de problème*,' said Trader Ryan, glad to make up for his mistake by updating the Monegasques on the use of the English vernacular.

While they were waiting for the police, the inspector photocopied the passport and put Trader Ryan's details on the casino's records.

The policeman was a tall young man who looked as if he had been here before.

'Where are the chips?' he asked in English.

Trader Ryan took them from his pocket and scattered them on the desk.

'There are only 500 francs,' said the inspector, laying them out.

'I had put 200 on the next spin,' Trader Ryan told him.

'What happened?' the policeman asked.

Trader Ryan told him the sequence of events. The policeman listened to this and nodded. Then he turned to the inspector.

'What's your name?' he asked.

The question seemed to rattle the inspector.

'You know me,' he said. 'I'm the inspector of the casino. You don't need to ask my name.'

A lengthy silence followed this as the policeman sat in judgement on the situation. Somehow, mysteriously, he reached the right decision. He made a gesture to the inspector.

'Give him the money,' he said.

Within a couple of minutes the 500 francs had been brought out from the cash desk and given to Trader Ryan. The inspector looked as if he was about to be taken seriously ill.

'Good afternoon, gentlemen,' said Trader Ryan, and followed Fred out of the office.

'You haven't been in Monte Carlo twenty-four hours and you're banned for life from the casino,' said Fred when they were outside. 'What are you going to do next?'

'Disembowel my wife,' said Trader Ryan.

In Le Gratin restaurant at the Beach Plaza Jeremy Tyrrell and Lena Ryan were having dinner – roast duck with peach and brandy sauce. They had moved their places so that they were no longer sitting opposite each other, but side by side. Earlier they had caught the train to Italy and strolled through the old streets of Ventimiglia, which provided a stark contrast to the polished refinement of its neighbour, Menton, on the French side of the border. Now they sat side by side and, occasionally, hand in hand, relaxing after a tiring day.

'This is the life, Popsy,' said Jeremy Tyrrell.

She loved his confidence and his youthful enthusiasm and wanted to share them but sometimes the gaping chasm of their ages prevented her from matching his exuberance.

'How long can it last?' she asked. That he could fly off at the age of twenty-four with a woman of forty with no thought of tomorrow still surprised her, although she knew now that he was older than his age, quite accustomed to choosing the most interesting option and pursuing it with an assurance and self-possession that came from his upbringing, his education or his money, or, quite possibly, from all three.

'It will last as long as we want it to last,' he said, pouring her some more wine. 'One of these days I shall be dragged screaming into the family firm and not let out until I'm seventy. I've promised my father to start taking it seriously at thirty.'

'He sounds very understanding.'

'He's ahead of his time, my old man. I think he regrets the youth he never had. He went into an office at eighteen and didn't even get abroad until he was thirty-six. Be happy is what he's always told me: "Life's too bloody short to economize on happiness, son."'

Lena Ryan loved his voice. It wasn't exactly posh, but it was loud and clear and correct. She could imagine him reading the news.

'What is the business exactly?' she asked.

'A printing works,' he said.

'You know about printing, do you?'

'Among other things.'

'What else?'

'I know about the great vowel shift of the fourteenth century and how to scramble eggs.'

'I'm speechless.'

'I like that in a woman.'

A waiter in a white jacket arrived to take their plates and, spotting a crumb, removed it. He produced a menu with a flourish and they both chose gâteau.

'Do you think your friend Fred will go to Nice Airport?' Jeremy Tyrrell asked when the waiter had gone. 'What does that bloke do, anyway?'

'Oh, I think he'll turn up all right. I saw a light in his eye when the name Kate Seymour was mentioned.'

'Why do they call him Cardboard Fred?'

'The man I am currently married to came up with that. His surname is Carton, although I think Dermot had rather more in mind when he coined the nickname. A certain vulnerability, the opposite of an iron man. He's the sort of chap who becomes depressed when he reads about an atrocity on the other side of the world. Most people take it in their stride; Fred takes it personally.'

'And what does he do?'

'He's done a bit of everything but nothing very much. He never really got into gear. But he's rich now. He was left some land. Do we have to talk about him?' She put out her hand and covered his and then, looking over his shoulder, saw her husband and Fred coming into the restaurant.

'My God,' she said. 'He's here.'

From the door of the restaurant Trader Ryan had seen his wife in a strapless black evening dress holding hands with the boy from Charterhouse, looking into his eyes, asking questions. Her face was as brown as he had ever seen it. Jeremy Tyrrell, in a light grey suit, white shirt and green patterned tie, was giving her all his attention.

'Let's join them,' said Trader Ryan. 'They've got two spare chairs.'

Fred, having promised his guest dinner, had been dragged here reluctantly, feeling that food and drama were best kept apart. But Trader was adamant that he must see his wife, that was why he was here, and the hotel was the only place that he could be sure of finding her.

He followed Trader across the crowded room and tried to compose his features into an expression that would conceal his anxiety about this misguided errand. When Trader Ryan arrived at the table he smiled down at the two diners, pulled back one of the empty chairs and sat down.

'Well, hallo,' he said.

Fred, embarrassed now, sat on the other chair and nodded at the couple whose cosy dinner had been so brutally interrupted. But Lena Ryan ignored him. She was looking at her husband with a mixture of incredulity and loathing.

'What do you want?' she asked eventually.

'What do I want?' said Trader Ryan. 'I want to know what you're up to, lover. I seem to remember that we got married. I've come to take you home.'

Fred heard this with a sense of shock. To see the man who had posed as a reluctant and ill-treated husband now assume the role of suppliant was not a development that he had expected. He looked at Jeremy Tyrrell and was astonished to see how calm he was: he looked as if he had been temporarily cornered by the office bore.

'Take me home?' said Lena Ryan, her voice raised just a little. 'If you take me home it will be in a coffin.'

Trader Ryan's face lost some of its initial cheerfulness at this. 'You think I'm going to let you run off with a randy teenager, do you?' he asked. 'I can see that you're getting younger every week but you're going to have to go some to catch him up.'

'You don't have to be abusive, Dermot. You just have to piss off,' said Lena Ryan. 'Why on earth are you here, anyway?'

Trader Ryan laid his hands flat on the table and looked into his wife's eyes – his wife's post-coital eyes, he now saw.

'I'm here to save my marriage, dear,' he said mildly. 'It's what devoted husbands do. Get your things, pack your bags and we'll go home. We all make mistakes. I've made a few myself.'

Lena Ryan wasn't listening to most of this.

'Save your marriage?' she said with a bitter laugh. 'When did you care about your marriage? You've treated me like a skivvy for twenty years.'

'I've looked after you for twenty years, Lena,' said Trader Ryan. 'I've fed you and clothed you and made you laugh. You don't think this public-school Lothario is going to look after you for twenty years, do you? When he's my age you'll be sixty.'

This shaft, touching on Lena Ryan's darkest fears, went in deeply.

'You drunken, disgusting bastard,' she said quietly. 'How could you hope to understand?'

For a moment they seemed to have run out of steam.

Fred said, 'Where's my dinner? We don't appear to be getting any service.'

'You won't,' said Jeremy Tyrrell, glad to find a conversation that he could join. 'You have to wear a suit in here.'

Fred looked round and suddenly realized how out of place he and Trader Ryan were, in their open neck shirts and old jeans. Dressing for dinner, an occasion which to be really enjoyed required comfort and informality, had always struck him as such a foolish idea that he had forgotten people did it.

Trader Ryan was not deflected by this peripheral chat. He looked at his wife but she refused to meet his gaze, staring instead at the gâteau that she had never started.

'Oh, I understand,' he said. 'I understand, you ungrateful slag. You're after sex and money before it's too late.'

'You filthy, revolting slob,' she said, not as quietly as before.

Trader Ryan leaned forward on the table. 'Listen to me, you rancid old crone. If you walk out on me now, you'll get nothing. Nothing from me and nothing from him.'

'Christ, that's a laugh,' she said, not laughing. 'What did I ever get from you apart from headaches, insults and ingratitude? Go home, you obnoxious pig, and give me some peace.'

'You venomous tart!'

'You odious creep!'

'You poisonous bitch!'

Adjectives hurtled across the table inflicting bruises that nobody could see. Fred had to admire the way that Jeremy Tyrrell's sang-froid remained intact during this fracas.

'Forty-thirty,' said Fred.

'Whose serve is it?' asked Lena Ryan.

'Yours.'

'You're a vulgar, moronic drunkard who should be living in a bus-shelter.'

The adjoining tables were occupied by a convention of Renault salesmen, who were slowly abandoning their own conversation in favour of something more interesting.

'I don't think she likes you,' said Fred.

'May I suggest you go now?' Jeremy Tyrrell asked politely. 'This doesn't seem to be leading anywhere.' It was as if he had been the phlegmatic chairman presiding over this contretemps and had now decided to call order.

'Don't suggest anything,' said Trader Ryan. 'When I've finished suing you for alienating my wife's affection you'll be taking evening classes on how to cut your throat.'

'It doesn't appear to me,' said Jeremy Tyrrell calmly, 'that there was any affection to alienate.'

Perhaps feeling that the debate had been thrown open to the floor, Lena Ryan turned to Fred. 'Can you imagine sleeping with him?' she asked. 'When he was drunk it was like being assaulted by a kangaroo.'

This was more than any of them wanted to hear, particularly Trader Ryan.

'You treacherous cow,' he said, as if his armoury of abuse was nearly depleted. 'Go home in a coffin? With your spreadeagled legs it will have to be one of Joe Orton's Y-shaped coffins.'

Trader Ryan's instinct, which he had brought with him to this table, was that here at least, in this decidedly classy restaurant, she couldn't throw a microwave at him or hit him with a sauce bottle. It had given him freedom to talk without fearing the violent reprisals which had so often disrupted conversations at home. But his confidence on this subject was founded on the thinnest of ice, and his final fusillade seemed to tip some balance in Lena Ryan's mind. In one swift movement – the more dexterous because she avoided soiling her own black evening dress – she slipped her hand beneath the plate that contained her uneaten gâteau, upturned it in mid-air and placed it, none too gently, on Trader Ryan's head.

The hush which had slowly grown at the surrounding tables was broken now by titters of laughter and, in certain appreciative quarters, robust applause.

Trader Ryan sat motionless for several seconds, and then slowly, as if he was very tired, took the plate from his head and put it on the table. His hair had been replaced by a curious *mélange* of cream, cherries, apricots, sponge and almonds.

'I take it,' he said eventually, 'that you're not coming home?'

'That seems to be the gist of it,' agreed Jeremy Tyrrell.

'Not now, not ever,' said Lena Ryan.

Trader Ryan turned to Fred. A piece of apricot slid slowly down one cheek.

'Do you fancy a drink?' he asked.

'You're psychic,' said Fred.

The two of them got up and left the restaurant without another word.

'Well,' said Jeremy Tyrrell when they had gone, 'what would you like to do now?'

'I think I'll have some gâteau,' said Lena Ryan. 'It looked rather good.'

In the King's Head an hour later, his hair still wet from a

quick shampoo, Trader Ryan said, 'I'm sorry for her really. What sort of future does she face?'

'One that she expects to be an improvement on her past, apparently,' said Fred. 'I sort of got that impression. You surprised me. You seemed so keen to get her back.'

Trader Ryan looked down at his pint of Pelforth Pale and nodded to himself. 'I'll miss her. I admit it. When you've been married for twenty years you get used to each other. I honestly thought she was enjoying herself. I thought she thought life was fun, like I do.' Now he shook his head. 'She was all right until she read that book.'

'I was also surprised,' Fred told him, 'that you didn't direct any of your fire towards Jeremy Tyrrell.'

'I'm not that much of a hypocrite. It's a man's job to chase women, a little duty imposed on him by nature. It's a burden I have always borne myself with great fortitude. But it's the woman who decides what happens next.'

'I see. That way you can always blame the woman?'

'Well, the woman is always to blame, isn't she?' he said, as if this were a self-evident truth requiring no further discussion.

'The woman must have standards, but men don't need any? I can see why Lena took to that book. The idea that your behaviour caused her behaviour hasn't crossed your mind.'

'Listen, you sex-starved ectomorph,' said Trader Ryan, waving a finger, 'you're going to end up in the marital mincer if you have thoughts like that. Obliterate them from your mind or you'll wind up with egg on your face, not to mention gâteau on your head.'

Fred couldn't help laughing at the picture this evoked. 'You realize that everything you've done so far has jeopardized my position as an officially approved resident of this Principality? You've got me banned from the casino and the Beach Plaza and that's just day one. How long are you planning to stay? Will there be anywhere left for me to go by the time you fly home?'

'I think that was the trouble with Lena. She found life with me too exciting.' He emptied his glass. 'Do they do food here? I'd like to get some grub inside my head instead of on it.'

Eating sandwiches, he remembered what Fred had asked him. 'I'll go home on Thursday. I've got to do the stall on Friday to pay for this jaunt.'

'Good,' said Fred. 'Kate Seymour arrives on Friday and I'm meeting her at Nice.'

'She's coming out to see you?'

'No, she's coming out to see Jeremy Tyrrell but I've been substituted. He doesn't want to see her.'

'Perhaps you can persuade her to put gâteau on his head.'

'There are lots of things I want her to do but that isn't one of them.'

Trader Ryan looked at him with a fresh expression of concern on his face. 'Before you get carried away you should read about this new survey they've done among a thousand married couples in Germany,' he said. 'They found that after marriage men become more miserable, get more headaches and higher blood pressure, but women bloom. They don't even get the illnesses they had when they were single.'

'I'm being told this familiar stuff by a man who has flown across Europe to try to save his marriage.'

'Well, I don't get headaches as long as I duck the missiles,' said Trader Ryan. 'And I want her back.'

# NINE

AÉROPORT Nice Côte d'Azur didn't seem like an airport at all. Huge jets from New York and Istanbul, Casablanca and Copenhagen, might be dropping on to its seaside runway less than a mile away, but in its sunny halls with its spotless floor and chic shops it didn't appear to be involved in the tension-filled business of international air travel. In the car park outside there were orange trees and palm trees. It was like approaching a pleasure dome.

Strolling among its cheerful arrivals and departures, Fred had to remind himself where he was. He hadn't taken off from many airports but had spent a lot of time waiting to meet people in them and none had ever looked like this. The feeling of strangeness wasn't helped by his clothes. His dress was normally so informal that it had in the past produced a response from sleepy doormen who had interposed their underworked bodies into the space where the door had been, reluctant to believe that this scruffy visitor had been invited to the proceedings inside. But today there had been a flurry of expenditure in the gilded boutiques of Monaco and now, catching sight of the stranger in a mirror, he felt his confidence grow. A short-sleeved silk shirt, Cerruti slacks and a pair of Cardin shoes had replaced the old shirt, jeans and sandals which were his daily wear, and the only doubt that bounced back from the mirror was whether he had already reached that awesome moment when his waist was bigger than his chest.

Other larger doubts remained unresolved even while Kate Seymour's aircraft was throwing its engines into reverse thrust on the runway outside. Should he announce his reserve status straight away, and let the bewildered new arrival know that Jeremy Tyrrell would not be seeing her? Should he pretend that he had been sent to meet her and that the man she was expecting to see would be appearing later? Or should he pretend that their meeting in this sunny building was as unexpected to him as it was certainly going to be to her?

These were the questions that had resolutely remained unanswered during a picturesque train journey through Cap d'Ail, Eze, Beaulieu and Villefranche, and they remained unanswered now. Each possible course of action created its own problems and unpleasant scenarios, usually involving Kate Seymour's rejection of Fred. He had seen too many men climb off the substitutes' bench to discover that they were going to get only five minutes on the field.

There was a time when a box of chocolates would have been an appropriate investment at this stage but in today's calorie-conscious climate, he imagined, it would be a *faux pas*, as they said in England. He toyed with the idea of flowers – there were enough shops around here selling them – but whether a young lady already burdened with luggage, handbag, air tickets and who knew what else would welcome fresh things to carry seemed doubtful. Flowers, anyway, could appear presumptuous at this delicate encounter; they could come later.

He strolled round to the area where new arrivals emerged from customs smiling with anticipation at the prospect of a stay on the Riviera; people didn't look like this when they arrived at Heathrow. He stood there watching them, feeling suddenly nervous and wondering what on earth he could say.

She came through the narrow hallway looking sensational, a white trouser suit, a red bow on her black hair, a snazzy suitcase. She put it down almost immediately and looked round the hall. Her gaze swept past Fred without a hint of recognition, and then came back to him as if his face had triggered a memory somewhere. He advanced, smiling.

'Hallo,' he said. 'Welcome to Provence.'

'Hallo,' she said. 'I know you from somewhere. I'm looking for a man.'

'I'm a man,' said Fred. 'It says so on my passport.'

She looked at him uncertainly. 'I didn't mean any man. Somebody is meeting me. I hope.'

'Jeremy Tyrrell is unable to get here,' he recited. 'He has asked me to meet you and take you to Monte Carlo. I'm Fred Carton. We met in the Cellar Bar earlier this year.'

At some time during an unconfident youth he had read a book on etiquette and learned that a man should never offer a lady his hand but wait until she offered hers; it seemed necessary now, however, to impose his presence on her and the situation. She shook the offered hand briefly, but looked perplexed.

'Where am I going to stay?' she asked. 'I hadn't expected this.'

'Follow me,' he said, picking up her case. 'You are booked into the best hotel in Monte Carlo, and your carriage is waiting outside.'

The trick now, he realized, was to make things happen so quickly that Jeremy Tyrrell would be forgotten in the excitement. Heli Air Monaco's white helicopter was waiting outside and soon they were soaring over the Mediterranean. A train might be good enough to get Fred from Monte Carlo, but he had decided that Kate Seymour deserved a superior form of transport. She gazed out of the windows in wonderment at the spectacle that unfolded before her now: the mountainous hinterland, the crowded shoreline, the blue sea stretching away to their right.

'That's the bluest sea I've ever seen,' she said. Her voice, affected perhaps by the flight, sounded sexily husky.

'It's what you artists call cobalt blue, isn't it?' said Fred. His faith in helicopters was not sufficient to ensure the cool aplomb which he had hoped to exhibit at this moment; around the precarious oil rigs in the North Sea, he seemed to remember, it practically rained helicopters. But insouciance was the word for what Kate Seymour was exhibiting. She leaned towards the window and looked down at the pleasure boats in a way that Fred feared could materially alter the flight path of the tiny machine that was holding them aloft.

Sweeping round Cap Ferrat they could see the rock of Monaco Ville in the distance. The heliport was at the water's edge on the reclaimed land at Fontvieille, and so Fred's relief at setting foot on solid land again was not as unqualified as it might have been: only a few years ago this solid land was water.

The taxi journey through a tunnel and round the port was sufficiently distracting to keep Kate Seymour's mind off the questions that Fred knew were coming. As they were driven up the incline of avenue d'Ostende they could see the huge Niarchos yacht, Atlantis 2, lying unused in the harbour, as it had been ever since Fred arrived. But as the taxi entered the place du Casino and stopped outside the Hôtel de Paris, the questions in her mind were joined by several more.

'Is this where I'm staying?' she asked. 'It looks more like a palace than a hotel.'

'It does, doesn't it?' said Fred. 'This is where the social élite snooze. Antique furniture, crystal chandeliers, ornate mirrors, paintings and statues, and, beneath this lot, 200,000 bottles of wine in a cellar carved from rock. I've had a look round. It seems OK.'

She looked at him as if he were mad. 'I can't afford this,' she said. 'I want to stay in Jeremy's hotel.'

'He's paid for you to stay here,' said Fred. 'You can't say no. It's the experience of a lifetime.'

She looked out of the taxi at the hotel's impressive façade and it occurred to him that it would take some confidence to walk into a hotel like this. While booking her suite he had contemplated the rotunda with its beautiful polychromed glass and felt quite out of place himself.

'What the hell,' she said suddenly, and got out of the car. He followed her quickly, paid off the driver and carried her suitcase up marble steps. The courtesy she received inside from a staff who had only dealt with the very rich seemed to reassure her. She also, he was glad to see, knew some French.

'When they've shown you your rooms, would you like to come over the road for a drink?' he asked.

'I don't seem to have anything else to do,' she said. 'I'm sorry. I don't mean to sound ungracious. I'm just wondering where Jeremy is.'

A man in a uniform picked up her suitcase and led her away. Fred looked at the luxury which surrounded him. In the entrance hall was a bronze horse whose fetlock had been turned golden by the good luck touches of superstitious gamblers on their way to the casino.

Ten minutes later she reappeared looking more relaxed. 'It's fantastic,' she said. 'I've never seen hotel rooms like that before. It must be costing him a fortune.'

He led her across the casino square to the Café de Paris, where they sat outside in the fading sun. She asked for a chablis spritzer. When the drink arrived she looked at Fred properly for perhaps the first time.

'The impression I had of you when I saw you in the Cellar Bar was of a sort of penniless poet, or certainly somebody who was out of work. Now you're whizzing around Monte Carlo in a helicopter. It's all a bit odd, isn't it?'

'Life's strange, isn't it?' he agreed. Sitting next to her now and looking into blue eyes which were set off dramatically by the darkest of eyebrows he had difficulty in assembling a coherent reply.

'Do you live here? Are you working here?'

'Yes and no,' he said. 'Yes to the first question, no to the second.'

'This is all very queer. I seem to have been put in the care of a man I don't even know.'

'Exciting, isn't it?'

'It's bloody peculiar, actually. Where is Jeremy? He's got a girl, hasn't he?'

He nodded. 'He brought her with him.'

'The bastard,' she said, but she spoke so nicely that it lacked venom. 'It's my fault really. After all, he didn't invite me to come down and see him. I just felt I needed a break. I was obviously putting more weight on our relationship than it could stand.'

'You don't seem too upset,' Fred suggested. He had

feared tears at this stage but now he saw how wrong he had been. Kate Seymour was a disciplined girl, cool, calm and collected: it would obviously take more than this situation to get her upset.

She shrugged and then picked up her drink. 'He was just a friend. At least I thought he was. Who's the girl?'

'Dermot Ryan's wife.'

'She's old enough to be his granny.'

'She's beginning to look younger than he does,' Fred told her.

This was the time in the evening when the rich began to appear in their Ferraris and their Rolls in search of the night life that had made Monaco famous. Cocktails at the Hôtel de Paris, dinner by candlelight in some roof-top restaurant with a breathtaking view of the harbour, and then the casino and a nightclub on the avenue des Spélugues, where the local sport of celebrity-spotting could carry on until dawn.

Fred, despite his new and expensive clothes, wasn't dressed for any of this, and he could hardly have met her in evening dress. He watched the crowds on their desperate quest for fun and ordered more drinks.

'What are you going to do?' he asked.

Kate Seymour smiled at him for the first time. 'That's just what I was wondering. My return flight isn't until Monday morning.'

'Why don't I show you the Azure Coast, as we call it in English?' He liked the way that he put himself forward as teacher and guide when he had seen little of the area himself. 'There's a lot to see and you don't want to waste the visit.'

The slightly concerned expression that she had worn ever since she arrived in Nice seemed to fade at this suggestion.

'That would be very kind of you,' she said. 'I'd enjoy that.'

'I'll be at your hotel at nine o'clock.'

'Are you sure you won't be bored? After all, you live here.'

He put his hand over hers and gave it a squeeze.

'Oh no,' he said. 'I won't be bored.'

The following morning she was standing on the steps of the hotel in white jeans and a sea-blue shirt, both of which revealed her figure more effectively than last night's trouser suit. He shook her hand very formally and then kissed it.

'What if it rains, Mr Carton?' she asked.

'Rain is an English phenomenon,' he told her. 'Down here the vegetation is kept fresh by the dew. How do you feel about trains?'

'Love them.'

'Good. That way we can drop off at lots of different places.'

'Let's go.'

In Nice they watched the gigolos with their immaculate white jackets and carefully coiffured hair drinking coffee on the front while they studied the passing trade and wondered where their next Armani suit was coming from. They had coffee themselves on the promenade des Anglais, a palm-lined, three-mile, eight-track traffic jam that separated the crowded capital of the Riviera from the beautiful baie des Anges. Afterwards they wandered inland and saw flowered gardens, modern fountains and Italianate arcades. In the old town beyond the cafés and the bistros they came to the vegetable market, where gleaming aubergines, courgettes and red, green and yellow peppers were piled perilously high. On the boulevard Victor Hugo, a tunnel of plane trees, they saw an old lady who lived out of a supermarket trolley, boiling her potatoes in a tiny saucepan on a tiny stove. From seventeen museums and galleries, Kate plucked the one devoted to Marc Chagall. Canvases which made up his *Biblical Message* occupied two rooms. Fred stared at his *Noah and the Rainbow* and foresaw difficulties in sharing her enthusiasm for great works of art: he fancied he had done better at school.

In Cannes they were surrounded by pigeons, poodles and poseurs. They dodged them along the pink Croisette, where people really did walk to be seen, and strolled along to the old port on the west of the town. The beach of imported sand was mostly private and stringently regulated, with expensive sunbeds arranged in neat, military rows, each with its own side table for the champagne. On the other side of the road some of the most luxurious hotels in Europe were finding no difficulty in filling their rooms. Cannes, sheltered by the hills, home of the mimosa, had been virtually discovered 150 years ago by an Englishman, a former Lord Chancellor, who was on his way to Italy. It was an unknown fishing village then, but today his statue stood, surrounded by flowers, just below the Palais des Festivals. Proud to have discovered some peace, he was saluted now for starting a stampede. Not far from the statue, they found the Bar Cristal, overlooking the port. It had stools at the bar and beer that came out of barrels, not bottles. Fred felt at home.

In Juan-les-Pins, where the distant memory of an old pop song had led them to expect the heights of elegance and sophistication, they found the boisterous haunt of the young, cacophonous music in the streets, gaudy shops, buckets and spades, outlandish beachwear – Blackpool without the rain.

And then from there in the early evening they got a taxi across the pine-covered peninsula to Antibes and found the best of everything: lovely old streets, stone castles, modern shops, a maze of tiny alleys, a covered market, a pretty port full of pleasure boats, and quiet squares with bars and restaurants whose pavement tables were sheltered by the palm trees. In the car-free rue de la République they sat outside the Bar François and watched a small white train bedecked with blue and white flags drag three carriages full of tourists through the narrow streets.

'I've discovered the secret of your slim build,' Kate said. 'You don't eat food.'

'I catch your drift,' said Fred, finishing his beer. 'Let's find a good restaurant.'

They walked through the *zone piétonnière* in the direction of the sea and came to the Place Nationale, where tourists sat beneath Heineken sunshades in the square enjoying an evening drink. Incongruously, among these old buildings, a digital clock announced the time from a lamp-post.

In a restaurant nearby the cuisine was *nouvelle*. Fred thought that it would please his artistic guest that the courses looked like paintings, with sunbursts of carrots, courgettes and celery, but he found it difficult to decide whether the lettuce was intended for nourishment or decoration.

'Would you like champagne?' he asked. 'You can get it in France.'

She raised one eyebrow. 'Can we afford it?'

'Why not?' he said. He didn't want this friendship to be

influenced either way by talk of money, but sooner or later she had to start asking questions. It turned out to be sooner.

'You're a mysterious man, Fred,' she said, when the champagne had arrived. 'What do you *do*?'

'Less than I should,' he told her. 'Mostly I sort of ponce about.'

'In Monte Carlo?'

'It's warmer.'

His answers were leaving her with more questions than she started with. She managed to smile and frown at the same time.

Drinking his champagne, Fred congratulated himself on the skilful way that he was conducting this affair. No fierce declarations of love were going to have Kate Seymour rearing like a startled horse. No outbursts of passion would disturb this civilized scene. His model here was Brer Rabbit, who found it helpful to disguise his wishes. Mature restraint and cool charm were intended to intrigue and then irritate and finally insult until curiosity about why he seemed impervious to her beauty would ignite feminine pride and provoke her into chasing him. If he held back long enough, he hoped, he would be dragged into bed. It was a strange approach but it had this to be said for it: it never failed.

He understood the boundaries very well, the perimeters and parameters within which he could perform without causing unease; so the fact that after his prolonged sexual dysfunction he could quite happily devote the rest of his life to kissing her bottom was information that it would be prudent at this stage to withhold.

'Why don't you work, Fred?' she asked now. 'It's none of my business. You don't *have* to answer.'

'I inherited some money,' he told her. 'The reason I'm here is to avoid a rather large tax bill. My mother died and was richer than I thought. I found that you don't appreciate your parents properly until they're dead.'

The reference to parents had a strange effect on Kate Seymour. The colour went out of her cheeks and she stared down at her food without looking at it.

Unnerved by this, Fred began to eat his meal as if he had never handled a knife or fork before, but had been led to believe, by someone he didn't really trust, that they were the agents that could be relied upon to get the food from his plate to his mouth.

'My mother died this year,' he said quickly. 'It sort of explains things. Are you OK?'

She nodded but didn't answer for some time. 'Something happened,' she said after a while. 'Can we keep off the subject of parents? It has a funny effect on me sometimes. Not always. Just sometimes.'

He flew from the subject like a man caught in the wrong bedroom. He found another.

'Tell me about your work,' he suggested.

Kate drank some champagne and it was a moment or two before she seemed ready to take on this new topic.

'I'm trying to do a children's book. It's just a little thing. It's called *Cockle the Emu*, a picture book with a simple story for the under-fives. I haven't even found a publisher yet, but of course I envisage a whole series of Cockle books, Cockle dolls, Cockle jigsaws, Cockle T-shirts.'

'And there's a fresh market every year with a booming birthrate,' said Fred, relieved to see her acting normally again.

'Cockle is my real work. The rest pays the rent, as they

say. The drawing is easy. It's thinking of the stories that takes the time.'

'I can think of stories but I can't draw,' said Fred. 'Perhaps we should go into partnership.'

'Go on then,' she said. 'Give me a story. I need it.' She seemed to be all right now and was giving him a challenging look.

'Well, I don't know the format,' he said, thinking immediately of a story.

'Twelve thick pages that children can't tear, with a colour drawing on each and words at the bottom. What I need is short simple stories that a child of three could follow. Come on, partner. Hit me with one.'

She was her normal confident self again now. Fred refilled her champagne glass. 'Every morning Cockle goes down to the pond to feed the fish. One day he goes out in a boat on the pond. But the boat breaks down and he is stranded in the middle. It starts to rain and he is cold and wet. Then the fish see him and together they push his boat to the shore because he is the one who gives them food.'

'That's almost perfect actually,' said Kate. 'Have you just thought of that?'

'Me and the champagne. Is the gregory in the post?'

'Gregory?'

The word distracted her, as he had intended it should; he could still hear her saying, '*Something happened.*'

'Gregory Peck, cheque,' he told her. 'Why don't you give me your address and I'll send you some more stories.'

She picked up her handbag. 'I'll give you my card at once.' It was a black card with gold lettering that said KATE SEYMOUR, FREELANCE ARTIST and gave the address of the studio where she worked and, apparently, lived. Fred pocketed it as if it was a map that showed where the treasure was buried.

As they strolled towards the station afterwards, she said, 'Will you join me on the beach tomorrow? I imagine the shops are shut.'

'Is it Sunday tomorrow?' asked Fred. 'In your company one loses track of time.'

Antibes station, with its palm trees and colourful banks of flowers, looked more like a horticultural show than a railway station. You couldn't imagine commuters waiting in the early morning rain at a place like this. Even now, in the late evening, some travellers were stripped to the waist, and the names of the stations on the line – Menton, Monaco, Villefranche, Nice, Cagnes, Cannes – did not sound at all like the list of dreadful dormitories drearily recited in the drizzle by a British Rail announcer with a speech impediment. When the train came in he took her hand to help her on and forgot to let go.

They had been on the beach for over an hour the following afternoon when they saw Jeremy Tyrrell and Lena Ryan arrive and take two sunbeds some distance away.

Kate was wearing a yellow bikini which confirmed what Fred had suspected about her body. Decorously concealed most of the time behind some floppy clothing was a figure that would stun a eunuch. Lying on her back her breasts retained the shape they would have had if she was upright, and she had a dancer's legs. Fred was delighted that every time he met her she was wearing fewer clothes than on the previous occasion and wondered tremulously whether she might go topless. Her mouth looked as if somebody should be kissing it.

'There's a friend of yours over there,' he told her.

Her curiosity made her sit up, and they watched Jeremy Tyrrell and Lena Ryan throw bright red towels on their sunbeds and then rummage in a large bag for a bottle of something and two glasses.

'That's no friend of mine,' said Kate. 'Is that really Mrs Ryan?'

'The redesigned version.'

'I hope I look like that at her age. What does she take – monkey glands?'

'I think what she takes is a toy boy. It's the new elixir. The years fall away with the clothes.'

She watched them pouring out drinks and then she lay back in the sun. 'I bought him a book by a Hungarian novelist at Easter. I told him he didn't read enough. What do you think the book was?'

'Hungarian novelist? That narrows it down a bit.'

'It was called *In Praise of Older Women*. Another of Kate's clangers. He obviously took it as Holy Writ.'

'He's seen us,' said Fred.

Scanning the beach, the way restless sunbathers do, his gaze had at last reached Fred and Kate. He peered, uncertain at first, and then gave Fred a little wave with the hand that wasn't holding a drink.

Kate asked, 'Is he coming over?'

'He's thinking about it.'

'He's got the gall. They pick it up at Charterhouse.'

Fred thought that it was most unlikely that Jeremy Tyrrell would want to face Kate now, and he was even more doubtful about whether Lena Ryan would favour the idea, but it was Kate's judgement that was swiftly vindicated. Jeremy Tyrrell put down his glass, stood up, adjusted his trunks, and ambled in their direction.

'He's decided to visit us,' said Fred.

'I'm not in.'

But when he came up to them she sat up and watched his approach.

'Hi!' he said. 'You made it then.'

'I seem to have done,' she told him. 'How are you?'

'I'm fine. Isn't this a great place? My God, why haven't I seen you in a bikini before?'

'Perhaps because it was winter in England, Jeremy. They're not worn much in the snow.'

Transfixed by her body, he didn't seem to notice this dig. Instead he asked, 'Would you two like drinks? Come over and say hello to Lena.'

Fred listened to this last suggestion incredulously. It required a sublime indifference to people's feelings to come up with an idea like that, but a certain cheerful insensitivity, he thought, was the precise characteristic that carried people like Jeremy Tyrrell through their clumsy lives. The people who got hurt were not even noticed: the focus of attention had moved on.

'Would you mind awfully if I didn't?' Kate asked. 'I'm quite happy where I am.'

'Oh, come and have a drink,' he said. 'Don't be a stick-in-the-mud.'

'A stick-in-the-mud? Is that a public-school expression? Jeremy, I can forgive your faithlessness, but being maladroit as well is going too far.'

Fred laughed aloud at this, which seemed to annoy Jeremy Tyrrell. He flushed slightly.

'Well, if you're going to be –'

'A stick-in-the-mud.'

'– unpleasant, I'll toddle along. See you, Fred.'

He turned to go but couldn't resist a final lingering

glance at Kate's body. When he had walked a few yards she remembered something and called after him.

'Thanks for paying for my hotel.'

He turned round. He thought she was being sarcastic. 'Why should I do that?' he asked.

'Didn't you?' she asked. 'Haven't you?'

He shook his head. 'Which hotel are you in, anyway?'

'The Hôtel de Paris.'

'Blimey! I wish I could afford an hotel like that.'

He wandered off, surprised at how unhappy he felt about this brief conversation. Across the sunbeds Lena Ryan was watching him and had watched him since he left her side. Seeing him returning, she waved a hand. Reluctantly he waved back.

Fred lay down and closed his eyes. He liked the way that Kate Seymour had handled a difficult situation.

Suddenly she was whispering in his ear, 'Did you pay my hotel bill?'

'Yup.'

'Why?'

He opened his eyes and looked at her. 'Because the first time I saw you I thought, that woman is exquisite.'

She lay back, closed her eyes and smiled.

Monday morning in Monte Carlo did not have the inherent gloom of Monday mornings in Britain. Only the sun began work promptly. On the Crédit Lyonnais building the time and the temperature flashed alternately: 10.58 – 24°.

They came into the town from the place du Casino, where the beautiful upper garden, still visible on postcards, was now a gigantic building site as scores of brown men in blue boiler suits worked on the construction of a huge underground car park. A bigger job, for somebody else, would be replacing the garden on top when they had finished.

Creating space where previously there had been none provided constant employment in this constricted neighbourhood. The noise of the drill was never far away as clapboard sprouted and cranes swung overhead. Nearby, the luxurious Métropole shopping centre was under construction, a de luxe project on three different levels. Above it there would eventually be a new hotel with more than 150 rooms; below it was a bomb shelter in the basement.

Although only half-built, it was already open and Kate led the way in. She had the idea that all foreign trips should end with a shopping spree. The world's newest escalators took them down three floors, where they found that in this sloping town they were not, as they had imagined, in the bowels of the earth, but at ground level for another street on the other side of the new development. The air conditioning was so powerful that Fred felt cold for the first time since he had arrived.

'What can I buy you?' he asked, and thought: a farmhouse in the hills? An engagement ring? A honeymoon in Hawaii? The moon?

'Buy me?' Kate said. 'I think you've spent enough on me this weekend.'

She had lingered beneath the chandeliers that illuminated the darker corners of this opulent new world, outside the Giovani shop. He suggested shoes.

'I would like to try those on,' she conceded, pointing at the window.

But when she had decided on a pair of Xavier Danaud's high-heeled, open-toed numbers in white leather that was made to look like Emu skin, she produced her own Access credit card.

'Do you know what Access stands for?' he asked.

'Tell me.'

'A credit card encourages silly spending. Let me buy them. A farewell present before you fly out of my life.'

She looked at him then. 'Who said I'm flying out of your life?'

'I've seen the air ticket.'

'Well,' she said, 'there are more where that came from.'

'Does that mean you might return to these parts? I should be terribly happy if you did.'

Today she was wearing a yellow dress which stopped an inch or two above her knees. Her legs, already brown, gave him the idea of going down on all fours and kissing them.

'I'd love to,' she told him. 'It's lovely here. Sun and sea. Little gardens full of exotic flowers where nobody is ever mugged. It's not the raucous seaside town I was expecting.'

He searched in vain for a hint that his own presence here might be a reason for her to return. 'Consider yourself invited,' he said.

The shop girl had taken her credit card and was now filling in the amount on the slip.

'Next time I'll sleep on your floor,' she said. 'That hotel bill must be enormous.'

And perhaps moved by this financial consideration she looked up and kissed him – on the cheek.

# TEN

NO sooner had Kate Seymour flown back to England than an engraved invitation arrived in Fred's apartment from several floors above his head.

*Mrs Amelia Fotheringay*
*requests the pleasure of your company*
*at a cocktail party*
*on Saturday, the ninth of July,*
*at six o'clock*

The sort of invitation that would have been hurled scornfully into the bin at home came to him here as a lifeline, a chance to meet somebody and an occasion to look forward to. Fred had his suit cleaned and, to his great embarrassment, arrived first.

Amelia Fotheringay was a plump, cheerful woman in her fifties. She wore a black silk-jersey dress with earrings, bracelet, necklace and a diamond pin in her hair.

'Come in,' she said. 'What's your name?'

'Fred.'

'Come in, Fred. I've seen you wandering around looking like Banquo's ghost.'

The apartment was three times larger than Fred's and lavishly furnished; the thick white carpet seemed too good to walk on. The paintings on the wall looked, to Fred's untutored eye, like the real thing; one, he was sure, was a Constable. Mrs Fotheringay led him out to the balcony, where a man in a white jacket presided over a table of drinks.

'This is Albert,' she said. 'He is my waiter for the night and will see that you don't run out of drinks.'

'It was kind of you to invite me,' Fred said, 'seeing that we've never met.'

'The reason I'm giving a party is to find out who the hell lives here,' said Mrs Fotheringay. 'This must be the emptiest apartment block in Europe. Have you noticed how few lights go on after dark? The buggers are all living up the coast surrounded by land now they've got an address for tax purposes.'

Fred took a glass of champagne from Albert and asked his hostess, 'How long have you been here?'

'Just a year,' she said. She took a glass of champagne herself but didn't drink from it. 'My husband was selling his business for rather a lot of money after two heart attacks, and his accountant told us to spend a year down here while the sale went through. As it happened my husband died two months after we got here and I haven't quite got myself organized enough to go home.'

The phone on the wall rang. She answered, 'Carruthers, MI5,' and winked at Fred. 'Send 'em up.'

Other people were already at the door and she swept across the room and waved them in.

'Have you been drinking, dear, or is that some cheap aftershave?' she asked a tall blond man with a moustache who seemed to have arrived alone. 'Never trust a man with a moustache,' she said to Fred. 'Just growing one is an act of deception.'

The man smiled at Fred. 'She's a gay old stick, isn't she? Philip Hunt is my name.' But before Fred could reply, Mrs Fotheringay had urged the new arrivals towards Albert and the drinks, and fresh faces loomed before him. In the corner of the room a man started to play a white piano, a slow, gentle tune that would not intrude on the conversation. The guests were all beautifully dressed, mostly middle-aged and nearly all in pairs. Fred looked round to see whether any beautiful daughters were in tow but couldn't see one. The room smelled of money but it was not an aroma that would ever reach the nostrils of the taxman.

When Philip Hunt reappeared he was telling a joke to a plump, prosperous looking man called Humphrey. They pulled up alongside Fred, as if men alone should stay together. Humphrey wasn't listening as Philip Hunt told his joke; he was thinking of the joke he would tell when this one was finished.

Humphrey, it emerged, was a designer or an architect, one of the absentee tenants of Park Saint Roman who had his place in the hills near Grasse, a farmhouse converted at great expense into the sort of Provençal retreat that would end up in a glossy magazine. His new swimming pool, they learned, was surrounded by palms, kumquats, magnolias and oleanders, and the view of the hills was glimpsed through cool gothic arches.

'I seem to be one of the few people who actually live here,' said Fred.

'I didn't realize that people actually lived here,' said Humphrey. 'I thought it was a postal address.'

'Well, I live here,' said Philip Hunt. 'It's not exactly a high-rise in Bermondsey. I find it very comfortable.'

'What do you do, Philip?' Humphrey asked, twirling a champagne glass that was already empty.

'I am *the* Philip Hunt,' said Philip Hunt.

'Really?' said Humphrey, looking baffled. 'Which Philip Hunt is that?'

'You mean you've never heard of me?' said Philip Hunt,

who seemed genuinely surprised at this gaping hole in Humphrey's knowledge. 'I'm the writer, the author of many novels. As a matter of fact, my last one, *Don't Put Your Daughter on the Worthington,* was shortlisted for a literary award last year until it was edged out in the final shake.' He stared around the room in search of material that would help him fill a book.

'Well, well,' said Humphrey, looking at him. 'I've never met a writer before. What do you do – use a word processor?'

'No, a Parker roller-ball,' said Philip Hunt reluctantly, as if this was classified information that was being prised from him with the help of red-hot needles beneath his finger-nails. Perhaps he imagined, thought Fred, that everybody would start writing novels if they knew that Parker roller-ball pens were how you did it.

'What else have you written?' asked Humphrey.

'*Across the Trees and into the River* did rather well. In fact, they're filming it.'

'Comic novels, are they?' asked Fred.

'Who's to say,' said Philip Hunt, 'what a comic novel is?'

Amelia Fotheringay was suddenly beside them now, in the company of a small Italian businessman.

'Filly Punt,' he said. 'In Italy we love your humour.'

'Mario is pissed as a handcart,' announced Mrs Fotheringay.

'He sounds sober to me,' said Philip Hunt, glad to have found a reader and not anxious to see his opinions dismissed as the maunderings of an alcoholic.

'Amelia, you are so unkind to me,' said Mario, 'and I have a most active libido.' He took hold of both her hands and kissed them. The red hair around his ears suggested that he was trying to postpone old age with the help of something from the *pharmacie*.

'You only want me for my Monet,' said Mrs Fotheringay, winking at Fred. 'I imagine that going to bed with you, Mario, is something a woman would hardly notice.'

'What else is there for you to do here?' asked Mario, with the help of some plaintive hand gestures that embraced both supplication and desperation.

'I have to feed my yucca plant twice a week,' said Mrs Fotheringay briskly. 'That's as busy as I hope to get.'

Mario abandoned his courtship abruptly and headed for the bathroom. Mrs Fotheringay watched him go.

'He's as incontinent as a dog in a lamp-post factory,' she said. 'How are you, Humphrey? Have you met Philip and Fred?'

Albert appeared now and filled all their glasses.

'I'm fine, Amelia,' said Humphrey. 'I've just been to England for my father-in-law's funeral. It's the wettest July there since 1939. They couldn't even finish Wimbledon on the right day.'

'When I went to my father-in-law's funeral they opened the window to let out his spirit,' said Mrs Fotheringay. 'Bloody odd, I thought. I hope it got caught in the fan. How are you, Philip? Are you a millionaire yet?'

'Writers don't get rich, Mrs Fotheringay. It's one long balls-aching struggle.'

'I seem to have read about some very rich writers,' said Mrs Fotheringay. 'What about Cecil Parkinson?'

'You mean Jeffrey Archer,' said Philip Hunt. 'But you take a writer like George Orwell. Do you know how much *Animal Farm* made him in its first year? £79. And what about Scott Fitzgerald? Three years after *The Great*

*Gatsby* he earned $31 from books in an entire year. No wonder they were both dead by my age.'

'If it's such a poorly paid business,' said Fred, 'how come you're a tax exile?'

'Exactly,' said Mrs Fotheringay.

'I told you, I sold some film rights,' said Philip Hunt. 'One lump sum I'm trying to hang on to. Next year I could earn two bucks.' He shook his head at the injustice of it all.

'And you, Fred,' said the hostess, 'what do you do?'

It was a bit like being on a chat show, he thought, with everybody being given their five minutes in the spotlight before public attention was abruptly yanked elsewhere. It was an experience he had yearned for, but now his mind jammed.

'I'm in the leisure business,' he said eventually.

'Really?' said Humphrey, as if this was something he knew about. 'How?'

'As opposed to the work business,' said Fred. 'It seems selfish to get a job when there are so many unemployed looking for work.'

'Unemployed but not looking for work,' said Humphrey. 'How do you think the government keeps getting re-elected with three million out of a job? It's the workless who vote for them. They've learned to appreciate leisure.'

'I've been trying to teach people for years,' said Fred. 'But they keep rushing into offices.'

'Well, I don't vote for them,' said Mrs Fotheringay. 'There's a cruelty at the bottom of Conservatism that I can't stomach.'

There were calls soon to transfer the party to the pool, which still glistened in the evening sunshine fifteen floors below them – calls which found sufficient support to produce space and seats in the apartment. Fred lowered himself into a white leather sofa and looked round the room. There seemed to be a lot of Swedes and Germans about, but Americans and French, who did not benefit from Monaco's tax-free ways, were hard to see. The pianist was giving them some Marvin Hamlisch.

Two women, not much older than Fred, took the vacant seats on the sofa. One of them passed him her empty glass and asked him to fetch a mint julep. Among the battery of ornaments on her dainty hand he thought he saw a wedding ring. He was so impressed by her haughty manner that he fetched her drink, refilling his own glass at the same time.

'You know Claud,' the lady was saying to her friend when he returned. 'He lives at Grimaud. He was telling us over dinner the other night that during the Occupation he had to eat his cat. His wife didn't know until he told us last week. She was appalled. "I always wondered what happened to that cat," she said. "You ate it in 1943," he told her.'

The woman took the drink from Fred without acknowledgement. He hung on for a while, hoping to lose the role of invisible man, but the conversation moved on without him to the subject of a forthcoming visit to the Monte Carlo Sporting Club by Sammy Davis Junior. He stood up and went out to the balcony. The cheerful sound of chatter and laughter rose from the pool, where a topless girl was the centre of attention. Fred felt himself pulled to this scene without even the conscious effort of making a decision, and soon he was sharing the lift with two old ladies whose aromatic perfume would have set him back in a high wind. The high wind, he remembered, was called the mistral, which howled down the Rhône Valley and knocked people's hats off, but even it, he reflected, would be hard pressed to dissipate the odour here.

At the forefront of the pool's spectators was Philip Hunt, who looked as if he had never seen a topless girl before.

'Jesus,' he said. 'Look at that chest.'

'I am,' said Fred. 'That's what I was doing.'

Philip Hunt was a tall, slim man with a gaunt look around the eyes, as if he had spent too much time in the feverish world of the imagination. Released temporarily from his self-imposed womb, he appeared perplexed, perhaps finding that the realities which confronted him now did not quite meld with the world that he had been creating with his roller-ball pen. He stroked his blond moustache nervously.

'She's Swedish,' he said. 'You can always tell. Sex starts at ten up there. It's the long winters. There's nothing else to do.'

Fred accepted this résumé of an entire nation's sex life without comment, but Amelia Fotheringay, who had now appeared behind them, said, 'What rubbish. If there's so much sex going on up there why are there only about twelve Swedes?'

'Prophylactics,' said Philip Hunt. 'Excuse my back, Mrs Fotheringay.'

'Excuse it? I prefer it,' said Mrs Fotheringay crisply. 'What's the matter with you boys? Haven't you seen a naked woman before?'

'Not lately,' said Philip Hunt. 'They seem to have improved them. My God, I'm forty-five. I could be a grandfather by now.'

'Stick to the books, Philip. They're far less demanding.'

This didn't seem to be the advice that Philip Hunt wanted, and he continued to watch the girl until she slipped into the water.

'I wouldn't mind taking her upstairs and bending her buttocks over the sink,' he said, almost to himself.

'That's where you take girls on a date, is it?' said Mrs Fotheringay. 'The kitchen?'

'I can't remember where I take them,' Philip Hunt said.

Fred wondered what sort of books this man could be writing in the monastic seclusion of his cell in the sky. The sex scenes, if there were any, would depend on a memory that was apparently faulty, and with no family or children his experiences would be far removed from the life of his average reader. Perhaps he wrote science fiction.

'In coming down to the pool we seem to have separated ourselves from the grog,' he said. 'This was a mistake.'

'You're not the first man to find himself in the wrong place through lust,' said Mrs Fotheringay. 'The sexual stupidity of men could be the subject of your next book.'

'When that girl was disporting herself in the pool it seemed like the right place,' said Fred. 'I remember the moment quite clearly.'

But the dilemma was resolved by Albert, who now appeared with a bar on wheels that he had brought down in the lift and set up beside the pool. Soon everybody had champagne again.

Fred sat back on one of the comfortable loungers that were put out around the pool each day, and watched others cooling themselves in the water. The suit which he almost never wore now felt as inappropriate as suits had always seemed to him, but everybody else was wearing one so he kept it on. From the bar in the corner of the garden came the music from *Watership Down*.

For the first time since he had arrived in Monaco, Fred felt that he belonged.

# ELEVEN

SOME habits had not survived Fred's journey south, an indiscriminate reliance on television to fill the empty hours being one of them. Others had endured as if he had never moved: one morning a week was devoted to shopping. With a little planning it was possible to make this exercise last three or four hours; he was learning how to fill his days.

On a Saturday in late July he left the apartment soon after nine and set off for the port, where he had a coffee at one of the open-air cafés at the water's edge. Tourists wandered aimlessly around him looking at the boats. As the English papers hadn't arrived, he bought the *International Herald Tribune* and *Le Canard Enchaîné*. This last purchase was a somewhat ambitious gesture for someone with his language problems, but he had hoped that the cartoons might leap the barrier. He was disappointed in this hope and turned to the other paper. There were fleeing Kurds in Turkey, epidemics in Bangladesh and looting in Rangoon, but it was news of England that he needed today. How were Sebastian Coe's preparations coming along for the Olympic games? Was it still raining? Which popular television star had most recently been exposed in the Sunday papers as a dope-taking pederast? What fresh strokes was Margaret Hilda Thatcher planning behind the sinister black bricks of 10 Downing Street? And was there beans on toast still for tea?

He finished the coffee and strolled away from the port

up the rue Princesse Caroline looking at the shops. He came to the English bookshop, Scruples, and went in. Almost immediately he spotted a paperback by Philip Hunt called *The Man Who Forgot to Breathe*. He bought it without a second glance.

In the Codec supermarket in the subway by the harbour he moved along the shelves with his list like an experienced housewife. The list was in two languages and drawn from a much longer list in the apartment that he had compiled soon after he arrived and had found himself trying to do the washing-up with a bottle of bleach.

Lunchtime drinking, one of the great pleasures at home, was another habit that had not survived the move. The temptation was too great and with this much leisure he could see himself spending most of his time either drinking or recovering from it. But on Saturdays he made an exception and ended up in the King's Head or the Bar Tabac chatting to strangers.

Today, as it was on his route home, he dropped into Flashman's for a few pints of Holsten. It took only two to push his thoughts in the direction of Kate Seymour.

She behaved like a girl who had never heard of sex. There was no hint in her behaviour that she had ever considered going to bed with a man and, according to Lena Ryan, she had not gone to bed with Jeremy Tyrrell. Fred found this unnatural and alarming. Perhaps she was the last 23-year-old virgin in Britain. Perhaps he was in danger of involving himself with a girl who would bring him nothing but mystery and frustration. The mystery of her reaction to talk of her parents worried him still. The trouble was that the very thought of her made him want to dance.

He watched as a man from the bank collected the bar's

money. He gathered that in Monte Carlo the bank collected the money from the businesses in the town, not caring to wait until the businessman took it to the bank.

The conversations around him were in several languages. The trick was not to look round when you heard them talking English, so they didn't know they were being eavesdropped.

His thoughts returned to the enigmatic Miss Seymour, and he wondered whether the twelve-year gap in their ages was a factor in her behaviour. It didn't seem to be important from where he stood, but to her it could be a discrepancy of laughable proportions. Perhaps his long wait for a conventional sex life would continue for several years yet. J. B. Priestley was making love at eighty-three and Charlie Chaplin, he recalled, was another geriatric leg-over artist. The English, like the Irish, matured later.

When he left the bar he saw that some people were finding partners. On Saturday afternoons a procession of cars, each bearing pink ribbons and sounding its horn, meant that another couple had just got married, and walking back to his apartment he counted four wedding parties.

The posters on show in the boulevard des Moulins told him that among today's diversions were Vivaldi at the cathedral, and L'Illusionniste at the Théâtre Princesse Grace. His own programme was less expensive. He put his bathing trunks on beneath his jeans and got the lift down to the pool armed with Philip Hunt's novel.

Discarding jeans and shirt he found a sunbed and pulled it up to the edge of the pool which was shaped, oddly, like a woman's brassière. He lay at the northern, left breast end of the water. On a litter bin a few feet from his head a notice said AIDEZ-NOUS A GARDER LE PARC SAINT ROMAN PROPRE MERCI. Cleanliness was everything here: at one end of the little garden the dog park was being obediently used by a white poodle. At the far end of the pool he could see Amelia Fotheringay in a deck-chair reading *The Times*. A bottle of something protruded from an ice bucket at her elbow.

Philip Hunt's slim volume, *The Man Who Forgot to Breathe*, was, he gathered fairly quickly, the story of a sexually frustrated 25-year-old, written, no doubt, by a sexually frustrated 25-year-old. The hero, Jed Wilmott, stumbled through 200 pages with an almost permanent erection, dealing single-handedly with his priapic problem in the most unlikely venues: on trains with no corridors, in taxis and darkened alleys, in lifts which he would jam between floors until the cadenza. He lurched through his concupiscent existence with one hand round a cigarette and the other in his trousers. It was not surprising if he forgot to breathe; he was coping with a more pressing need. There was a single endorsement on the back: 'Poignant' – *The Lady*.

Fred was half way through Jed Wilmott's solo performance when a shadow fell over the page and he looked up to see Philip Hunt standing beside him in blue bathing trunks. He was embarrassed to meet the author of these reminiscences, if they were reminiscences, and faintly uneasy if they were not. If Philip Hunt had spent his formative years crouched over his parts with his elbow going like a piston it was not something that Fred wanted to know.

'Filly Punt,' he said. 'I'm reading one of your books.'

'That little *conte*,' said Philip Hunt. 'I always thought it was going to win the Booker McConnell prize.'

'It would have been a cert for the Wanker McConnell prize,' said Fred. 'It reminds me of *Portnoy's Complaint*.'

Philip Hunt looked hurt at this. 'I think if you look at the date in the front you will find that it was published twenty years ago when I was twenty-five. In 1968. *Portnoy's Complaint* came out the following year and then Brian Aldiss did a book in 1970 called *The Hand-Reared Boy*. No, I pioneered masturbation as a literary metaphor, no question. I never got the credit I deserved.'

Fred could not imagine what credit would be appropriate. An OBE for services to hand-jobs would be a bit of an eye-opener, even with the dubious standards of today's honours lists.

He said, 'A bit difficult to film it.'

'It gets easier every year. Another ten years and it will be prime-time television. Fancy a dip in the pool?'

He slipped into the water without waiting for an answer and crossed the pool with a slow crawl. Fred, reassured that it was a suitable depth for a non-swimmer, entered the water more cautiously. Many residents from the apartments had come down to the pool to cool off, while others sat drinking at the bar in the corner of the garden.

Philip Hunt swam alongside him and stood up. 'What are you doing tonight?' he asked.

'I'm going over to the King's Head,' Fred told him.

'What's it like?'

'It's like a pub. You give Roy money, he gives you pints of beer.'

Philip Hunt nodded as if he had vaguely heard about this arrangement.

'Do you mind if I join you? I've got writer's block and a few drinks might shake up the cerebral cortex.'

When he walked into the King's Head that evening Fred saw Lena Ryan sitting alone at the bar. She was wearing a rather smart blue jacket with a tight white skirt, and smoking an extra long cigarette. The smile that she gave him was several degrees warmer than her recent welcomes.

'Thank God you've come in,' she said. 'I sat in here all last night and you didn't show up and when I went over to your apartment the security man wouldn't even tell me your phone number.'

'You could have waited in reception,' Fred told her. 'Your husband did.'

'He wouldn't let me do that, either. He thought I was a whore. They certainly cosset you in that place.'

Fred could see why the security guard would make such a mistake: few women this old looked this sexy unless it was their job. The blue jacket, neatly buttoned, revealed plenty of cleavage and the crossed legs on the stool – or rather two of Roy's tiny stools – revealed inches of thigh. The streaked hair and the suntan, with some very artistic make-up, combined to give the impression of a young woman with one thing on her mind.

'What will you drink?' he asked. She was nursing an empty glass.

'Gin,' she said, 'with tonic.'

Roy, who had already pulled a pint of Pelforth Pale for Fred, produced a gin and asked, 'Are you any good at running, Fred? We've got a good fun run coming up to Biot golf course.'

'You should pack it in, Roy. It's lethal,' Fred told him. 'What happened to that bloke Jim Fixx who wrote the definitive book on jogging? He dropped dead jogging.'

Roy wanted to answer this but was called away to the other end of the bar. It looked as if Saturday night was a busy time in the King's Head.

Fred turned to Lena Ryan. 'Well, now that you've found me, darling, what do you want? You're not concealing a gâteau on your person, are you?'

She smiled at the memory but the smile was short-lived.

'He's left me,' she said. 'He's buggered off and I don't know where he is.'

'When did this happen?'

'I went out yesterday morning to the chemist and when I got back to the hotel he wasn't there. Then I realized that his clothes had gone and all his things. Shaver, toothbrush, the lot. I couldn't believe it. He had been perfectly all right when I went out.'

'How extraordinary,' said Fred. 'What a bastard.'

'You don't know how big a bastard. He hadn't paid the bill.'

'What – any of it?'

'Oh, he's had to pay weekly but he hasn't paid this week's and it's a bloody expensive hotel.'

'How much?'

'I don't know. It must be around £1,500 a week for the two of us. I'm in the cart, Fred, and you're the only person I can turn to.'

'What do you want to do?'

'I just don't know. I don't know which way to turn at the moment. The only thing that's concerning me is not getting thrown into their small prison for an unpaid bill. I gather that they're pretty hot on debts in Monaco.'

'They are,' said Fred, reaching for his beer. 'I've got money I don't know how to spend, but I can't get my hands on it till Monday. Can you stall till then?'

'That's lovely, Fred,' she said, and kissed his cheek. For a moment, he thought, she was beginning to look her age, but now she was the new young Lena again. 'I shall never be able to repay you, and I mean that literally.'

'I must admit that I shan't enjoy settling Jeremy Tyrrell's half of the bill. Where do you think the little creep is?'

But even now, particularly with her anxiety removed, Lena Ryan couldn't bring herself to accept this description of her former lover.

'He was a nice boy,' she said. 'I don't know what happened. He seemed so happy.'

'Do you think it was money?'

'It could have been. Perhaps he couldn't bring himself to tell me that he had run out.'

'Was there any contact with home?'

Fred was wondering whether Jeremy Tyrrell's father had called in his credit and demanded his return, but the question was no sooner out of his mouth than he thought of Kate Seymour, an even more potent reason why he might have flown back to Britain.

'There were no phone calls that I knew of. Of course I knew he would leave me one day, but not like that.' She looked across at the French boys who were playing darts in the corner as if there might be a replacement among their number. 'He told me once that he never wanted to go home.'

Fred could well imagine Jeremy Tyrrell's cultured tones murmuring this or something like it after a sexual convulsion in the Beach Plaza; what was surprising was that Lena Ryan should believe it. But while she was upset at the melancholy void which the absconding toy boy had left behind him here, he was much more concerned about the mischief that he could be creating at home. He could see quite clearly now what had happened: one glimpse of Kate's body in a bikini and he had bolted.

'I suppose you think I've made an idiot of myself,' said Lena Ryan, lifting a glass that was already empty. Fred dragged himself away from a picture of Jeremy Tyrrell beating frenziedly on the door of Kate's studio, his trousers round his ankles.

'As a matter of fact I thought you were rather brave,' he replied. He picked up her glass and emptied his own and then looked for Roy, who was leaning through a hatch to the kitchen where his mother produced pies. 'I thought you might become a heroine for the country's housewives: the woman who said, "Enough is enough",' he told her.

'And I thought Dermot was your greatest friend.'

'Oh, he is. I love him. But I should hate to be his wife.'

'As a matter of fact it was wonderful for the first few years. We had such fun.'

'What went wrong?'

'I grew up and he didn't.'

'Well, you've got your own back now. You look more like his daughter than his wife.'

'I meant mentally. He's got the mentality of a teenager. It can get a bit trying when your husband behaves like a naughty son. You start to treat him like one.'

Roy came over and served their drinks and then busied himself with switching the music which filled the bar to Radio Riviera. A chirpy announcer told them that tomorrow would be very hot.

'I must admit that I have never seen much virtue in growing up myself,' said Fred. 'Where does it lead to but the grave?'

'That probably accounts for why you get on so well with Dermot,' she said. 'Two boys together not wanting to become men.'

Fred thought this was a little harsh on somebody who

had just promised to give her anything up to £2,000, but was prevented from saying so by the arrival of Philip Hunt, who came through the crowd wearing a pale-blue lightweight cotton denim suit and a red shirt.

'Hi,' he said. 'Do you know I've never been in here before? I get nervous if I step out of my tax haven. This is Roquebrune, isn't it? "Brown rock."'

'Philip, this is Lena Ryan,' Fred said. 'An old friend of mine.'

'She doesn't look that old to me,' said Philip Hunt, smiling at her.

'This is Philip Hunt, a world-famous novelist of whom nobody has ever heard,' Fred told her.

'Well, I've heard of him,' said Lena Ryan. 'I've even read him. Dermot had some of his books on the stall.'

Philip Hunt smiled at this news, managing remarkably to give the ambivalent impression of a man who had learned humility and is very proud of the fact.

'Which ones have you read?' he asked.

'I remember one that made me laugh. Wasn't it about a man who kept playing with himself?'

'Only in the sense that *Major Barbara* is about a girl who plays the tambourine,' said Philip Hunt, a trifle stiffly. 'My novel was a sparkling foray into the turbulent mind of a young man who was struggling towards maturity, according to the *Guardian*.'

'Blimey,' said Lena Ryan, 'all I remember was a chap jerking off all over the place.'

'I've noticed before that what a reader gets out of a book is often quite different from what an author puts into it,' Philip Hunt said, turning to Roy for a drink. 'What can I buy you two people?'

Fred thought that Lena Ryan's succinct synopsis of

*The Man Who Forgot to Breathe* was a masterpiece of brevity and precision, but he didn't want to get involved in a discussion because he hadn't finished the book. He imagined that it was going to end with men in white coats carrying the impotent hero from the page but he preferred to find that out for himself.

'Pelforth Pale is what I'm drinking,' he said. 'Lena seems to be on gins.'

Philip Hunt, competing with the music from Radio Riviera, transmitted this order with some difficulty. 'I sometimes think that the reason why young people like very loud music is that it makes it impossible for them to attempt the painful process of thinking,' he said. 'An entire generation is being cretinized by amplified music.'

'And then they won't read your books?' said Lena Ryan.

'They can't read now without moving their lips, can they? Half of them can't find Britain on a map. The democratization of our educational system will finally have been accomplished when absolutely everybody is pig-ignorant.' He picked up a large whisky that he had ordered for himself, shrugged light-heartedly at the idiocy with which he was surrounded, and said, 'I'm not really pompous, Fred.'

Fred was slightly taken aback at this. He had just been wondering whether Philip Hunt was a shade pompous. Perhaps this was what they called the perceptive power of the novelist.

'What are you doing here, Lena?' he asked. 'You're not working, you're not on holiday and I don't think you're a tax exile. The only thing I can think is that your husband works here.'

'Have I still got a wedding ring on?' she said, consulting

her left hand. 'Well that can come off now.' She removed the ring with a struggle and dropped it into her bag. 'Tell him my story, Fred. If you sell the film rights I want Jane Fonda to play me.'

Out of loyalty to Trader Ryan, Fred's account of the Ryans' recent past omitted no details: microwave ovens bounced off heads, husbands were consigned to tents, slices of apricot slid down blushing cheeks, and randy toy boys zipped up their trousers and flew without so much as an *au revoir*.

Instead of reacting to this troubled saga with a display of sympathy and understanding, Philip Hunt produced a small notebook from his jacket pocket and started to scribble furiously.

'Terrific stuff,' he said. 'I can definitely use that husband in the tent bit.'

'Are you sure you don't want to know the make of the microwave?' Fred asked. 'We're dealing with human tragedy here.'

'I'm a puddle of tears,' said Philip Hunt, 'but I've got to get it down first. How come he had a tent, anyway? It isn't something that most people have among their possessions.'

'Dermot's idea of a holiday used to be a camping trip to North Wales, preferably pitched fifty yards from a pub. We couldn't afford Antigua.'

Philip Hunt scribbled some more: there would be no unexplained tents wandering fortuitously into his narrative. He snapped the notebook shut and returned it to his pocket.

'What are you going to do?' he asked.

'The immediate plan is another gin,' said Lena Ryan. 'After that, who knows? Life's a problem, isn't it?'

'Life is hope, disillusion and tears, in that order,' said Philip Hunt, shaking his head. 'That's my conclusion after considerable study.'

Lena Ryan looked at him. 'Are you not enjoying Monte Carlo?' she asked. She could see in this lugubrious writer a certain wistful charm.

'Monte Carlo is a diorama,' Philip Hunt announced. 'It makes it manageable and I like it. But it's only a small chapter in my gruelling life. What does tomorrow hold?'

'That's what I ask myself, but when I say tomorrow I mean tomorrow.'

'Is there any chance that you'll go back to live with your husband?'

'There's more chance of Ian Paisley going to live in Dublin,' she replied. 'The trouble is that financially he's not even worth divorcing.'

As her glass was empty, Fred bought three more drinks despite still having a full glass himself. The faces in the bar were beginning to become familiar now. The King's Head clearly had a regular clientele of people who lived and worked here and did not depend on itinerant tourists – most of whom would never find the place.

'As Jim Fixx spent most of his time jogging, there was a good chance that that is what he would be doing when he died,' Roy said as he took the money. He had waited a long time to get his answer in and seemed very happy with it.

Philip Hunt was stroking his moustache and studying Lena Ryan in much the same way, Fred thought, as he had looked at the girl in the pool.

'How would it be,' he said, 'if I invited you out to dinner tomorrow evening?'

'It would be lovely,' she said almost girlishly.

'The Belle Époque at the Hermitage, I think. *Un restaurant élégant*.'

'A word of advice,' said Fred. 'Go for the cheeseboard. It doesn't stain as much.'

# TWELVE

ONE afternoon Fred arrived back at his apartment slightly buzzed from the consumption of two litres of Tuborg, to find that somebody had penetrated the vaunted security system sufficiently to slide a note under his door. The note, written in capital letters on Loews Hotel notepaper, said: COME TO ROOM 444 AT EIGHT O'CLOCK AND GET A SURPRISE. Life wasn't so packed with incident that he could afford to pass up invitations like that but his curiosity about its origin could not survive the sleep-inducing qualities of four pints of Tuborg and he was soon lying dressed on his bed dreaming about Cockle the Emu.

He had broken his own rules about lunchtime drinking in the Bar Tabac, where he had sat at one of their little round marble tables and written a letter to Kate. The alcohol was supposed to be an aid in this creative endeavour and up to the third glass it had been. But the fourth glass contributed a poetic and drunken passion to his prose which jarred hopelessly with the delicate and virginal stage which their relationship had reached – if they had a relationship, he thought.

'How are you?' he wrote, and knew immediately that this wasn't going to be an easy letter.

It seems a long time since you flew out of my life and I wait here daily for you to fly back. The sun is still shining and the beach is hotter than ever, but we exiles are prone to boredom and need a little excitement in our lives. Is it Cockle the Emu who is keeping you from me? It would be just my luck to have an emu for a rival. Jeremy Tyrrell, the former toy boy, vanished a couple of weeks ago, leaving Lena in the lurch. Has he come home? Have you seen him? I got the impression that it was the sight of you on the beach that unsettled him. It certainly unsettled me. Could you come here and do it again? Of course, if you found Monte Carlo too claustrophobic, I would be happy to meet you in Nice or Antibes. Or Santiago or Kinshasa for that matter. I know an air ticket shop. Tell me when you are coming and I'll send you one. I find that my life is better when you are around.

This short letter, interrupted as it was by glances at the world going by outside and the frequent struggles to get the waiter's attention, took an hour and a half. Sentences that struck the wrong note had to be ruthlessly deleted, as did others that had taken him quite a long way in the wrong direction before he realized the destination they had in mind. Affectionate with a light touch was the mood he was seeking; if he presumed too much, it might alarm her. Now all he had to do was write the whole letter out again without the deletions.

He imagined that she was working. The self-employed usually were. But if his encouragement could get her back on a plane, here it was. Buried in the letter was the question that nagged him. Had Jeremy Tyrrell arrived at her door with flowers? The unwelcome possibility had given Fred the idea of flying home. After all, he was allowed ninety days in Britain during this year's exile. But he decided reluctantly that he would look rather foolish if the two of them were together again and even more foolish if they weren't.

The previous afternoon, when a rare collection of clouds

had gathered over Sospel or L'Escarène and then drifted south to obliterate the sun, he had sat in his most comfortable chair and finished *The Man Who Forgot to Breathe*. His journey to the final page had been impeded by a repetitionary quality in the story of Jed Wilmott, although he had to admire the sheer inventiveness of the author in thinking of so many ways in which the frenetic hero could deal with his problem. Fred had been quite wrong, he discovered, in expecting Jed to be carried off, impotent and deranged, by men in white coats. He ended up working in a palatial hospital in California earning a small fortune as a sperm donor. This brought Philip Hunt to the only joke in what had developed into a surprisingly solemn book. When Jed Wilmott refused to produce until they increased his pay, the more entertaining English newspapers all chose the same headline: SEMEN STRIKE!

When he had finished the book he went out on to his balcony to see whether the clouds had moved on. He was now keeping a 'list of things to do' to keep himself active. He had once thought that sitting here alone for a year would turn him into a cabbage; the reality was that he was much busier than he had ever been at home. At the top of his list was a visit to the exotic garden which was described as one of the wonders of Europe. The garden, on a rocky hillside that protected it from both the north wind and the mistral, had its own microclimate, which produced the huge plants only otherwise seen in Africa or Mexico.

On the balcony he found that the sky was blue again and he saw Philip Hunt and Lena Ryan lying by the pool. It was the first time he had seen them since he had introduced them; filled with curiosity, he hurried to the lift.

They were lying on sunbeds, a small table covered with

drinks between them. When Fred arrived neither seemed capable of moving from a prostrate position.

'Hi,' said Philip Hunt, opening one eye. He was wearing a new pair of blue boxer shorts and looked even more gaunt than usual.

'I've been looking for you,' Fred said, pulling up a chair.

'But you couldn't find us?' said Lena Ryan. She had a new bikini and looked fairly tired herself. Fred thought that they had probably been frantically occupied in the bedroom. Philip Hunt's next remark reinforced this suspicion.

'We haven't been out much. How are you? Have a drink.'

Fred picked up a bottle of Cordon Rouge and poured himself a glass. 'I was looking for Lena mostly,' he said. 'You wanted me to do something for you.'

'Was that the money?' Philip Hunt asked. 'Don't worry, I've taken care of it.'

He had clearly been not in the least discouraged by the fact that Lena Ryan had arrived in his life with a £1,500 bill round her neck. He sat up now and refilled her glass.

'I'm not in the hotel any more, Fred, so you wouldn't have found me,' said Lena Ryan. 'I'm a resident of Park Saint Roman, and a very nice place it is.'

He could imagine them on that first evening, dancing to a cream piano at the *bar terrasse* at the Hôtel Hermitage, the tinkle of music amid the marble columns, and the air heavy with longing and anticipation. Had two people ever needed each other so much? It would be impossible to say who was hunting and who was hunted.

'It was a *coup de foudre*,' said Philip Hunt.

'That's French, Fred,' said Lena Ryan.

'I thought it might be. What is it, some sort of cake?'

'It means love at first sight,' said Philip Hunt. 'My God, even people in England know that much French.'

Lena Ryan sat up and reached for her drink. 'We're going to get married, Fred. What do you think of that?'

'I think Trader will be fairly surprised. He's under the impression that you're his wife.'

'He's riddled with misconceptions, that one,' said Lena Ryan. 'I'm about to disabuse him of several.'

She sipped her champagne and looked very much like a woman who had organized her life to her complete satisfaction. Fred had to admire the nifty transition that she had executed so smoothly. In his more drunken moments Trader Ryan had often hinted that his wife was remarkably bright but until now Fred had had only the somewhat unpersuasive evidence of her marriage to Trader Ryan to go on. Today's news provided belated confirmation of what Trader had told him; if they were about to confront each other in the divorce courts it would be more one-sided than Mike Tyson versus Andy Pandy.

He said: 'Where's the wedding to be?'

'Where else but here?' asked Philip Hunt. 'A romantic setting and a cloudless sky.'

Fred poured himself some more champagne. This lovesome twosome had raced ahead so quickly that they were practically on the verge of issuing invitations.

'Philip is one of the very few men I have met who believes that men treat women badly,' Lena Ryan told Fred now. 'It isn't a very fashionable view at the moment, is it?'

'Women have been used, abused and discarded for years,' said Philip Hunt, 'and if they are not exactly left for dead, they have certainly been abandoned as silent partners at the other end of the dinner table.'

'I think you'll make an excellent husband,' said Fred. He couldn't imagine Trader Ryan making a speech like this. 'Do you anticipate any problems with the divorce?'

'None at all. This Dermot chap has a history of adultery and drunkenness, and I have a very good lawyer in London.'

'But Dermot is in the family home. Lena has deserted it and is living in Monte Carlo with you.'

'She was driven away by his behaviour. Oh, the court will see it our way, I've no doubt. No doubt at all.'

Fred had heard enough stories from the divorce courts to believe him. He couldn't see how they could now prove adultery if Trader Ryan denied it, and flying microwave ovens, he thought, should also be part of the story that the court was obliged to listen to, but he didn't want to dampen this romantic couple's spirits by raising the topic today.

'I've finished your book,' he said instead. 'A very enjoyable read. How's the new one coming along? Have you got over your writer's block?'

'Book?' said Philip Hunt. 'I haven't had any time to write books.'

Waking up on his bed fully dressed and feeling inordinately vague, Fred's befuddled brain grasped at one coherent thought: he would stick to the *eau minérale* tonight. But when he had finally hoisted himself upright he saw the mysterious note inviting him to meet somebody at Loews Hotel and realized that the shape of his evening was not in his hands.

Half an hour later, after a shower and a shirt change, he was cutting through the gardens to the avenue des

Spélugues. The name referred to the underwater caves that abounded in the area.

Bizarre edifices from another age shared the cramped street space here with more modern architecture. The avenue, slanting down towards the sea in a savage U-turn, was the home of several night-clubs and a restaurant, Rampoldi, where the stars were reputed to gather, which Fred kept meaning to visit. At the foot of the avenue was Loews.

There wasn't really room for the Loews complex in Monaco and so it overhung the sea, supported by huge piles that had been driven into the sea-bed. It was a futuristic polygon – hotel, conference centre, casino – decorated in American colonial style with a colourful six-sided piece of art work on the conference-centre roof. The hotel itself was enormous, with five restaurants, three bars and a nightly international cabaret. Walking into the building, Fred had the feeling that he had entered one of the new indoor shopping centres rather than an hotel. Crowds hurried about talking in several languages and once again most of the men, flown here at their employers' expense, wore their names on their lapels.

Fred found the lift and wondered what to expect. For a brief moment during the long walk from his apartment – he now walked almost everywhere in the hope that it was doing him good – he had nursed the happy idea that Kate Seymour was playing a little game and was waiting for him now, suitably unrobed, in Loews. But the writing was not a girl's, and certainly not a girl with artistic talents, and he walked on mystified. He framed a list of the people who could possibly be waiting for him, and then was able to cross each one off.

He reached room 444 and knocked firmly on the door.

From within there came the sound of a glass being placed on a glass table. On these lush carpets there was no sound of footsteps and the next thing Fred heard was the door handle. The door was opened to reveal a smart man in an immaculate grey suit, white shirt and pink silk tie. Fred was about to explain who he was when he realized that the man was Trader Ryan.

'I thought I'd surprise you,' he said.

'You did it. What's going on? Have you had a head transplant?'

'Come in, Fred. Let me tell you.'

He ushered Fred into a five-star room and headed immediately for the champagne. A glass for his visitor was already waiting. Fred looked at the huge double bed, the expensive armchairs and the superb bathroom next door and then went across to the window to admire the view of the Mediterranean.

'You mean you didn't like sleeping on my sofa?' he said.

'That's all behind me now, as the man with haemorrhoids said. Drink this, kid. I'm going up in the world and I owe it all to you.'

'I think I'd better sit down.'

He took the champagne and sat in an armchair. He was having some difficulty in convincing himself that this really was Trader Ryan. Not only had his taste in clothes changed; his greying hair had been cut and brushed back. The impression was of a reasonably successful lawyer.

'I'm rich, Fred,' he said, slumping into an armchair himself. 'I was dead right about the options market. It's absolute magic.'

'How much did you make, for God's sake?' Fred asked. He was thinking that luxurious Loews was about as far as you could get from a camping holiday in Wales.

'The profit was £130,000. That is without the ten grand you were kind enough to lend me and which I have for you here in the form of a bank draft.' He removed an envelope from the inside pocket of his jacket and handed it to Fred.

Fred looked at it and looked at Trader Ryan.

'Tell me what happened,' he said. 'I don't suppose I'll understand but you can tell me slowly.'

'There's nothing to it. The shares went up from £2.60 to £3.20, but the options went up from 5p to 70p. It was just the sort of thing I had been reading about.'

Fred tried to understand. 'I can't even remember how many options you bought,' he said.

'I spent all your money on them – 200,000 at 5p each. I sold them for 70p each. Profit: 65p times 200,000. I've sold the stall.'

'Sold it?'

'I'm going to make the crash helmets. I'm talking to business people about it. Hence the suit.'

'I think I'd better have some more champagne.'

Trader Ryan jumped up and refilled his glass. 'I flew in this morning and crept round to your place hoping to God I wouldn't see you. I wanted to surprise you here.'

'How did you get the note under my door?'

'I gave the security guard a few francs to do it. You can make things happen when you're rich.' He went over to the window and looked at the sea. 'I honestly think this is the happiest moment of my whole life. What was yours?'

'I haven't had it yet.'

'And I had you down as a pessimist! But here I am – a five-star hotel, the fairy-tale princedom, £130,000 in the bank!'

'A new suit,' said Fred. He was finding it more difficult

to adjust to the suit than to the money. 'I've got to congratulate you. It just shows what a man can do when he's got some capital.'

'I always told you, didn't I? Now I move into phase two. The world's scooter-riders and motor-cyclists will all be wearing my patented crash helmet and I'll be a zillionaire.'

Fred's state of shock was such that he was finding it hard to share his friend's enthusiasm. At the same time he was now capable of believing anything. He drank some more champagne and remembered that he had promised himself an alcohol-free evening. Fat chance.

'How long are you here for, Trader?' he asked. 'Or do I call you Dermot, now that you're a tycoon?'

'I suppose Mr Ryan would sound too formal? Why don't you call me "sir"?'

'I'll call you Dermot.'

'Compromise – call me Sir Dermot. How long am I here? I've booked in for a week. I rather took to this place, so I thought I'd come down and give you the good news, not to mention repay your kind loan. Also there's Lena. Are they still here?'

'There's some news on that front,' said Fred. 'She's getting married.'

Trader Ryan put down his glass and looked at Fred. 'What do you mean, she's getting married? She already is married. I was there at the time.'

'Some people do it twice.'

'She wants to marry Jeremy Tyrrell?'

'Good God, no. Things have moved on since then.'

'What's she doing – working her way through the Côte d'Azur?'

'She's met a man called Philip Hunt. He's a writer. You used to have some of his paperbacks on your stall.'

Trader Ryan looked confused. 'Where's Jeremy Tyrrell in all this?'

'He went off suddenly, leaving your wife with a four-figure hotel bill.'

'Well, of course. What did she do?'

'She was stranded and I was going to give her some money. But then she met Philip Hunt and he coughed up. Now she lives with him in my apartment block.'

'I want to see her,' said Trader Ryan.

'You might need one of your crash helmets. What are you – some sort of masochist?'

'Distance, as they say, is a great promoter of admiration. I suppose she looks about eleven now?'

'She looks pretty contented. I should keep well clear of her. She's got things she hasn't even hit you with yet.'

Trader Ryan sat down again and poured them both some more champagne. 'It's different now, isn't it? I'm not the man she knew. Do I look like the man she knew? I've got a lot of money. I've got myself a new image.'

'You seem very keen to get her back.'

'She's about the only woman I've ever met who you can actually talk to. That's why I married her. Where can I find her?'

'In Park Saint Roman.'

'I can see her up there now, shaving her legs and swilling her Pill down with Chablis.'

'If I were you, I'd meet her in a missile-free area. The Gobi desert would do nicely.'

'You don't seem to think that she's going to be impressed by this prosperous, well-dressed man.'

'The trouble is,' said Fred, 'she's already got one.'

When the champagne bottle was empty Trader Ryan suggested a move to livelier parts. He delved in a new, grey suitcase, found an envelope and transferred a fistful of 500-franc notes to his wallet. Then he disappeared into the bathroom and emerged with his hair freshly combed.

'Aftershave without the shave,' he said. 'We businessmen don't have time for the minutiae.'

In the fourth month of his exile, Fred had become accustomed to an alien lifestyle in which he was not forever checking his watch. Shops were open in the evenings, bars were open in the afternoons and some places didn't open at all until nearly midnight. If anybody was working, they were discreet about it, like a man with a secret vice, and Britain's most familiar artefact, a circular screen in collapsible form, raised on radial ribs and attached to a central stick, would be as incongruous here as an Eskimo on the Costa Brava. He was beginning to wonder now what the point would be in rushing home when he had served his year.

As Trader Ryan consulted what Fred saw was a new Lassale watch, Fred drew his attention to some of this.

'We can eat first and drink later, or the other way round,' he said. 'You're not in England now. You can dance at two o'clock if you want to.'

'Let's eat. I owe you a five-course dinner for those sandwiches you bought last time.'

They went out into a humid evening and made the slow, uphill trek to the Rampoldi, where they were surprised to get a table. The speciality was pasta, but they ordered steaks and a bottle of red wine. Glancing round for the celebrities who were supposed to gather in this establishment, they saw only a dissolute pop star whose stellar evolution had ended, as some stars' did, in a black hole. His nose seemed to be collapsing, too, its septum burnt away by years of snorting cocaine.

Trader Ryan worked his way through a first course of tuna fish and beans, and asked, 'What's Philip Hunt like?'

'He's a frustrated 45-year-old, desperate for a partner. It was like introducing a kid to ice-cream. But he seems a nice enough chap. I think he spends most of his time wondering why nobody appears to have heard of him.'

'I read one of his books once and thought it was bloody brilliant, but I'm quite prepared not to like him. Wives dislike the men their husbands knew before marriage, and husbands dislike the men their wives meet after it.'

'In my opinion you'd be better off trying to find a new lady.'

'An ambitious project at my age, Fred. I'm so old I have to put my glasses on to find out whether I've got an erection.'

'You're no older than Philip Hunt.'

'It sounds as if he has been saving himself.'

Their plates were removed and the steaks arrived. Outside, taxis were stopping on the hill to drop off well-dressed customers, who arrived in pairs and received an effusive welcome at the door. It was a continuous ceremony that Fred was nervously monitoring – this was just the sort of place that Philip Hunt might bring Lena Ryan to if they could prise themselves apart for long enough to eat, and the prospect of the Ryans kicking lumps out of each other was not one that he contemplated with any great pleasure. He filled their wine glasses and kept one eye on the door.

Philip Hunt and Lena Ryan were dining at Le Bistroquet. The dinner was a celebration. That afternoon they had dropped into a *bijouterie* near the port and bought an engagement ring which, much in evidence tonight, seemed to give them both a new confidence.

'I've never had one of these before,' she said, holding up her hand, fingers splayed. 'Dermot couldn't afford it. In fact for the first two years of our marriage I was wearing a borrowed wedding ring.'

'Our wedding ring is going to be something special,' Philip Hunt promised. 'White gold with diamonds.'

The very words thrilled Lena Ryan. She had only encountered them before in women's magazines.

'And where will we live, Philip?' she asked. 'Have you thought of that?'

Philip Hunt had rented a basement flat in Earls Court for years, a commitment he was only too happy to relinquish when the film money came through. It was conveniently near his publishers and his agent, and London provided the material and the people that he needed for his books. He had always fancied living in Dorset but was frightened to take himself that far from where he perceived the action to be: in Dorset he might find himself writing about people who had sex with sheep.

'Why not here?' he said. 'If I get a decent advance on the book I keep not writing it could be possible to stay on. The rent's expensive but I wouldn't be facing a tax bill every six months.'

The idea of living in Monte Carlo appealed to her greatly, but there were other considerations.

'You should buy a house,' she said. 'Get your money into bricks and mortar. You rent a place for years and what have you got to show for it? Nothing. Buy a house and your money doubles every five minutes.'

He could see what she was thinking and he didn't blame her. A woman needed financial security.

'That means England,' he said. 'I could never afford to buy in Monaco. Even half a million pounds doesn't get you very much. Could you stand the weather at home after what you've found here?'

'It doesn't rain in bed,' she told him.

Outside they strolled hand in hand across the place du Casino, avoiding the Rolls-Royces that cruised hopefully towards sparkling social functions, and decided that their evening could not end without a drink. Philip Hunt found himself slipping all too easily into a cycle of pleasure that he would never have permitted in his disciplined past, when he could only relax at all if he had written his daily three pages.

Flashman's was crowded but they eased their way through the chattering drinkers and reached the counter. Immediately Lena Ryan saw Fred talking to a businessman on stools a few feet away. She took Philip Hunt's hand and pulled him in that direction: she had to show someone her engagement ring. She put her right hand on Fred's shoulder. He turned to see a left hand held up for his inspection.

'Hallo, Lena,' he said uneasily. 'That looks like a sort of engagement ring.'

'You've got it, Fred. I knew you weren't as daft as you look.'

She turned to include the businessman in this celebration and suddenly realized that he was her husband.

'Good God!' she said. 'What happened to you?'

Trader Ryan swung round on the stool, took in his wife, the engagement ring and, lurking in the background, Philip Hunt, and said, 'Hallo, darling. How are you?'

'Philip,' said Lena Ryan. 'This is my first husband.'

Philip Hunt said nothing but extended his hand, which Trader Ryan shook without a trace of embarrassment.

'What's happened to you, Dermot?' Lena Ryan asked. 'You look as if you've been refurbished.'

'A new image, darling. I've struck it rich. I'm a businessman now. The stall has been sold and I am into other enterprises.'

'What do you mean, you've struck it rich?' she asked suspiciously.

'Just a hundred grand or so. In fact, rather more than that. I've been dealing in the options market. I believe I told you about it, and you were kind enough to offer a little encouragement. "Don't be a prat all your life" were your words, I seem to remember.'

He threw a broad smile at Philip Hunt who, somewhat confused, smiled back. This man did not fit at all with the picture he had been given. The husband he was going to put into a tent in his next novel did not look a bit like this. He decided to buy drinks.

Fred and Trader Ryan wanted pints of Holsten, but Lena Ryan asked for a large whisky. Philip Hunt decided to have one too. Ryan, he thought. There must be some Irish blood with a name like that. They were an unpredictable species.

'Is he kidding?' Lena Ryan asked Fred.

'He's rich,' Fred told her. 'He must be. He's staying at Loews.'

'Has he really sold the stall?'

'So I understand. In today's cliché, he's upwardly mobile.'

'I always knew that success would come for me,' said Trader Ryan, as if he were holding a press conference that had been hastily convened to satisfy a world greedy for his secret. 'Ideas, hard work and a little capital are the ingredients that you need. I expect you found that yourself, Philip?'

His tactics tonight, Fred thought, were quite different from those he had deployed at the Beach Plaza. Affability and charm were being thrown into the battle to save his marriage, the sort of qualities that he imagined were to be expected from a rich man in a new suit.

'I only needed the first two,' Philip Hunt said briefly.

'I needed the third,' said Trader Ryan. 'It was a lack of capital that held me back, wasn't it, darling?'

'That and the thirst of a camel,' Lena Ryan said. 'A tendency to be unconscious at crucial moments during the day was a bit of a drawback, too.'

Trader Ryan joined in the laughter that greeted her observation, but he looked as if he only vaguely remembered this unfavourable picture from the past.

'I *did* behave like that once, didn't I?' he agreed. 'My God, I was an irresponsible youth.'

Lena Ryan, having almost recovered now from the shock of her husband's news, was in no mood to see history being rewritten under her nose.

'A youth aged forty?' she said, glaring at him. 'It doesn't sound quite right.'

'Well, we all break out occasionally,' said Trader Ryan amiably. 'It's a response to the pressure.'

'The only pressure you ever knew was when they were trying to shut the pub,' said his wife. 'You were a junk dealer, Dermot, not the chairman of Shell.'

Trader Ryan paused, wondering what he could say that would not attract such barbed retorts. 'It's not what you were that matters, it's what you are,' he said mildly.

'And what are you?' asked his wife. 'How are we describing ourselves this week?'

'I'm a tycoon in the making, Lena, an entrepreneur. I have a brilliant idea and I have capital. The rest is a doddle.' He picked up the glass that Philip Hunt had filled for him only moments before and emptied it in three gulps. 'Who wants another glass of analgesic?'

He ordered another round of the same drinks from the French girl behind the bar and realized that his miraculous transformation and dazzling prospects had failed to produce the desired reaction in his wife. He knew now that if popular acclaim had swept him into 10 Downing Street, she would resolutely refuse to be impressed. The realization depressed him more than he could have imagined, and drained away his reserves of charm.

He turned to Philip Hunt. 'I gather you want to marry my wife?' he said.

Philip Hunt, only slightly fazed, nodded. 'We plan to get married, yes,' he said.

'Bigamy's OK in Monaco, is it?' Trader Ryan asked.

'I'm divorcing you, Dermot,' Lena Ryan said.

'Oh no, you're not,' he told her. 'You haven't any grounds. I've got the grounds but I'm not divorcing you.'

'I think this conversation is best conducted through solicitors,' Philip Hunt said. 'There's not much point in discussing it here.'

Lena Ryan ignored this appeal for temporary peace. 'Not got grounds? I've got acres. I've got hectares. When the court hears my story I'll get compensation for having been married to you in the first place.'

'I agree with Philip,' said Fred. He had been here before and could see too easily how this was going to end.

'I'm supposed to sit here and let this stranger walk off with my wife, am I?' Trader Ryan asked.

'Your wife had already walked off,' Philip Hunt told him.

'Yes, with somebody else. How long do you think you're

going to last? You'll need new testicles by the end of the year. The middle-aged nymphomania of Mrs Ryan. It'll end up as a novel by Muriel Spark or Brian Moore – or Philip Hunt.'

'Well, I don't have to stay here and listen to this,' said Philip Hunt finishing his drink. 'I had hoped we could handle it in a more civilized fashion.'

'Civilized? With Dermot?' said Lena Ryan, seething now at his dig about nymphomania. 'You've got more chance of playing chess with a pig.'

Trader Ryan shrugged, almost helplessly. 'What an evil bitch you really are,' he said quietly.

The word bitch was one insult too many for Lena Ryan.

'A bitch, am I?' she said, picking up Fred's new untouched pint and emptying the glass over her husband's head. 'I'll tell you something, Dermot,' she said as the beer ran down his face and drenched his new suit. 'The other day you weren't worth divorcing from a financial point of view. Well, now you are.'

She turned then and followed Philip Hunt, who was already making a nervous exit.

# THIRTEEN

THE following morning on the train that carried them west through sixteen stops Trader Ryan finally resigned himself to the fact that his marriage was over.

'I married a terrorist,' he said. 'How do people get to be as violent as that?' He was wearing a newly bought white lightweight suit that made him look, if anything, even smarter than he had last night. Yesterday's suit was being restored to pristine condition by the hotel.

'Frustration,' said Fred. 'The same thing that creates real terrorists. All things considered, I'd say you're lucky not to be in a body bag.'

They were heading for Cannes, a destination that Trader Ryan had chosen having seen it once on television. He wanted a quick look at the Côte d'Azur before cutting short his visit 'to pursue business interests'. The train gave them a fine view of red rocks tumbling into a blue sea, which they would have missed in one of the local high-speed taxis.

'It must have been building up for years and I never noticed it,' he said. 'She's certainly changed a lot in the last twelve months. When I first married her she thought weekly sex was overdoing it. Now she's rarely upright.'

'You're sure that what you were doing *was* sex? She's behaving as if she's only just discovered it.'

'It felt like sex to me. You both hang from the rafters by your ankles – is that right?'

'Don't ask me,' said Fred. 'My memory isn't what it was.'

They walked down to the front from the station at the back of the town, pausing for an hour on the rue d'Antibes, the main shopping street, where Trader Ryan cast a professional eye over the windows as if there were bargains hidden here that he could sell at a profit on the stall he no longer had. But he regretted the time he had spent on this when they reached the Croisette and he saw the topless girls on the beach.

'They're showing their bits and pieces,' he said. 'I think I'll sit here for a moment.' The panorama of brown bodies that strolled almost naked not only on the beach but also between the pink parasols of the beach restaurants seemed to paralyse his faculties. 'We didn't get a lot of this when I was camping in Wales,' he said. 'From the back they look completely naked.'

'Sexual pleasure is for the rich,' Fred told him. 'You know what they say – the upper class have orgasms and the working class have babies.'

There certainly seemed to be an aura of money about the people who sauntered along the front. The pink stones of the Croisette had been laid for Gucci shoes.

'I think it's nearly time for my ham sandwich,' said Trader Ryan consulting his new watch.

'Ham sandwich?' said Fred. 'You don't come to Cannes to eat ham sandwiches. Truffled pâtés, fish terrines and confits are what this place is all about.'

'Let's have lunch at one of these beach restaurants then. I might get nudged by a naked breast.'

They went down some steps to the sand that had been imported from Fréjus and found a table in the shade of a parasol. Soon they were eating grilled langoustines with a garlic mayonnaise dip and salad.

'Is this how the rich live?' asked Trader Ryan. 'I keep

forgetting I'm not poor any more.'

'You look rich in that suit. But weren't you worried about what Lena said last night?'

'Which bit? Nearly everything she said worried me.'

'She's going for your money, Dermot. Her divorce lawyer is going to skin you.'

Trader Ryan stopped eating for a moment. 'How do you mean?'

'Your windfall has arrived a few months too soon. She's entitled to a slab of it.'

'She can't do that. It's my capital. It's my launching pad.'

'I think you're going to find that it's her capital, too. She's still your wife. You were silly to tell her about it.'

'I had to tell her. I was trying to get her back.'

'Well, I told you that was a forlorn mission.'

A bottle of wine arrived a little late, and Fred poured some out. A tall girl, naked except for a golden G-string, sashayed past their table.

'You've really depressed me now,' said Trader Ryan, barely noticing her.

'Well, let me depress you some more. Have you heard of the Inland Revenue?'

'Who are they?'

'Very sinister people, Dermot. They watch out for people who have been earning money and come round and take it. That's why a lot of people don't bother to work any more in Britain. You can keep it if you've stolen it or won it or conned somebody, but if you've earned it, they take it.'

'It seems a strange system to me.'

'A mite bizarre, I grant you. I've become quite an expert in it. That's why I'm a tax exile. What you've made is £130,000. The Inland Revenue will want 40 per cent of that in capital gains tax. That's £52,000, Dermot. I've worked it out for you. Lena's lawyers will swoop next and if you've got enough left to open a pie stall I shall be surprised.'

'But I've never had money before. If you spread it over my working life it doesn't come to £6,000 a year.'

'That's not how they tax it.'

Trader Ryan poured himself some more wine and thought of the implausible past and the now improbable future. The naked flesh that drifted past him was ignored as he stared into his wine, twisted the glass, drank from it and then twisted it again.

'Is this what they call the enterprise economy?' he asked, looking sick.

'That's it, kid. The Inland Revenue show the enterprise, and you make the economies. The first thing you need to do when you get home is see a lawyer and, after that, an accountant.'

'And after that an undertaker.'

As they walked along the Croisette afterwards Trader Ryan's plans for the day began to fall apart beneath a cloud of gloom. He had wanted to see Cagnes, where Renoir lived, and the pretty little town of Biot, dominating the valley of the Brague. They got as far as the old town in Cannes, Le Suquet, and looked at the eleventh-century watchtower that stood above all the other buildings, and eventually Fred got him into the museum below it. There they pondered over an Egyptian mummy's hand and a Japanese warrior's costume, but items like these, which would have enthralled him in the days when he had his own junk shop, left Trader Ryan unmoved.

'Let's get drunk,' he said, as if this was an idea that had never occurred to him before.

'That was always your reaction to a problem, Dermot.'

'Well, it's got me this far.'

They strolled down from the old town to the port and along to the Bar Cristal where Fred had drunk with Kate Seymour, and when they had got themselves some seats at the bar he remembered her sitting on the same stool in her white jeans and sea-blue shirt, laughing happily at his jokes.

'I came here with Kate,' he said, when their pints had arrived.

Trader Ryan turned to him on his stool as if he was glad to have something else to think about.

'I've been so preoccupied with my own domestic joys I forgot to ask. How did you get on with her?'

'Wonderfully – up to a point.'

'The point being the bedroom door.'

'How did you know that?'

'No one ever goes to bed with her. There's a dark secret in her past.'

Fred felt the hairs on the back of his neck stand up. 'What? What do you mean?'

'Oh, just stories you hear. I don't even know whether they're true.'

Fred put his drink down. 'I think you'd better tell me, Dermot. Even if they're not true.'

Trader Ryan was drinking seriously now and couldn't reply for the glass at his lips. He waved his free hand dismissively.

'Forget it,' he said when his glass was half empty.

'I'm not going to forget it now, am I?' said Fred. 'Tell me what you heard. What is she supposed to have done?'

'It's not what she did, it's what her father did.'

'What?'

'Went to bed with her. Or so they say.'

'Her father?'

'He's her step-father, actually.'

'He's the vicar of Arton.'

'Well, most vicars are loopy, aren't they? You've got to be a bit loopy to think you know something that the rest of us don't know. Usually it's a mental-home job, but some slip the net and harangue people from a pulpit.'

Fred wasn't listening to this. He was trying to assimilate what Trader Ryan had told him. In his long exposure to gossip and rumours his experience was that the more unbelievable stories were the true ones.

'Do you mean with her consent?' he asked.

'Good God, no. Look, Fred, I don't know whether any of it's true and I certainly don't know what happened if he did get into her bed, or if anything happened at all. The story is that Kate kept quiet about it for her mother's sake. She was a widow who had only just married the vicar and she worshipped him. Kate told her best friend some time afterwards. That's the source of the story, I believe, but it could be all lies. OK?'

Not OK. Not OK at all, thought Fred. He stared at his drink but couldn't trust himself to pick it up. The story was obviously true. It fitted exactly with Kate's strange reaction in Antibes. *Something happened.*

At first he felt too sick to drink his beer but when he eventually picked up the glass he emptied it quickly.

'I shouldn't have told you,' said Trader Ryan. 'I can see that now.'

'I'm shocked.'

'You look it. You haven't fallen in love with her, have you? That *would* be a triumph of hope over experience.'

Fred was holding his empty glass aloft to attract the barman's attention. 'She's the best thing I've ever met,' he said. The barman came up and refilled their glasses.

'The vicar of Arton,' said Fred. 'I'm going to murder the bastard.'

'That might not be what Kate wants.'

The cheerful crowd that bustled in here to escape from the sun did not expect to find two men looking so depressed. They came in with their children, tired and thirsty after boat trips to one of the islands where they had visited the dark and smelly prison of the man in the iron mask who had been locked up there 300 years ago. Nobody today knew who he was but the most popular theory was that he was the illegitimate brother of Louis XIV. Listening to the tourists chat about it, Fred thought that the prison would make a suitable home for the vicar of Arton.

'Now that we've thoroughly depressed each other, let's try to look on the bright side,' said Trader Ryan.

Fred abandoned a pleasant picture of the vicar in an iron mask. 'Where's that?' he asked.

'I should have thought that what you have seen between me and Mrs Ryan lately would have been enough to convince you that I was right about marriage. My own misogynist beliefs are firmly back in place. You're lucky, Fred. You're single.'

Fred considered this argument, but for it to have had any validity he would have to be able to imagine Kate Seymour hitting him with a microwave oven. His mind baulked at the idea.

'I've decided that being a bachelor isn't much fun,' he said. 'I've tried it for long enough. I'm thirty-six next week, I've got a million in the bank and most of the time I've got nobody to talk to, no one to cherish.'

'Cherish the peace! Do you know how long the average marriage lasts these days? Nine years. The game's up. The bubble's burst. Marriage is *vieux chapeau*, as they say in Cannes.'

'You would never have guessed it from the way you've been chasing Lena.'

'I was chasing the woman, not the wife. Whose round is it?'

'Let's say mine.'

Trader Ryan picked up his new pint. 'Here we are in the south of France, money in the bank, free time and plenty of sunshine, and we're both as miserable as sin. It doesn't seem right to me.'

It was another two hours before they felt optimistic enough to stumble out into the sun. A tired pianist in the next bar was playing some Andrew Lloyd Webber.

Trader Ryan, venturing a dance to this familiar music, tripped over a chair on the pavement and sprawled full-length among the litter. For a moment he seemed to be considering staying there but he eventually responded to Fred's half-hearted suggestion that he get up. He brushed down his new white suit but there were some marks he could not erase.

'I'll be glad when I'm fed up with this drinking lark,' he said.

When Fred's birthday arrived the following week he wasn't quite sure what to do with it. He had never shared the enthusiasm of others for celebrating these milestones to the grave, and yet they were not occasions that he felt he should ignore.

Trader Ryan had flown home with a worried expression

on his face that had not been helped by the size of his hotel bill. His departure seemed to have created a vacuum that Fred hadn't noticed before he arrived.

He left the apartment when he was sure that some English newspapers would have reached Monte Carlo and walked along to the Bar Tabac for coffee. He didn't feel a day older than yesterday but he had, according to the Bible, just moved into the second half of his life, if he hadn't already been in it. In fourteen years' time he would be fifty. How long was fourteen years? He went back that far into his past and remembered his twenty-second birthday. It seemed like the day before yesterday. He had been working in St Ives in Cornwall, doing a summer job in an hotel. It was an hotel in which any member of the staff might be called upon to do any job; only the chef was allowed to pursue a single occupation. Sometimes Fred had been up at six o'clock, cleaning all the shoes before breakfast; on other days he had been the barman, serving drinks until midnight to florid-faced northern businessmen whose wives' aversion to flying had cruelly restricted their holiday options. But there had been plenty of time for the beach and the bars and the barbecues that were constantly being organized by the other holiday workers – students, nurses on a sabbatical, poets, misfits, and it had been a memorable summer. It was an experience that people in regular employment never had.

The *Daily Mail* had arrived at the news-stand and he took it into the Bar Tabac. Normally he liked this paper, finding that its coverage corresponded to the amount of time he wanted to spend on reading about the day's disasters, but today it was obsessed with pollution in the North Sea. There was no more boring sight in British journalism, he thought, than the *Daily Mail* with a bee in its bonnet. He turned to the inside pages. In America an election was moving towards its climax. A man who repeated the old saying, 'If you can't stand the heat, get out of the kitchen,' was apparently going to replace a man in the White House who repeated the old saying, 'You ain't seen nothing yet.' The country that produced great writers was bent on electing leaders who couldn't even find an original sentence. The paper's back page was even more depressing. Britain's athletic selectors had come up with the bright idea of leaving Sebastian Coe out of the British Olympic team. Fred thought that Coe was the most successful sportsman that Britain had produced in this century. He had won the Olympic 1,500 metres gold medal twice, which no human had ever done, and he was the only Briton to even win it once. Fred threw the paper on to another table and drank his coffee. Fred Perry won Wimbledon three times, he thought, but they were wearing long trousers then. Who else was there? The competition for Britain's most successful sportsman of the century wasn't exactly a crowded field.

None of this made enjoyable birthday fare. He left the Bar Tabac and decided that a new, short haircut would be a suitable move given his advancing years. There was a salon on the boulevard des Moulins where middle-aged ladies absorbed the instructions in a dozen foreign tongues and then did it their way. He led them in his direction by using his fingers as scissors.

He hadn't been sitting there long when Philip Hunt came in. Holding his head at the angle demanded, Fred didn't see him but he recognized the voice.

'Hallo, Fred. Has Dermot gone yet?'

'He's flown home,' Fred told him.

'Oh, good. We can come out now.'

'Have you been hiding?'

'I wasn't keen for us to bump into him. Something explosive seems to happen when the Ryans meet.'

'I noticed that.'

When the lady, restrained from her own creative ideas by Fred's finger language, had finished with him he looked in the mirror at a brown-faced, short-haired man whom he hardly recognized.

'*Bon*,' he said, giving her a tip.

He waited while Philip Hunt had a gentler cut and then he waited a bit longer while he had his moustache trimmed to his own meticulous specifications.

'How's the book going?' Fred asked when they were both in the street.

Philip Hunt looked blank. 'I haven't written a word since I met her. There doesn't seem to be time. I'm beginning to wonder how married men write books.'

'Well, they probably don't on honeymoon,' said Fred, but his remark didn't elicit the lubricious information that he had mischievously sought.

'What have you got planned?' Philip Hunt asked instead. 'I suppose every day's the same for you retired folk?'

'Today ought to be different. It's my birthday.'

'Oh, I must buy you a drink then. Let's go to Roy's.'

Fred had managed not to drink at all since the departure of Trader Ryan. Instead he had read books and struggled to master swimming in the pool. But as today was his birthday, a drink seemed almost a duty.

In the King's Head Roy was fixing up a video recorder beneath the television so that that evening he would be able to show the local French boys who were addicted to his dartboard how the game was really played with a tape of a darts championship taken from British television and sent out by his sister.

'Jim Fixx was fifty-two when he dropped dead jogging. I looked it up,' Fred told him. 'Lots of non-joggers last longer than that.'

'How long would he have lasted if he hadn't jogged?' Roy asked.

'Longer,' said Fred.

Philip Hunt produced a wallet full of notes and demanded champagne.

'Where is Lena?' Fred asked.

'She's writing to my solicitor, who is now her solicitor, about a divorce. Do you think her husband is going to be difficult?'

'I think it's finally got through to him that his marriage is over. He got one bruise too many. You haven't noticed any missiles whistling past *your* ear, I suppose?'

'Oh, come on, Fred. That's not the real Lena.'

'The microwave seemed awfully real to Dermot.'

Roy appeared with a bottle of champagne.

'What are we celebrating?' he asked.

'My birthday,' said Fred. 'We're looking at thirty-six wasted years here. People have been born, grown up, had children, become rich and famous and expired while I've been wondering what to do.'

It was true. Entire lives, successful and fulfilled, had reeled past while he had been waiting for things to start. The realization of how short the whole business was became more vivid to him every week.

That morning he had lain in bed and worried about his money. He was beginning to feel guilty about having so much when he needed so little.

'When you decide what you are going to do with your

life, let me know,' said Philip Hunt. 'It could be grist to my mill. I've never met anyone who spent thirty-six years growing up before.'

'I'm thinking about giving my money to charity and becoming a saint,' Fred told him. 'Having kept it out of the wasteful hands of the Chancellor, there must be something useful I could do with it. I don't need it, you see. I don't know what to do with it. When you've never had any money you don't develop the tastes that only money can satisfy. Luxury remains a mystery. What would I do with a huge car or a vast house? I even prefer Roy's Pelforth Pale to this champagne, which tastes like cider to me.'

'Pearls before swine,' said Philip Hunt. 'Give the money to me. I can be relied upon to spend it intelligently.'

'On what?'

'I think I'd start with a three-month round-the-world cruise. There's 90 per cent of this planet that you and I have never seen, Fred.'

'I'm not sure I want to. Arabs cutting each other's hands off, Indians living in cardboard boxes, Poles queueing in the snow. In Pakistan girls who have been raped are locked up for five years for committing adultery. Why should I want to set foot in an evil country like that? And do you know why Jesus wasn't an Australian? Because they couldn't find three wise men or a virgin there.'

'Xenophobia running rampant,' said Philip Hunt. 'It's dismal to listen to.'

'Anyway, you can afford to pay for your own world cruise. You don't give money to a tax exile.'

'I'm not that rich, actually,' said Philip Hunt, pouring more champagne. 'Dermot Ryan has apparently got more money than I have.'

'But he's going to have to pay tax on his.'

'Tax and alimony. Lena's working on it.'

'I thought she might be. You'll get your world cruise after all.'

'If I can keep my strength up.'

'Demanding, is she?'

'She has a certain inventive quality. I can see why her husband was so reluctant to let her go.'

When they had finished the bottle Fred suggested that he should buy another but Philip Hunt was already looking at his watch.

'Lena will be expecting me,' he said. 'I'd better get along.'

Fred didn't want to spend the afternoon drinking, either. He was keen to get back in the pool and continue his struggle with the mysteries of swimming. And when he got back to his apartment, he was glad that he had. A birthday which seemed to have arrived without cards or presents had a treat for him after all.

The letter, from Kate Seymour, had been written with a purple felt-nib pen that demanded large handwriting so that three pages were needed to say very little.

Cockle the Emu has been welcomed with great excitement by a clever publisher and the first book is now being produced with your story. I thought we should celebrate this and am going to bring the proofs down to show you on Sunday 4 September, same flight as last time. Could you meet me at Nice?

Love, Kate

P S Thanks for your nice letter.

Happy birthday to me, he thought. Her letter, brief and businesslike though it was, provoked a small dance around his apartment. He had wondered whether she would write at all and he had only the faintest hope that if she did she would announce a visit. He found his swimming trunks and towel. This development could best be considered in the cooling ambience of the pool.

Amelia Fotheringay, sitting in the shade of her *ombrelle* with a book, saluted his arrival with a wave and he went over to her.

'I'm reading one of Philip's novels,' she said. 'He's a dirty sod, isn't he?'

'Which book is that, Mrs Fotheringay?' he asked, but he could already see. 'Yes, I've read that one.'

'It's disgusting.'

'You seem to have almost finished it.'

'Well, I've got to find out what happens to the poor devil. I imagine he sprains his wrist.'

He sat down on the grass beside her. She seemed a lonely figure. The usual dozen or so were splashing in the pool. They were mostly German. Others sat drinking at the bar in the corner of the garden. They were mostly Italian. Only the British and the Scandinavians seemed to favour prostrate solitude.

'Why don't you get married, Fred?' Mrs Fotheringay asked, looking down at him. 'That's what proper human beings do.'

'Do you recommend it?'

'I can't say I do. The man wants one thing, the woman wants another. Their preferences seldom coincide. But people do it, don't they? The life of the single man isn't exactly a bowl of cherries judging by this poor bastard's story.' She reached for a pina colada at her elbow. Beside it was a brie-and-apple sandwich.

Fred said, 'I read once that every woman should get

married but no man ever should.'

'Well, I must admit that I wouldn't have liked to stay single. My life was better because I got married, despite the fact that my husband was a somewhat morose man. He used to get through two bottles of wine a day, although I suppose it would be more accurate to say that two bottles of wine got through him. But he was pretty witty. He once had the idea of writing a book called *Indoor Games for Flag Days*.'

'He sounds a bit of a joker.'

'Oh, we had fun. I used to love staying at five-star hotels and mingling with the very rich. Now you only mingle with a bunch of insurance salesmen at an expenses-paid conference.'

'I see,' said Fred. 'It's not fun being rich any more?'

'It's certainly no fun on your own. That's why you should get married, Fred. I think you would make an excellent husband and it grieves me to see you floating around here on your own. Haven't you a girl?'

'I'm trying to acquire one, Mrs Fotheringay.'

'Introduce me to one and I'll tell her about your virtues.'

He went over to the pool and got in. The water was warm. His frantic efforts at swimming took him a few yards before his head sank slowly below the surface. He squatted shoulder deep in the water and considered how to handle Kate's visit.

The first thing he was quite certain about was that she should stay in his apartment and not on her own in an hotel a mile away. The second thing was that they should go to bed and make love. The third was that he should get her to talk about the incident with her step-father. Catharsis, abreaction, release.

Sitting in the pool, it all became quite clear to him. It didn't need the tortuous advice of a head doctor to show him that what was required to banish the memory of her family nightmare and prevent it spoiling her life was a normal sexy relationship with a normal sexy man.

He looked across and saw that Philip Hunt and Lena Ryan had found themselves sunbeds next to Mrs Fotheringay, who was holding up his novel and reading excerpts from it. Lena Ryan was chuckling delightedly at these extracts.

Fred got out and went over to them.

'This pornographer has found himself a wife, Fred,' said Mrs Fotheringay. 'You see? It's not difficult.' She turned to Lena Ryan and asked, 'Why didn't you come to my soirée, dear?'

'We hadn't met then,' Philip Hunt told her.

'And now you're getting married? Perhaps you could give Fred some lessons in high-speed romance.'

Lena Ryan smiled at Fred like a flirtatious teenager. He wondered if she knew that she had left her husband for a poorer man.

# FOURTEEN

A sixteenth-century olive mill that had been converted into one of the most fashionable restaurants on the Côte d'Azur seemed a fitting venue for his reunion with Kate, and so he booked a table at Le Moulin de Mougins.

Mougins was an ancient fortified village in the hills behind Cannes. From its hill-top position it provided astonishing views of the Grasse countryside and the panorama continued all the way to the foothills of the Alps. Dotted about the dark surrounding greenery were magnificent hidden villas, including Picasso's last home. The village itself, with its narrow lanes and fifteenth-century fortified gate, had been miraculously restored and the white-walled, red-roofed houses looked as if they were part of a film set.

The old mill, a jigsaw of massive stone walls, had crushed olives for their oil for 400 years until it was converted into a gourmet's paradise only twenty years earlier. Hot canapés accompanied the aperitifs, and the food itself arrived under domed food-covers of pink and white pottery.

Fred had swept Kate to this elegant eating-house within an hour of her arrival and bustled her through the restaurant's creeper-covered entrance. She was still a trifle breathless when they sat down.

'This is to celebrate *Cockle the Emu*,' he told her. 'It should be the best meal you've ever had.'

'Blimey, Fred,' she said, in a mock East End accent, 'you know how to look after a girl.'

She was wearing the same white trouser suit that she had arrived in before, which was a relief to him: he was wearing the same Cerruti slacks and Cardin shoes. The gentle tan that had begun in Monaco had faded under Britain's moist summer, and there was a tiredness about her eyes that had come from hours of drawing and re-drawing in the studio where she struggled towards success. Fred envied her this more than he could bear to admit – a career, a talent, an ambition and the will to achieve it. Her success had softened her in some way and through the tiredness he could see that she was more relaxed.

'They're awfully enthusiastic,' she said. 'They think Cockle will end up with one of those five-minute slots on children's television. Eat your heart out, Postman Pat.'

'Did they give you money?'

'A thousand pounds so far. It's an advance against the book's royalties. They're publishing in December to catch the Christmas stockings.'

'I thought you were just beautiful. I didn't know you were clever as well.'

Kate glowed. 'May I ask where I'm sleeping tonight?'

'There was some loose talk last time about sleeping on my floor.'

'Yes, I did say that, didn't I?'

Fred's initial hope about the dinner was amply fulfilled: it was the best meal that either had ever had, although in his case this did not present the kitchen with an insuperable challenge. Breton lobster arrived in a delicate saffron and orange sauce. It was followed by a mouthful of grapefruit and vermouth water-ice, and then duck with wood mushrooms in a Margaux sauce with apples. They both finished with the restaurant's own speciality, a nougat glacé.

Fred had always been a bit paranoid in restaurants, becoming convinced quite quickly that the waiter despised him. Once, feeling himself placed thoroughly in the wrong, he had even apologized for leaving an unsatisfactory meal. But the service tonight made him feel important. He produced a wad of notes which seemed to convince the staff that he really was.

During the long taxi ride back to Monte Carlo he held her hand as if she might de-materialize in the darkness.

He asked: 'Did Jeremy Tyrrell come to see you?'

'Twice,' she said immediately. 'Once drunk, and once sober to apologize.'

'What did he say?'

'He said that the Mrs Ryan business had been a terrible mistake and that he was in love with me and would marry me tomorrow.'

'Where did this poignant scene take place?'

'At the door of my studio. I wouldn't let him in.'

'He didn't mention that he scarpered leaving Lena Ryan with no money and a huge hotel bill, I suppose?'

'Good God! What did she do?'

'Oh, she's all right. She's engaged to a writer now.'

'She doesn't hang about, does she?'

'The sun makes people romantic.'

He showed her round his apartment nervously, scared that she might feel cornered and demand the independence of a room in an hotel. But she happily took off her jacket and opened her case as if this was her home.

'Have a look at this,' she said, pulling page proofs from her case.

They sat on the sofa and examined beautiful colour pictures of Cockle the Emu in a rowing boat, being pushed to the side of the pond by six smiling fish.

'The pictures will be on the right-hand pages and the words on the left. What do you think?'

'Wonderful,' he told her. 'How many books have you done so far?'

'I'm going to do four a year. I've finished the March one and am working on one that will come out in June.'

He went out to the kitchen to make them coffee and wondered what the sleeping arrangements were going to be. Should he leave her alone and let her recover from her work and her flight? Or would he find, as he had found in the past, that if he didn't make a move tonight, it would have become twice as difficult by tomorrow – separate sleeping would have become a custom that could not easily be changed?

'I've made your bed,' he told her. 'You have silk sheets.'

She looked up. 'Where are you going to sleep?'

'On the sofa?'

'Will you get any sleep?'

'I could sleep on a brick wall,' he promised.

But when she had disappeared into his bedroom he didn't find that sleep came as easily as usual, and it wasn't entirely due to the strangeness of the sofa. Lying there with the balcony doors open and the distant hum of the night traffic on the corniche drifting up to him with the hot air, he realized that she had not expected this gentlemanly arrangement, which thoughts of the vicar of Arton had nudged him towards, but was prepared for something quite different. He had read it in her eyes too late. When he finally sank into a disturbed sleep he was immediately unfaithful to her, dreaming of wild sexual episodes with Lena Ryan, to whom he was not even attracted. He fell off the sofa twice.

Kate Seymour emerged the following morning in a

thigh-length white bathrobe, her hair pinned up attractively on the top of her head. She announced her intention of taking a shower.

'Are scrambled eggs and ham OK?' he asked.

'Lovely.'

'Tea or coffee?'

'Tea. This place is as good as the Hôtel de Paris.'

Breakfast on the balcony gave her an idea. Gazing down at the oddly shaped pool, she decided that she could quite happily spend the day lazing beside it. She wanted to see Antibes again, but that could wait.

'Let's call today a rest day,' she said.

'I like resting,' said Fred. 'It's what I'm good at.'

It was eleven before they got down to the pool. Kate had to iron some clothes that had become creased during the flight out. She seemed surprised to find that Fred possessed an iron. He didn't tell her that he had only bought it the previous day to press his trousers before meeting her at Nice.

Mrs Fotheringay was in her usual position, and she couldn't disguise her curiosity when the two of them came out of the building. She waved an invitation to them across the water.

'Is this the young lady you mentioned?' she asked. 'She looks like Brigitte Bardot.' Having completed her disconcerting tour of Philip Hunt's manual stimulations, she had retreated to the territory she knew: the book on her lap was Agatha Christie. 'And do you like it here, my dear?' she asked when Fred had introduced them.

Fred was waiting for Kate to discard the bathrobe and reveal the bikini, but it was a development that the conversation delayed. She sat on the next sunbed but only removed her shoes.

'I love it,' she said. 'France seems such a happy place.'

'I don't know about that,' Mrs Fotheringay said. 'Three people a week commit suicide under the Métro trains in Paris. They are so used to it that the trains are running again in fifteen minutes. The great thing about Monaco if you're a decrepit old dear like me is the absence of crime. I got mugged on Waterloo Station once.'

'What happened?'

'Oh, nobody took any notice. You'd have to be doing something pretty odd at Waterloo for anybody to take any notice. Buggering a melon might do it.'

'What happened to the muggers?' Fred asked.

'I tried to kill them with my hat pin.'

'Good Lord,' said Kate.

'Oh, I had no compunction at all. I would rather be tried by twelve good men than carried out by six, but they got away with my purse. You don't have that sort of experience here.' She turned to the glass on her table and took a sip. It reminded Fred to order something. When he returned with a waiter who carried champagne in an ice bucket, Kate had shed her robe to reveal the briefest white bikini, which he hardly dared look at: he was so frustrated now that even Mrs Fotheringay's strange idea of buggering a melon wasn't entirely devoid of appeal.

'Kate has been telling me what a sensitive person you are,' Mrs Fotheringay told him. Kate blushed slightly at this revelation, which had obviously been intended to go no further, but Mrs Fotheringay was not acting thoughtlessly. She was helping things along. 'I've told her that if she's got any sense, she'll marry you. Sensitive and rich? What more does a girl want? When I was young you'd settle for a bloke who cleaned his finger-nails if you could find one.'

'Would you like some champagne?' Fred asked her.

'Would a cat like milk?'

He poured three drinks and lay back on his sunbed. Sensitive and rich? He could have reeled off a dozen adjectives to describe himself, several of them by no means complimentary, and not thought of either of those. It was astonishing how the fact of the money had disappeared so completely into the basement of his brain that he never thought of himself as rich at all. He never wondered what luxuries he could provide himself with; he only bought something if he really needed it. Shop windows were still, as they always had been, a temptation he ignored, and a silly price label attached to something that he did want produced the same scornful laugh that it always had. The only item he had bought in weeks was the iron, and that was the cheapest in the shop.

And yet, he guessed, he was now making £3,000 a week in interest, £1 million in five or six years, given the complexities of compound interest. He itched now to give some of it away but had little enough faith in the more famous charities. What percentage reached the desired destination? And what destination should he choose? Abroad, one famine followed another: in that bottomless pit his contribution would disappear without touching the sides. At home, the old and the sick were crying out for help but the government, who could provide it from their back pocket, preferred to squander billions instead on military hardware, convinced, apparently, that the Russians were anxious to march into Basingstoke or Tunbridge Wells.

But the growing sense of guilt that accompanied his multiplying fortune made him recoil from Mrs Fotheringay's adjective and want to disown it. Somewhere in

Britain there was an old lady who couldn't afford to keep herself warm. But how could he find her?

Unsettled by these thoughts, he turned to a much prettier picture at his side but she seemed to be asleep. This at least gave him a chance to study the voluptuous contours of her body without embarrassing her.

It wasn't only the sun that drove him into the pool. If he didn't cool down, he would soon be behaving like a character in a Philip Hunt novel. Splashing around in the water, which this afternoon was almost deserted, he found that he could now swim ten yards or so before he was below the water rather than on it. He surfaced spluttering to see Kate diving in. She swam towards him easily and then floated just out of his reach.

'I couldn't make out whether you could swim or not,' she said.

He stood up in the water and waded towards her. 'First I can swim, then I can't swim. At that stage I sink,' he said. 'I'm working on it.'

'Let me help you.'

He lay on his stomach on the water and she held him up.

'Use your legs,' she said. 'Pretend you're a frog.'

'Kiss me. I want to be a prince.'

'Princes can swim. It's all part of the royal training.'

It was difficult for him to concentrate with her hands on his body, but soon he found that the hands had gone and he was swimming laboriously across the pool on his own.

'Very good,' she said. 'It's just a question of confidence and then it comes naturally.'

When they returned to their sunbeds he ordered more champagne.

'That's very kind of you, Fred,' said Mrs Fotheringay. He filled her glass. It was Kate he wanted to drink it, and when she had done he filled her glass again.

'How's the book, Mrs Fotheringay?' Fred asked.

'I'm beginning to think that Agatha Christie lacks the febrile imagination of Philip Hunt.'

'He will be pleased to hear that.'

'What a wonderful life you people lead,' Kate said dreamily. 'The sun, the champagne, the pool.'

Fred poured her some more champagne. 'This is about as stressful as it gets,' he told her. 'But we put our shoulders to the wheel and soldier on.'

'Put your shoulders to the sunbed and soldier on.'

Lunch seemed to be forgotten in the heat that hung over the garden. There was no wind but the faint odour of suntan lotion drifted round the edge of the pool. At the bar in the corner the Italians were becoming noisier with the drink but elsewhere the sun had reduced the residents to an uncommunicative silence and even the waiters were able to sit down. He would have been quite happy to abandon this torrid setting but the cloudless sky was a novelty that Kate seemed reluctant to forsake. Lying beside her, he knew that if he didn't make a move soon, he never would. Their relationship would have skimmed irrevocably into a platonic realm where any attempt at sexual coupling would not only come as a rude shock but actually be slightly embarrassing. Sex, he thought, should come quickly or not at all.

An hour later when the ferocious sun had begun to turn her nose red she was glad to follow him upstairs into the cool of his apartment. She stood in her bikini in front of a full-length mirror and said, 'I hope I haven't overdone it.'

'You need cream,' he told her, and found some. Rubbing it gently into her shoulders and back while she watched him in the mirror, he undid the top of her bikini and let it fall to the floor. She stood there bare breasted, looking at herself in the mirror.

'You really wanted to see them, didn't you?' she said.

'I did rather fancy a glimpse,' he said laughing. They seemed to him to be remarkable: they had survived the removal of their support without any change of shape. He put some more cream on his hand and rubbed them gently.

'They're not sunburnt,' Kate said.

'So they're not. I'm getting confused.' He knelt down in front of her and rubbed cream into the tops of her thighs where the sun had been particularly cruel and then he found that the bottom of the bikini had to be taken off for him to do the job properly.

'What happens now?' she asked shyly as he kissed her stomach.

'It's just a question of confidence and then it comes naturally,' he told her.

She remembered saying it. 'Do you mean that one good lesson deserves another?'

'Just pay attention,' he said. 'I shall be asking questions afterwards.'

He pulled off his trunks and she stared at him with an expression that was a delicious mixture of fear and fascination. 'You'll never get that in me.'

'Well,' he said, laughing again, 'I'm going to have a bloody good try.'

He leaned back on the arm of a chair and pulled her on to him. His hands were cupped round buttocks made of silk. She winced as he slipped into her and then she gasped.

'You *are* a prince,' she said, and then she was moving too. 'Christ, I could get to like this,' she whispered. He tried to hold his climax but there had been too many celibate months: he seemed to explode inside her.

'Is that it?' she asked when he slowed up.

'That was the *hors-d'oeuvre*,' he said, standing up and carrying her towards the bedroom. Her legs were round his waist and when he untangled them and laid her on the bed he saw blood. The vicar of Arton hadn't been so successful after all.

'Something happened?' he said to her the following day in Antibes. They were having morning coffee at a table on the pavement outside Le Glacier bar restaurant in a corner of the main square. The square was called la place Général de Gaulle. The French, Fred realized, loved to name anything – streets, squares, stadia, airports – after generals, particularly this one.

'What do you mean?' she asked. 'Something happened?' She looked remarkably fresh this morning for a girl who had just spent ten hours in bed, not many of them sleeping. In fact she didn't seem to be quite the same girl. She was more cheerful, more outgoing, more talkative; the introspective streak that had been there like a barrier in front of him had been dispersed by a night of passion. 'Do you mean last night?' she asked. 'Something definitely happened last night.'

'I remember,' he said. 'Shall we do it again tonight?'

'Do we have to wait that long? It's legal in the streets of France, isn't it? They're big on *l'amour*.'

He wondered seriously whether he would be ready for more by this evening, let alone now. Four orgasms in one night had certainly taken the edge off his lust. Steak and wine, he had once heard, was the remedy.

He told her, 'I was talking about something you said when we were in Antibes before. You didn't want to talk about parents and you said that something happened. I'm curious about what it was.' His instinct was that at last, after last night, she would be prepared to talk about it.

She looked at him and then at the little brown wobbly table where their coffee cups were almost empty.

'It's a gruesome story but I don't mind telling you if you think you want to hear it. Shall we have another coffee?'

Fred turned round and beckoned to the waiter. Above a solitary palm tree he could see a plane from Nice climbing into a blue sky.

'My father died when I was twelve,' she said when their cups had been refilled. 'I've since been told that that is almost the worst age for a girl to lose her father. Three years later my mother married again. We were living then in a small village in Wiltshire and my mother, who had not seen the inside of a church when she was married, seemed to find some solace in religion when my father died so unexpectedly. He was a fit, vigorous man who loved sport and the outdoor life, and then suddenly one day he keeled over with a heart attack. We were both shattered. I'm told that I became moody. My mother started to go to church. There was no reason for it at all – she was as cynical as my father. There wasn't a single idea that they couldn't demolish between them, and then suddenly he was dead and she needed something to cling to. Well, you guessed the rest. She married the vicar.'

She stopped talking and picked up her new coffee.

'To provide me with a father, she says now, but I don't

know. He was a handsome man, still is, I suppose. She probably fancied him but I'm quite sure that she hasn't been very happy.'

She drank some coffee, put her cup down and looked round the square. Across the road the pigeons fluttered around the black wrought-iron balconies of the Société Générale offices.

'That's not the end of the story,' Fred said. 'Something happened.'

'So it did. It's something I prefer to forget and now I almost have.'

'Tell me.'

'It was seven years ago, when I was sixteen. They had been married for a year and my mother, after a lifetime of disbelief, had taken to the role of vicar's wife like a duck to water. On this evening she had been kept late at a charity meeting at the church hall, and I'd gone to bed early after a day of O-level exams. I woke up to find a naked man in my bed. There were hands on my breasts, hands between my legs. There seemed to be hands everywhere. I screamed and began to fight and it was a moment or two before I realized that this man was the vicar. All he said during the whole time was, "There's no point in screaming. The house is empty." He was excited and was trying to rape me.'

Her face had become pale during the telling of this story and she no longer looked at him, but concentrated on a small square of sunlight between their coffee cups.

'What I did was get my teeth into his left shoulder. I thought I was going to tear a chunk of flesh away. The noise that he had been making changed quite dramatically – a low, groaning noise became the most frightening wail. In the end he was trying to get away from me and my teeth were the only thing that was holding us together. When I let go he rolled out of the bed on to the floor and lay there groaning. Then he got up and shuffled stark naked from the room with blood running down his back. I lay in bed and didn't sleep again that night. The following day I failed my history exam.'

'What happened afterwards?'

'Nothing happened afterwards. I never said a word about it to him nor to anybody else, except a long time afterwards to my best friend. Thinking about it that night in bed, I knew that the only thing that would be achieved would be the emotional destruction of my mother. I don't believe that she would ever have recovered from the misery that night would have caused her and there had been enough sadness in her life. So I said nothing, and he said nothing. I imagine that she has noticed a certain coolness between us. We don't talk unless we have to and, of course, I've hardly lived there since. I was off to art college very soon afterwards and then I got my own studio flat with money my father had left me. But we both remember and he treats me with respect despite the coolness. I sometimes wonder whether he isn't puzzled about why I never reported him to somebody. I bet he believes that God fixed it for him.'

'And it put you off sex,' Fred said.

'Yes, it did,' she said instantly. 'Not half. What happened that night was very ugly and not at all what the magazines had led me to expect. I lost interest in the whole subject and concentrated on work. Jeremy Tyrrell used to call me frigid, and I expect that I was instrumental in driving him into the arms of Mrs Ryan. You've exorcized a ghost.'

'My pleasure. You're bloody good in bed, by the way.'

'Is that what gentlemen are supposed to say to ladies?'

Behind the ramparts erected to protect a port which had endured assaults since the fifth century was the Picasso Museum, housed in a castle on a terrace overlooking the sea. Beneath its Romanesque square tower was a collection of paintings, drawings, engravings and lithographs that in the inflationary world of art had now moved from the very valuable to the priceless. Picasso had used the premises as a studio after the war and left the works behind in gratitude when he moved on.

While Kate studied these treasures, Fred walked several paces behind her like a royal consort. As a figure of contemporary significance, he found the vicar of Arton more thought-provoking than Pablo Picasso. The violence, the selfishness, the hypocrisy boggled his mind, and the man was at large still, rebuking the ungodly, his saintly reputation firmly intact among the villagers.

As they walked down plant-bedecked alleys to lunch in the old port, he asked, 'Do you need to go home?'

She stopped walking. 'What do you mean?'

'Stay here with me. Move to a brighter, warmer world.'

'Say goodbye to a good night's sleep. I can't do it, Fred. I'm building a career. I've got a contract to fulfil. I need a studio.'

'OK,' he said.

She took his hand. 'It's a lovely idea but I can't think about it now. There's Cockle the Emu to consider. It's time you thought up another story, by the way.'

'How about Cockle and the Vicar?'

'That doesn't sound like a story for the under-fives to me.'

'In the world of the under-fives the vicar is always a good man?'

'Of course. Children aren't equipped to deal with evil.'

'Have you ever read a fairy tale? It's all horror. Little Red Riding Hood, Snow White, who nearly got murdered, the Three Little Pigs, two of whom got eaten. Tell 'em early that vicars are people too. They can handle it. It'll save them getting duped later on.'

'Why don't you stop talking nonsense and buy me lunch?'

He led her into the Chez Felix by the port. They seemed to be sitting in somebody's large front room. Fred ordered steak and wine for himself and felt the stirrings of desire.

The following morning he took her to Italy. The train sped east for a change, through four stops and twelve kilometres, and dropped them in the sunshine at the border town of Ventimiglia, where they needed both tickets and passports to leave the station.

They walked out into the old streets with tall brown buildings that were older and dirtier than the ones they had become used to, and they were surprised at the contrast that an invisible border could provide.

'It must be a bit like this when you go into Mexico from California,' Kate said. 'I don't seem to be surrounded by money any more.'

'Be nice to these people,' Fred told her. 'They strung Mussolini up on a meat hook.'

He was feeling surprisingly buoyant after another night of protracted sexual activity. At some time during the course of it he had convinced himself that he would need a wheelchair to get around in the morning, and then two hours after that he doubted whether he would have enough energy left to climb into one. But now he felt wonderful and decided that it must all be a question of training. Kate, too, seemed to have gained a new vitality from her unusually busy nights. A personality had been liberated by love. She hurried round the shops in Ventimiglia with a spring in her step that Fred was certain had not been there before. He noticed another change, too – she let him buy her a dress. She had come out in jeans and blouse but was transformed in the shop by a short, pink dress with a two-tier frill at the bottom.

They found a little restaurant on the seafront for lunch and decided that as they were in Italy they should have spaghetti.

'I can see the attractions of this place,' Kate said, looking out at an expanse of sand that was more a car park than a beach. 'Yesterday, Antibes. Today, Italy. Tomorrow?'

'St Tropez?' suggested Fred.

'England.'

'I was hoping you might change your ticket.'

'I wish I could. But I have to meet the publishers on Thursday in London. Come with me.'

'It would cost about £600,000 if I stayed too long. And I wouldn't want to leave. I'm not saying you're not worth it, of course, but if I'm going to give that much away the Chancellor of the Exchequer isn't the person I would choose to give it to.'

'Who would you give it to?'

'That's what I'm trying to work out.'

# FIFTEEN

A FEELING that he should rid himself of some of his money began to obsess him. While old people, who had given their lives to helping others, couldn't afford to put the coins in the meter that would provide the heat to keep them alive, he was sitting in the sun in this millionaires' enclave with more money than he would ever need. That he had hung on to the extra £600,000 when he already had a million began to fill him with disgust.

Alone again, with the October days shortening and the sun not quite as fierce as it had been only a few weeks earlier, he sat at the table in his apartment one evening and drew up a plan.

September had slipped past in a haze of heat broken only by darkened assignations with a television set, sometimes alone, sometimes in company, to follow the Coe-less Olympic games in Seoul. It was a dispiriting experience watching Britain's highest hopes being outrun by unknown athletes, and what little enjoyment there was had not been enhanced by a commentary in French. The high point had been Mrs Fotheringay's fascination with the sprinter Carl Lewis, whose bouncing body seemed to enthral her.

'This gentleman,' she pronounced, 'wants to strap that tackle up.'

Fred's plan was to find a man who could give away money. Giving money away, which sounded like one of the world's easier tasks, was fraught with problems if you were fussy about who the recipients would be. In the end he drafted an advertisement which he proposed to send to *The Times*. For reasons that were probably already dated, he imagined that a middle-aged man of integrity and dedication might be discovered among that newspaper's readers.

He wanted a man in his fifties, perhaps somebody who had retired early and was finding, as some newly retired men did, that without the stimulant of work their life was losing its impetus. He would be a man with a social conscience and sufficient energy to spend much of his time travelling. He would be familiar with the intricate structure of the social services, and would have the rare talent of understanding, when a bureaucrat was speaking to him, what the man or woman was actually talking about. The job would be well-paid and last a maximum of two years.

Fred imagined this man touring the country and finding in its poorer quarters old people whose needs were not met by government hand-outs and whose lives were a constant search for fresh economies. Their diet would not be adequate, their clothes would be worn thin, their house would need painting, and some of their furniture would need replacing. Their black and white television sets would be straining their eyes and it would be many years since they had had a holiday.

Finding the man who could carry out this mission without succumbing to the temptation to pocket some of the money himself would not be easy. He could see that he was embarking upon something that was not short of pitfalls but, he told himself in a mood of self-congratulation, nobody had ever said that giving away half a million pounds was easy.

The idea removed a burden of guilt that he had been carrying around for weeks. He had never had any money and had always identified with those who were in a similar position.

Several drafts of his advertisement lay in front of him and he selected the best and re-wrote it until he was satisfied that this would unearth the paragon he sought. He asked for a box number and put a blank cheque and his address in the envelope and then worked his way through the pile of old newspapers that had accumulated in one corner of the room until he found a copy of *The Times* and its address.

In the cool of the evening, with the letter posted, he developed a passion for cannelloni and, sauntering along Roquebrune's litter-filled street, he decided that he deserved it. He loved it that the shops were still open at this time with the fresh vegetables still piled in boxes on the pavement and old ladies slipping out of their brown houses to find the final ingredient for their evening meals. In England towns died at five o'clock and stayed dead for sixteen hours out of twenty-four.

He went into the Italian pizzeria and found a small table against the wall. No sooner had he sat down than he saw Lena Ryan and Philip Hunt beckoning to him from a larger table in the middle of the room. He got up and joined them.

'Great news,' said Lena Ryan. 'Philip is writing again.'

'Oh, good,' said Fred. 'I thought you had writer's block.'

'I've put the book I was working on to one side and started a new one,' he announced. 'It seems to have done the trick.'

He smiled happily at Lena Ryan, who was now unknowingly the poorly disguised prototype for Roxanna, the heroine of his new novel, which he was calling *The Pope's Daughter*. Roxanna, a woman with a nameless grievance, had a penchant for throwing things at her impotent husband who, many thousands of words later, would take up residence in a small tent on the back lawn. Philip Hunt was picking his way towards this delicious denouement with a single-minded commitment that stemmed largely from sexual exhaustion.

'How are you doing, Fred?' he asked. 'Given away your money yet?'

'I've figured out how to do it,' Fred told him. 'I'm going to advertise for a man.'

'You're going to hire a man to give away a fortune?'

'That's the plan.'

'You've got a higher opinion of the honesty of the human race than I have.'

'Well, they can't all be dishonest or the system wouldn't work.'

'The system doesn't work,' said Philip Hunt. 'That's why you and I are sitting here.'

A waiter appeared and took their orders.

'We eat here a lot,' said Philip Hunt when he had gone. 'Never let Lena near a cooking utensil, it might become airborne. Eat out and stay safe, that's my motto.'

'Have you heard from Dermot?'

'No, but he's heard from my solicitor,' said Lena Ryan. 'I expect I'll be hearing from his. Divorce is a great boon for the post office and the legal profession.'

'What is your solicitor telling him?' Fred asked.

'He's telling him all about how he is going to be a bankrupt bachelor. He's telling him he's going to be free like a tramp is free.'

'Poor Trader.'

'He won't even notice. He used to be young and crazy. Now he's old and mental.'

The cannelloni arrived with two pizzas that the others had ordered and two bottles of wine. The restaurant was filling up with the French locals, which Fred took to be a recommendation.

He attacked his cannelloni which, as always, were too hot, and wondered how the lawyers would disentangle the marriage of Trader Ryan. He had heard enough domestic inquisitions over the years and over the beers, usually conducted in a mournful atmosphere of baffled self-pity, about how somebody's marriage had come apart at the seams and taken the money with it, to understand that any adultery had to have taken place within six months of the petition being filed. But Lena Ryan, whose contact with the lawyers seemed to have added a cheeky self-confidence to her recently acquired girlishness, could not know what her husband had been doing in this time.

He poured their wine and asked, 'What exactly are the grounds for divorce?'

'I'm glad you asked me that,' she said, picking up her wine. 'I've become an expert very quickly. It's filed under Section Two of the Matrimonial Causes Act of 1973. Unreasonable behaviour is the answer to your question. This takes in drinking, vanishing, unspecified whoring and falling over in a drunken stupor. Farting and belching are unfortunately not admissible but I'm sure that you recognize the man.'

'It sounds a bit like Trader. Is he going to fight it?'

'That's what I'm waiting to hear. My solicitor thinks not. Financially it will be worth his while to co-operate.'

Fred looked at Philip Hunt. He thought the sound of warning bells would have drained the colour from his cheeks, but then he realized with some amusement that he was listening to this conversation as a writer, learning, memorizing, gathering material.

'Will there be a court hearing?' Fred asked. He half expected Philip Hunt to produce a pad and start making notes.

'Not if Dermot co-operates. It could all be quick and easy. If our solicitors agree, I could have a decree nisi by Christmas, and you can apply for the absolute six weeks after that. Philip and I could be married by February.' She found this idea so entrancing that she kissed him on the cheek. The gesture hauled him back from the realms of fiction and he nodded appreciatively.

'February?' he said. 'That's fine. I can't think why I ever liked living alone.'

Fred thought of the fate that was in store for Trader Ryan and then he thought about Philip Hunt, this late convert to matrimony. Both were so anxious to keep Lena Ryan in their lives. He wondered what she did in bed.

'We're going for a drink afterwards at the King's Head,' she told him. 'Would you like to come?'

'I've arranged to meet Amelia Fotheringay there,' said Philip Hunt. 'She's a witty old thing and I'm going to put her in a book.'

'You follow her around with your notebook, do you?' Fred asked.

He couldn't imagine Amelia Fotheringay in the King's Head; it wasn't her sort of place. But she was sitting at the bar with a nearly empty glass in her hand, looking round at an almost empty room. Roy, they learned, was fending off the years by running to Biot golf course.

'Why have you invited me here?' she asked. 'I feel as if I am in England.'

'I thought you might be feeling homesick, Mrs Fotheringay,' said Philip Hunt. 'Or have you gone off England?'

'I've gone off the England of today. Thrift, hard work, the importance of family life. The Thatcherite virtues. And I don't believe in any of them. They all overlook one cardinal fact – you're going to die.'

'You don't look as if you're going to die to me,' Fred told her.

'A lot of people have managed it. It shouldn't be beyond me, although they say a creaking gate hangs on the longest. Is anybody going to buy me a drink or is this a dehydration contest?'

A French girl took Philip Hunt's order for two large gins and two pints of Pelforth Pale.

'Why are you drinking beer, Philip?' asked Mrs Fotheringay. 'Why don't you get plastered like a proper writer? I suppose it's because you're an improper writer. Your book was rather good, by the way.'

'You didn't find it too . . . raunchy?'

'Not at all. My husband once founded a Society for the Preservation of Erotic Reading Matter in response to all that clean up TV nonsense. I believe it wasn't entirely fortuitous that the acronym was SPERM. Anyway, the books he brought home during that little phase made your stuff sound like Enid Blyton.'

'I don't remember Noddy behaving like that,' said Lena Ryan.

'Hyperbole, dear. But the world is getting ruder. I gave myself a treat today and went into Nice to do some shopping. Have you noticed that the bottles of women's deodorants are now shaped like the male sex organ? I suppose it gives them two chances of a sale.'

'Are you sure?' asked Philip Hunt, pulling a notebook from his pocket.

'You writers,' said Mrs Fotheringay. 'If you kept your eyes open you wouldn't have to make it up. I suppose that when you get married you'll be able to stop writing about onanism?'

'I wrote that book twenty years ago,' said Philip Hunt, looking hurt. 'My life hasn't been entirely celibate.'

'Just as well,' said Mrs Fotheringay. 'Marriage has got little enough to do with sex in my experience. In fact I'd say that marriages are to sex what tortoises are to hang-gliding, but don't let me put you off, Fred. Are you going to beat this writer up the aisle?'

'Apparently not. Kate went home.'

The news silenced Mrs Fotheringay for a moment. 'What do you mean?' she asked eventually. 'In preference to staying here with you? You haven't been buying the wrong soap, have you?'

'She has a career. She has ambitions.'

'But you have money, Fred. There's no substitute for money.'

'There is if you're an artist. It's called job satisfaction.'

'Really? I must say that today's young people seem a strange bunch to me.'

Radio Riviera's music which filled the bar stopped briefly for a news item. In some less fortunate part of the world, hijackers were throwing alcohol out of a plane and demanding instead copies of the Koran.

This information seemed to outrage Mrs Fotheringay.

'There's nothing like religion for destroying a man's mind,' she said. 'Hindu, Buddhist, Christian, Moslem, Shinto, Judaic. Bugger the lot of them. They're all raving mad.'

'You're in great form tonight, Mrs Fotheringay,' said Lena Ryan. 'Why do you get so angry?'

'The older I get, the angrier I get. You find more to get angry about. Don't you ever get angry?'

'I did once throw a microwave oven at my husband's head.'

'Unthinking violence. I'm afraid I find that disgraceful as well.'

'I know what will please you,' said Fred. 'I'll buy everybody a drink.'

Mrs Fotheringay smiled at him. 'I always thought you had the right idea, Fred. Spread a little happiness. Your girlfriend must be mad.'

# SIXTEEN

WHEN November arrived and the sun ceased to be the cynosure it had been since early spring, Fred found himself contemplating a sheaf of letters. They had presumably waited at *The Times* until there were enough replies to justify the postage and suddenly he was submerged in eager applications for the strange job he had outlined so briefly.

Just over 100 people were sufficiently intrigued by the prospect of a well-paid two-year spell of employment to send him the triumphant story of their careers along with such evidence as they could scrape together of a vibrant social conscience. They included a peer of the realm, a retired bank manager, a long-forgotten television personality, an executive in a nationalized industry who had been unseated in the drive towards privatization, and another victim of the same unstoppable force, a Labour MP of forty-five who had been swept out of the House of Commons and into the dole queue by the Thatcher revolution. 'Two years would be just right,' he wrote. 'By then the public will have spotted their mistake and returned me to Parliament.'

Studying these applications, Fred concluded that Philip Hunt had been unduly cynical: many of these people had a lifetime of honesty behind them, and credentials that easily surpassed his hopes.

He had never received so many letters in his life and having been conspicuously unsuccessful at finding a good job himself, he was fascinated to see how other people approached the problem. There was no room for modesty in this sort of missive and yet it had to be balanced, paradoxically, with a measure of obsequiousness. Neither boastfulness nor bootlicking had ever come easily to him: he could see where he had been going wrong.

When he had read every letter the applications covered the table and he read each one of them again placing them afterwards into 'possible' and 'impossible' piles. Then he read the possible pile again and did the same. Two hours later he was left with two applicants. Attracted as he was to the idea of employing a Lord, he decided eventually on the former MP, partly because he was a socialist and might be expected to be in sympathy with Fred's philanthropic aspirations, and partly because a man who was planning an early return to the House of Commons was hardly likely to be caught with his hand in the till. His name was Adrian Broatch.

Fred sent him an invitation to fly to Monaco as soon as possible, a request that he phone immediately with the date so that Fred could book him into an hotel, and a cheque for £2,000 to cover his expenses but with a suggestion that he would appreciate some change. Fred was interested in the change.

It was only when he had finished this task and was clearing up that he realized that there had been more in the post than this: letters that had arrived without the help of *The Times*, which he had not noticed. One was from Cedric Pringle, a friendly note congratulating him on the stoicism with which he was enduring his exile, and reminding him that it would be quite in order for him to spend Christmas in England should he want to. 'You wouldn't recognize your field now,' he added. 'It is a building site full of half-finished houses and half-finished roads, but it is being tastefully done and will certainly not be a blemish on the coastline.'

The other letter, he realized with delight, was from Kate, but he decided to make himself a coffee before he settled down to enjoy that. When he had done so, and had started to read it, he wished that he had prepared a stronger drink.

'When you so generously introduced me to this sex business there was one aspect which you completely forgot to mention,' she began in the large copperplate which was now in itself sexually provocative. The felt-nib pen, fuelled by magenta ink, had covered three sheets of stiff pink notepaper. The exotic effect was to make the letter seem more like a present that should be unwrapped rather than merely opened.

Two home pregnancy test kits from the chemist suggested that I should toddle along to see my doctor. He was quite excited about his findings until he asked whether I was married. I am going to have a baby in June and thought you should be the third to know. I have rung you a couple of times without success. Can you find a place in your heart for this baby?

Love, Kate

When he put the letter down he was surprised to find that its last sentence had brought tears to his eyes. He sat there for some time trying to digest the significance of this news and then he got up and took a can of beer out on to the balcony. The pool was deserted now but a gardener was conscientiously seeing that, whatever the season, the apartments' gardens remained immaculate.

Fred's picture of the future, hazy though it was, had not included a baby, probably because the present never seemed to include a girl. But now that the possibility had appeared he could feel enthusiasm flooding in. Having made so little of his own life, he could devote himself to someone else's. That was what parents did – grafted their failed ambitions on to their children, who were burdened with other people's lofty expectations before they had climbed out of their cots. But he suspected that as a father he would be a soft touch.

Clouds were drifting down to the coast now from the hills to the north and he went back inside and found his writing paper. The letter wrote itself and was the quickest he had ever completed. The sudden prospect of fatherhood seemed to have galvanized him.

Your news is wonderful. I hope that you think so too. Please ring me around six o'clock your time on the first possible evening. I am enclosing a 1,000 franc note towards your phone bill, chemist bill and postage bill.

I love you.
Fred

This was somewhat briefer than he wanted but he felt that what they had to say to each other now needed a telephone.

Four days later it rang at five past seven. In England it was five past six and Fred was already seated beside the phone, anxious to hear her voice.

'Mr Carton?' said a man with a West Midlands accent. 'Adrian Broatch.'

'Oh, hallo,' he said, confused. Now Kate would ring and find his number engaged.

'I have a flight booked for next Wednesday,' said the voice. 'It all sounds very intriguing.'

'I'll book you an hotel, Mr Broatch. There will be a driver waiting for you at Nice. What time do you land?'

Mr Broatch told him the flight number and time immediately. He sounded like a man who was used to winging his way round the globe. Fred wondered whether he had ever paid for a ticket himself.

'I think you'll find it interesting,' Fred told him. 'And very satisfying. I'll meet you at your hotel on Thursday morning at nine o'clock. What return flight have you got?'

'Thursday evening.'

Fred replaced the receiver and struggled to get himself into the mood for a quite different call. When nothing happened he fetched a can of beer. Even allowing for the idiosyncrasies of the postal service it seemed likely that if his letter had reached Adrian Broatch today, then Kate would have heard from him too. But after a quarter of an hour's silence he found his thoughts turning to the call he had just had. There was a modest hotel on the boulevard des Moulins, he had noticed, which would provide suitable accommodation for the once and future MP. Luxury would not be appropriate. All he had to do then was find a taxi driver who would stand at Nice airport holding a card with Mr Broatch's name on it. He was wondering why, with organizational talents like this, he hadn't been sucked long ago into the higher echelons of British industry, when the phone rang.

'It's me,' said Kate. 'I rang and you were engaged and then I had to let a woman have the phone box and she talked for twenty minutes.'

He took a deep breath. 'Marry me,' he said.

'Really?' she replied. 'Why?'

'It's what people do.'

'OK,' she said. 'If you feel that strongly about it.'

Her voice sounded so close it was hard to believe that there were 700 miles between them.

'How are you, anyway?' he asked. 'Are you OK?'

'I'm fine. Are you fine?'

'I'm delighted. Listen, I can't get home just yet. I've got a man coming out to see me. But I'll be there for Christmas and the New Year. Shall we get married in January?'

'Are you sure about this?' her voice said in his ear. He could imagine her in a phone box, her blue eyes, her hair pinned up. 'You're not feeling pressured, are you?'

Her voice now sounded faintly uncertain and then it faded behind some electronic disturbance.

'Are you still there?' he asked, and heard a distant, 'Yes.'

'I wanted to marry you anyway,' he shouted. 'That's what I wanted to do, for Christ's sake. I love you!'

Her voice, suddenly loud again, said: 'There's no need to shout, or they'll all know. Will you write me a nice letter telling me what a wonderful life we will have together?'

'I'll start it immediately. How's Cockle?'

'December 12 is publication day. I'm going to have drinks with my publishers. Will you escort me?'

'It would be a privilege,' he told her, but the line suddenly went dead and he waited in vain to see whether she had the coins to make another call.

Adrian Broatch sat in the lounge of the Hôtel du Louvre in a worn blue suit drinking coffee. He couldn't imagine what had brought him to this bastion of privilege and capitalism; it was so different from the bleak back streets of his old constituency that it was hard to believe they were on the same planet, let alone continent. But he could imagine the people who lived here: dubious tycoons, property developers with secret accounts, pampered film stars, preposterously wealthy aristocrats and, among the ranks of the reviled tax exiles, absurdly overpaid sports stars.

His distaste at this environment was equalled only by his fear of being recognized or, worse, photographed in it. There was a type of gossip column that would derive malicious pleasure from revealing that Adrian Broatch, the doughty defender of the poor, was staying at an hotel in Monte Carlo.

He watched nervously as a man came into the lounge wearing jeans and a short-sleeved shirt. He was tall and thin and very brown and he was carrying a supermarket carrier bag.

'Mr Broatch?' he said. 'I'm Fred Carton.'

Adrian Broatch stood up and they shook hands. This was not the sort of person he had expected to meet at all, but Fred had recognized the former MP immediately. He was short and stocky with a black moustache, the man Fred had frequently seen on late-night television berating plump Tory ministers with a fury that almost made the picture jump. He knew other things about him, too, now that he could put a face to the name. He was so incorruptible that when journalists wrote to him with a stamped addressed envelope he returned the stamp.

'Let me begin by giving you this,' he said, handing Fred a cheque. It was for £1,850. 'I got a cheap flight, the hotel is 400 francs a night and I gather that I can get a train back to the airport.'

'I'm very impressed, Mr Broatch,' said Fred, putting the cheque in the back pocket of his jeans. 'I chose you from 112 applicants and you're obviously the man for the job.'

Adrian Broatch stared at Fred keenly. 'All I want to know,' he said, 'is what the job is.' He had a rough edge to his voice, as if he had shouted outside too many factory gates.

Fred ordered two coffees and delved into his supermarket bag for some notes he had made. He could tell that his coffee companion was more accustomed to seeing people extract documents from a brief-case.

'I want to give away half a million pounds, Mr Broatch,' he said. 'Or, to be precise, I want you to give it away. The job is to find the right people to give it to – old folk who eat cardboard, can't afford a television, and die of hypothermia. That's the target. You can give £1,000 to 500 people or £5,000 to a 100 people. It's up to you how it splits, and allow for your salary from the total.'

Adrian Broatch looked as if Jesus Christ had just wandered in and turned all the water into Mouton Cadet.

'Did you say half a million?' he asked.

'It's some of the money I have saved by being a tax exile, Mr Broatch. We do have a conscience, you see. But I don't trust the Chancellor to spend it properly.'

'With this Chancellor you've got a point,' said Adrian Broatch. 'You're not pulling my leg, are you?' He looked round as if he was beginning to wonder whether a secret television camera was covering this meeting for one of the joke programmes. There were quite enough people in the media who would love to make him look a fool.

'No joke. If you agree to take the job on, it's just a question of arranging the money transfers.'

'Oh, I'll take it on. Nothing would give me greater pleasure.'

'No publicity and, of course, you'll have to keep out of your own constituency.'

'I will. It would be tantamount to buying votes. It's sad, though. I know many deserving cases there.'

Fred consulted his notes. 'I suggest you take £25,000 for the first year, plus your expenses, and then we'll see where we are at the end of twelve months. It may only take a year. You will have to decide how people are paid, cash or cheque, and I'll have the money transferred to a joint account we will open.'

'Nobody ever compared me to Father Christmas when I was in the Commons. Are you a Labour supporter, by any chance?'

'No, I'm not. I hate them all. The only thing your lot can ever do is raise taxes, when they're not stabbing each other in the back. Then they waste the money on wrestling mats for one-legged lesbians or some such insanity and have to borrow abroad. They're an embarrassment.'

Adrian Broatch had been replying to attacks like this for years and with a venom that made his assailants blanch, but this didn't seem to be the occasion for that sort of response. Instead, he said, 'Our heart is in the right place, Mr Carton.'

'Oh, the heart's in the right place but the brain's in neutral. What you and I are engaged in here is the real thing. A little intelligent redistribution of wealth. The only wastage will be what you waste and if that comes to more than 10p I shall be surprised. I'll be in England next month and we can meet up then to see how you are getting on. Any questions?'

Adrian Broatch had never had a conversation like this before. If he hadn't been sent a cheque for £2,000 when he was in England, he would now be convinced that he was talking to a madman.

'Just one,' he said. 'What's your job? I mean what were you doing before you came out here?'

'I was one of the unemployed,' said Fred.

'You were on the dole? So am I at the moment.'

'As a matter of fact I never went on the dole. If you'd given up your job it was only about £20 a week for the first six months, and I was always giving up jobs. I used to borrow when I was out of work and try to pay it back when I had a job.'

'And now you're rich?'

'I seem to be. But you're going to help make me less so.'

Adrian Broatch laughed for the only time. 'That's what socialism is all about, Mr Carton.'

Fred flew to London on an Air France flight on a day in early December. The Côte d'Azur was looking its sunniest. He could imagine the depressing contrast awaiting him after this short journey when he began to descend through the layers of cloud that seem to hang permanently over Heathrow.

His newspaper was filled with the story of an earthquake in the Soviet Republic of Armenia, which had killed an estimated 80,000 people and toppled every building higher than two storeys within a radius of thirty miles. It was just the sort of disaster that he didn't want to hear about when he was hanging precipitately in mid-air, at the mercy of a thousand unknown gremlins. To make matters worse, it had been a year of horrendous accidents, all of which he had studied with an anxious fascination. In the Gare de Lyon two commuter trains had collided, killing fifty-six people. In the North Sea an explosion on an oil rig had killed 167 and injured many more, while in the Arabian Gulf an American warship had shot down an

Iranian aircraft killing 290 passengers and crew. At an airbase in West Germany nearly fifty people had died when a mid-air collision during a demonstration by the Italian aerobatics team sent a burning jet cart-wheeling into the crowd; and in the Caribbean, Hurricane Gilbert chomped through Jamaica and the Yucatan peninsula killing 100 people, and then crossed the Gulf of Mexico and drowned 200 more.

This was neither the time nor the place to reflect on the vulnerability of the human race and, as an air hostess provided him with a gin and tonic, he struggled to fill his head with other thoughts.

The previous day he had dropped in on Philip Hunt to ask him to keep an eye on his apartment while he was in Britain. The author had been writing at a table in his spare bedroom and emerged blinking, as if nothing here was as real as the world he had just left. Lena Ryan was sitting on a sofa in the main living-room, her feet resting on a pouffe, reading an expensive magazine. They looked like a couple who had been together for years.

'When will you be back?' Philip Hunt asked him.

'Some time in January. Just as soon as I've got married.'

'Are you getting married?' Lena Ryan shrieked. 'To Kate? I don't believe it!'

'Soon there'll be three,' Fred told her.

'What a matchmaker I am,' she said. 'I was the one who suggested that you meet her in Nice.'

'And in return I introduced you to Filly Punt.'

'I hope you'll be back in time for our wedding,' said Philip Hunt. 'You might be called upon to make a speech.'

'And people say weddings are going out of fashion! How's the book coming along?' He had noticed now that the walls were adorned not with pictures but with the dust jackets of his earlier novels.

'*The Pope's Daughter* is half-written,' said the author stroking his blond moustache. 'Marriage under the microscope. I tell you, when it's published weddings *will* go out of fashion.'

'I hope it's not anti,' said Lena Ryan. 'Romance is what's lacking in this world.'

'I'm romantic,' said Philip Hunt. 'The book isn't.'

Fred left them to ponder this problem of literary creation and went back to his apartment to write a note to Adrian Broatch, telling him of his dates in England. The former MP had flown home with a bank draft for £50,000 to open a special account from which he would also draw his own salary and expenses. Detailed account sheets, showing where every penny had gone, were to reach Fred at the end of each month.

On the plane somewhere over Lyon or Clermont Ferrand, Fred's mind approached the bewildering thought that he would soon be a husband and a father, not the carefree and careless agent he had been for most of his selfish life. It was impossible for him to imagine himself in this role after years of living on his own. He could see the duties and responsibilities but he could see the pleasures too. He had probably had less experience of children than any man outside a Trappist monastery, but the prospect excited him.

The big event before that was something that he would be glad to have behind him. A sterile room in a register office, a humourless registrar with a large book, intoning words that would sound just faintly familiar. He and Kate in the front seats, relatives and friends sitting in uneasy silence behind. But what friends? What relatives?

The vicar of Arton?

He drank his gin and looked down from his window at what he took to be the Loire. Dusk was falling now and it would be dark before they landed in London. He would get a taxi to the country and book himself into the hotel. Tomorrow morning he would brighten Kate's day by turning up at her studio. She didn't even know that he was on his way home.

# PART THREE

Money, it turned out, was exactly like sex. You thought of nothing else if you didn't have it and thought of other things if you did.

James Baldwin
*Nobody Knows My Name*

Too many people have decided to do without generosity in order to practise charity.

Albert Camus
*The Fall*

# SEVENTEEN

HE knew from the light that he was back in England directly he opened his eyes. A low, overcast sky was offering very little help in illuminating the room and it was only when he stretched out an arm to flick a switch that he remembered that he was in an hotel and not his old flat. There was no switch to flick, only a light that came on over his head when he tugged a cord. When he got dressed he found a thick green sweater that he had hauled unnecessarily all the way to Monaco.

The first compensation for being in this country arrived in the shape of breakfast, a huge meal of cereals, egg, bacon, sausages and tomatoes, unlike anything he had seen in the morning for months. The early delivery of the morning paper, which he read over his breakfast, was another civilized bonus. The pink restaurant, with two chandeliers, an ornate wood-frame ceiling and a big, old fireplace, was a quaint reminder to the weary traveller that this was a very old building. Fred had been using it for years but had seldom penetrated further than its Cellar Bar. Eating breakfast here was a novelty that he enjoyed.

He strolled out into the town afterwards and felt as if he had never been away. Christmas decorations hanging across the streets were battling with the cold air in a struggle to attract some early-morning shoppers. Fred was surprised at how empty the town was, but a much bigger surprise awaited him when he had walked a few yards down the street.

There, on his old site and with his old stall, was Trader Ryan. He was wearing the dirty army greatcoat that had appeared every winter for years and blue woollen gloves. He stamped his feet as if he had already been out in the cold too long. He didn't seem to be doing any business.

For a while Fred stood and watched him from the cover of the shopping arcade that ran along to the junction, refusing to believe that Trader Ryan was back in this pitiful predicament. Was time standing still or had the events of the summer been only a dream?

He walked across to the stall; Trader Ryan seemed real enough.

'Cardboard Fred,' he said. 'The reluctant revenant! How the bloody hell are you? I have to tell you that there is something slightly ridiculous about a suntan in December.'

'What are you doing, Trader?' Fred asked. 'What's a rich man like you doing selling baubles?'

'I'm not rich, Fred. I'm broke. If I don't do this I don't eat. In fact, I'm so broke I couldn't even afford to buy the stall back. I'm renting it.'

Fred looked down at the strange assortment of goods that were laid out in front of him. They seemed vaguely familiar.

'What happened?' he asked.

'Well, you know what happened,' said Trader Ryan. 'I took your advice and saw an accountant and a solicitor when I got home. The next thing I got was a capital gains tax bill for £52,000.'

'You still had £78,000.'

'And then my wife and I started to communicate through lawyers. The most expensive way of chatting, incidentally, since Armstrong phoned the White House from the moon. Anyway, both lawyers agreed that she was entitled to half my money.'

'You still had £39,000.'

'You're forgetting the house, which is in both our names. I might still be paying a small mortgage, but the bloody thing is now worth £100,000 and I've got to give her half that. Given your way with figures, you'll have already worked out that I'm £11,000 adrift.'

'I don't believe any of this. She beat you up. She deserted you. She ran away with a toy boy.'

Trader Ryan shrugged. 'That was afterwards. Anyway I don't fancy standing up in court and telling them all that. I can hear laughter. I can see headlines about tents. She wants a quick divorce without any argument and in return will give up all future claims to money or property.'

'It doesn't sound as if there is any more money.'

'Well, she can't come back when the house has doubled in value, or if I make another pile.' He picked up a small bronze statuette of a horse and looked at the price on its foot. 'By this route it could be a long journey.'

That so much money could vanish quite so quickly frightened Fred. He had always attributed a certain solidity to large amounts of cash, which smaller sums never managed to achieve. His own seemed to just sit there and grow. He had joked about Trader losing chunks from his windfall but even his most pessimistic predictions had not envisaged him ending up in debt.

'That was unusual twenty years ago,' he said, 'the house being in joint names.'

Trader Ryan looked at him. 'You don't think I had £1,000 for the deposit, do you? Her father coughed up the money on condition that it was in both names. He thought I was a bad bet for a son-in-law.'

'He didn't?'

'The idea shocks you, I can see.'

'Shrewd bastard, was he?'

'That's why he was the one with the spare thousand.'

'Still, if you hadn't made a fortune on the options market, you would have had to sell the house. Look on the bright side. You'll be sole owner of a property worth £100,000.'

'And I can't afford a steak, I owe £11,000, and I'm going to have to increase my mortgage to raise the money.'

An old lady in a fur shawl was rummaging through the paperback books on the stall, and she picked up a novel by Philip Hunt.

'Have you read this, Mr Ryan?' she asked.

'He's a pornographer, madam. Why don't you take the Graham Greene?'

She dropped the Philip Hunt quickly and picked up *The Honorary Consul*.

'It's set in Argentina,' Trader Ryan told her. 'Much more your sort of thing.'

She gave him 10p and walked off slowly towards the Christmas lights and the shops, where 10p wasn't going to buy her anything very much.

'You ought to be making money out of Philip Hunt,' Fred said.

'Not if I have to praise him. I suppose this weather is a bit of a shock to you.'

'Not half as big a shock as seeing you back on this bloody stall.'

Trader Ryan looked depressed then. Fred suddenly realized that the big appearance change of Monaco had been discarded and he had reverted to his original persona.

His silver hair, no longer brushed back, fell forward again in an untidy fringe, and he needed a shave. The brief flush of late youth had faded as suddenly as it had appeared and he looked even older now than he had before it.

'That's marriage,' he said. 'I can't pretend I didn't know. I've been warning people for years.'

'It sounds brutal to me, particularly as Lena has a rich lover.'

'I don't blame her even now. It's the rules of the game. You shouldn't get married if you can't take a joke. What have you come over for, anyway? Christmas parties?'

'I'm getting married,' said Fred.

'We have a problem,' said Kate an hour later when he had arrived on foot at her studio flat. The walk out of town was longer than he had expected and much colder than he had hoped, but once he had started he had to push on; he was beyond the reach of alternative transport.

Kate's flat was at the top of a converted hop kiln. The largest of five flats, it occupied the space immediately under the roof. Most of it was her studio. In the centre was a large tilted drawing board where she was working on *Cockle and the Easter Egg* with the help of pencils, rubbers, fine-line pens, set squares, compasses and cow gum. Nearby was an easel where she did the occasional painting, the most recent being a flattering portrait of Fred. At one end of the studio was a small kitchen, an even smaller bathroom, and a large bedroom with a low double bed at the foot of which was a portable television.

She was wearing paint-stained jeans and an old sweater, and her hair was swept up at the back and held by two bright red combs. Fred thought she looked wonderful.

'Am I relieved to see you,' she said. 'I thought you'd done a bunk.'

He hugged her and kissed her and wondered how he had managed to stay away for so long. He decided that the back of her neck was an erogenous zone that needed kissing.

When he let go, she dived into a large box on the floor and produced several copies of *Cockle and the Fishes*. Its title was in blue letters above a drawing of Cockle the Emu and underneath, in smaller letters, it said, Kate Seymour.

'On Monday the shops will be full of them,' she said excitedly.

'And in two weeks the Christmas stockings will be full of them. It looks terrific.'

She decided to make coffee and he followed her into the kitchen.

'What a nice place,' he said. 'Roomy and light.'

'I want to keep it, Fred, if we get married. It will always be my workplace.'

'We'll buy a house nearby. So I can come and watch. How are you, anyway? Is everything OK?' He was having difficulty in keeping his hands off her as she poured their coffee.

'I throw up every morning. It's what you get for teaching a chap to swim. Do you take sugar? I ought to know that if we're going to get married.'

He realized that she wasn't really expecting them to get married at all.

'Why do you keep saying *if*?' he asked. 'I've come here to marry you. That's why I'm visiting this benighted country.'

She put the coffees on a small table in the corner of the kitchen and they both sat down.

'Where would this amazing event take place?' she asked. 'Have you thought of that?'

'Thought of it? I've dreamed about it. There are places called register offices. You go in single and come out hitched. It's quite painless by all accounts.'

Her face looked strained. 'We have a problem,' she said.

Fred wanted this brushed aside immediately. This was the year in which problems had disappeared from his life. They had been replaced by something much more pleasant.

'I talked to my mother and the vicar. They were going to know sooner or later, so I thought I'd get it over with.'

Fred had spent a lot of time contemplating his marriage, and his life with Kate afterwards, but he had not given this couple a thought. Having no relatives himself, he was apt to forget that other people still had them.

'How did they take it?' he asked.

'I think they were more surprised than angry. It wasn't what they expected to happen to me.'

'So what's the problem?'

Kate looked at the floor. 'They want us to get married in church – with the vicar officiating.'

Fred stared at her, wide-eyed. 'They want *what*?'

'I know,' she said. 'It's out of the question. But how do I tell my mother *why* it is?'

'Tell her you're an agnostic. Tell her you prefer weddings in a register office.'

'I mentioned a register-office wedding and she went mad. "Your father is a vicar," she said. "Of course he must conduct the service. We would look stupid if he didn't." '

'What did you say?'

'"My father is dead." It didn't go down very well, as you can imagine. The vicar left the room, and my mother went into a long sulk, which she's quite good at. But as I was leaving, she said, "Don't forget, Kate. You must be married in church here. You'd better talk to your friend and give us a date."'

Fred finished his coffee and went out to the studio to think. He couldn't picture Kate sitting in an old vicarage having conversations like this: it was like something from another century. The prospect of the evil vicar's influence reaching out to contaminate Kate's big day was unthinkable.

'Are you working today?' he called.

'Not any more. Why?'

'We have two little jobs. One, buy an engagement ring. Two, visit the register office and see what the formalities are. I bet it's a minefield of red tape.'

'I think I'll get changed for this. It sounds important.'

She disappeared into her bedroom and he sat down at her drawing board and studied her painstaking handiwork. He marvelled at the care and patience that went into one little book and hoped that the world's children were going to appreciate it. She seemed to have a very special talent and he was going to take care of it.

She came out in a short red coat and green trousers.

'It's strange seeing you dressed for winter,' he said. 'You look sort of huggable.'

'Let's get the engagement ring first. A single girl could get into trouble with passionate blokes like you about.'

They went out of the flat and down steps that ran down the outside of the building like a fire escape.

'How do you get into town from here?' he asked her.

'I've got one of those,' she said, pointing at a little blue car. It was a Metro and evidently stood outside in all weathers.

'You drive?' he said. 'I didn't realize.'

'I'm a lady of many talents.'

'Just what I need, having none myself. Kindly drive me to the register office.'

'And what are we going to do about the vicar?'

'Forget the vicar,' he said. 'I'm going to fix him.'

At six o'clock he met Trader Ryan in the Cellar Bar. Coming down from his comfortable bedroom upstairs was a much better approach to a drink than battling for half a mile through the cold wind.

Trader Ryan was already sitting at the counter with a nearly empty pint glass of lager. He was scribbling some figures on the back of an old envelope.

'It's pretty slim pickings on that stall in this weather,' he said. 'And the man who ran it this summer was charging too much and lost customers.'

'You'll survive,' Fred told him. 'How about a drink?'

'Only one?'

'To start with.'

The bar was crowded with early-evening drinkers who fell into the room from their offices for a quick session before hurrying home to an evening in front of the television with their families. They drank too quickly and kept a nervous eye on their watches in the hope that punctuality would avoid at home the friction they had endured at work.

Trader Ryan put his financial calculations back in his pocket. 'I got soaked walking home at two this morning,' he announced.

'You should have been in bed.'

'I had been. Then I got up and went home. It's an advantage not having a wife keeping an eye on your movements all the time. Lena had the 360° vision of a woodcock.'

Fred caught the attention of the barmaid, a woman in her thirties wearing a jade-green silk jersey and brown skirt. She had the sort of face that was sexy without being pretty – smouldering eyes and a big mouth. He ordered two pints of lager, and said to Trader Ryan, 'I'm glad you're not going without.'

Trader Ryan silenced him with a look and managed to convey without speaking that it was the barmaid who had been his enthusiastic partner in the early hours of the morning.

'I used to chase beautiful girls and find that their sexual requirements failed to match my own wild desires,' he said when his new love had moved down the bar. 'Now the world is full of liberated women whose sexual demands expose my deficiencies. Funny that.'

'I'm glad you find it so. You need a laugh.'

'Did you see Kate?'

'I bought her a ring.'

'Love in haste, detest at leisure,' said Trader Ryan. 'No army can stop an idiot whose time has come.'

'I thought it was stop an idea whose time has come?'

'It used to be. What have you and Kate got in common apart from an affection for you?'

Fred thought about this and couldn't think of a single shared taste. Champagne? Sunshine? Fillet steak? Breathing? He said, 'More than I expected.'

'Be warned. A woman will enthusiastically share your interest in all sorts of things before you're married. This interest will vanish as she comes down the church steps.'

'She's not going to come down any church steps, although the vicar seems to be expecting it.'

'The vicar,' said Trader Ryan. 'There's another complication.'

'He's not a complication, he's an irrelevance. In the meantime, I've just thought of something that Kate and I have in common. We're going to have a baby. Well, she's going to have it, and I'll sort of watch.'

Trader Ryan's expression moved from disbelief to horror. 'I think I'd better buy you a drink. This is a horse of a different colour. Lorna, my sweet, a quart of your best lager.'

'Did you stay awake today?' she asked him. At the end of somewhat delicate wrists she had the hands of a steeplejack.

'All day,' he told her. 'It's hard to drop off when you're standing in the street.' He pulled out a wallet that was unusually thin. 'I don't know why I'm buying drinks. I can't afford Christmas this year.'

'It's because I'm going to be a father,' Fred told him.

'So it is. Congratulations. I couldn't be more surprised if Maggie Thatcher turned out to be a woman. What made you do it? Did you think the world's population needed a boost?'

'Demography didn't come into it. I saw Kate in a white bikini.'

'Thus concupiscence doth make paupers of us all. My goodness, look who's just come in. Jeremy Tyrrell, posing as a human being.'

Jeremy Tyrrell, in a smart grey suit, was standing by the door looking round the bar. When he saw Fred he came across.

'Hallo, Fred, I saw you in town from my car this

morning,' he said. His eyes flicked uneasily to Trader Ryan and he nodded. 'Are you still living in Monte Carlo, Fred?' he asked. 'Is Lena? I don't seem to be able to get hold of her.'

'We're both still there.'

At this he took a wallet that was almost bursting with banknotes from his inside pocket. 'What a survivor that woman is,' he said. Suddenly he was counting £50 notes on to the counter and they both watched silently until he reached forty. A gold watch sparkled on his wrist.

'I'm rather ashamed of what I did but I had my reasons,' he said, picking up the £2,000 and giving them to Fred. 'I owe her this. Will you make sure she gets it?'

He left immediately, reluctant to face their questions. When he had gone Fred handed the money to Trader Ryan.

'I think this is yours,' he said. 'It sounds as if Lena will get it in the end anyway.'

Trader Ryan looked at the money and then he looked at Fred. 'Is this honest?' he asked, putting the money quickly into his wallet.

'Quite honest,' Fred told him. 'I know about these things. I'm in the wealth redistribution business.'

'I suppose, when you think about it, that you're not exactly a stranger yourself to the seductive defeatism of failure.'

'You didn't fail, Trader.'

'Well I turned £130,000 into bugger all in six months. There must have been some fiduciary incompetence somewhere.'

'You're never going to be head-hunted,' Fred agreed.

'I'm often willy-hunted, though, which is much more fun.'

'What you should be concentrating on now is a new money-making idea.'

Trader Ryan finished his pint and pushed the empty glass towards Fred. 'Why don't you fill that up? It's the alcoholics who have all the best ideas. The trouble is that they have forgotten them by the time they sober up, so nobody has ever heard of one.'

Fred called Lorna, who was chatting coquettishly with a lonely council officer, not knowing that the man's single attempt at sexual gratification had had a dramatic sequel in court, where the lurid evidence of thirteen boy scouts had removed him for some time from the town's social whirl. She filled their glasses and winked at Trader Ryan.

'I have a wedding date,' Fred told him. 'Friday 6 January. Will you be free on that day?'

'You want me to be your second?'

'Witness it's called, actually.'

'It would be an honour, Fred. I can get my Monte Carlo suit out again.'

Fred tried to picture Trader Ryan in the subdued atmosphere of a register office. It was as far from his natural environment as it would be possible to take him, and then there was his instinctive aversion to the ceremony that would be taking place.

'I know it's a bit like inviting a vegetarian to an abattoir,' he said, 'but you're my best mate, see?'

'*Noblesse oblige*,' said Trader Ryan. 'Where is the female lead in this forthcoming extravaganza, anyway? Shouldn't she be here, catering to your every whim and laughing loyally at your feeble jokes?'

'She's on her way here. We're dining in this very hotel and we would both like you to join us so that we can check up on your table manners, that sort of thing.'

'There's nothing wrong with my table manners, as it happens. I read a book once. Don't pick your nose with the spoon handle, always take your hat off when you belch. You'll find me quite civilized.'

And when Kate arrived Fred was surprised to see him segueing into another role: a man of charm and civility with impeccable manners and a graciousness that almost overwhelmed her.

In the dining-room he told her, 'I'm delighted that Fred is getting married. Now that women are the hunters, getting married is the only way of keeping them off.'

Fred was amused to hear him talk like this. His ability to contradict himself without a flicker of embarrassment would qualify him for high government office if only the right people were aware of his talent.

'The girls pester him, do they?' Kate asked.

'They've never left him alone, Kate,' Trader Ryan told her. 'Letters, phone calls, pathetic lunges at his body in the street. They can't help themselves, you see.'

'If only it were true,' Fred said. 'I wasn't even on the phone. My sex life made a monk look debauched.'

'He certainly wasn't sexually exhausted when I met him,' said Kate. 'I got the impression that he had been saving it up for rather a long time. What sort of father do you think he'll make?'

'He'll be a pussy cat. The kid'll be running him within two years.'

'That's what I think,' said Kate, and they smiled conspiratorially.

Fred could see why Trader Ryan had attracted so many women over the years: their approval was important to him and he worked hard to win it.

In the car park afterwards she threw her arms round

Fred's neck and said, 'Can you tell me something? Why are you sleeping in an hotel when I'm sleeping alone at the studio?'

He disentangled himself and jumped into the passenger seat of her car. 'I was only waiting for the invitation,' he said.

# EIGHTEEN

THE vicarage at Arton was a sombre building that lay back from the road and the smooth village green that faced it. The front garden, if it ever had one, had been laid to gravel and the house itself was built of forbidding grey stone.

Fred was brought to this rural outpost by a garrulous taxi driver who wanted the world to know how disappointed he was with an abrupt change of plot in a television soap opera that Fred had not heard of. His attempts to share the man's disgruntlement were less than convincing.

Mrs Cattermole, who had once been Mrs Seymour, was a small, attractive woman in her early fifties who looked as if she had missed a night's sleep.

'So you're Fred,' she said. 'You look much younger than I had expected.' She ushered him into a cheerless house of rugs and old furniture, and said, 'I'm afraid Kate isn't here.'

'I know,' said Fred. 'She's working. I want to see the vicar.'

'Well,' she said, and leaned against a chair to look at this man who had arrived from Monte Carlo without a job to marry her only daughter, whom he'd already made pregnant. 'He doesn't like to be interrupted when he's in his study working on his sermon, but I'm sure he'll be happy to see you. We've both been so curious about you. Kate tells us you're a tax exile. That must be a lovely thing to be.'

She seemed reluctant to let him out of her sight; she just stood there and stared at him as if she was fearful that he might pinch the spoons.

'It has its points,' he told her. It was hard to imagine that this little lady in a thick grey skirt and a pale-blue cardigan was Kate's mother. Uncertain of his reception here, he had decided to exhibit a cool politeness, but Mrs Cattermole seemed friendly enough. 'Why don't you come down?' he said. 'Kate loves Monte Carlo.'

'I'm sure I would, too,' she replied, 'but we never go abroad and if we did, it would be to somewhere less expensive. Vicars aren't among today's super-earners, you know.'

Fred felt that an offer of financial assistance was called for here but he decided against it: she might bring her husband. Instead, he said, 'What do you think of Kate's books?'

'Aren't they wonderful? We're very proud of her.'

At this moment a door opened behind Fred and a man came in. He was wearing a black cassock. Alexander Cattermole was a big man with greying hair and piercing eyes that were faintly disturbing, like a baby's squint.

'Do I gather that this is our future son-in-law?' he asked in a voice which Fred could imagine would carry without difficulty to the farthest pew.

He offered a handshake that was both bony and cold as Mrs Cattermole introduced them. She addressed her husband as 'Hun' and for a moment Fred wondered crazily whether there was Asiatic blood in this man before realizing that it was her loving truncation of 'Honey'.

'I came to talk to you,' Fred said, 'about the wedding.'

The vicar nodded slowly. He hadn't shaved since dawn and his five o'clock shadow looked like early-morning frost. 'Of course,' he said. 'There are things to discuss.'

'Perhaps you should go into the study, Hun,' suggested Mrs Cattermole. 'I'll make a cup of tea.'

'Come with me, Mr Carton,' he said, although his wife had introduced this unexpected visitor by his Christian name.

As they left the room Fred noticed a huge wood-burning stove at one end; there was something rustic about the rest of the house, with its dark walls and chintz curtains. The study had a stone floor and very little furniture. A packed bookcase covered one wall, another was bare except for a crucifix above an empty fireplace. There was a big desk against the third wall and it was here that the vicar sat, shuffling loose sheets of paper in front of him, the notes for his next sermon.

'Pull that chair up,' he said, pointing to a lonely chair at the door. 'Kate has many fine qualities,' he went on as Fred carried the chair to his desk. It sounded like a prepared speech. 'She is a hard worker, she's ambitious, she cooks well. Understand why I say it, you're a lucky man.'

Fred looked at the vicar without saying anything. He had always found it difficult to take a man seriously if he had to wear a uniform.

'I believe you met her in a bar?' he asked, having failed to draw a reply with his earlier observations. 'People stop drinking when their lives become happy.'

'We all need our props,' Fred said. 'I use lager. Some go to church.'

'Well, as we approach the third Christian millennium, let's see how long lager lasts, shall we? I've seen the damage that alcohol can cause. In my youth I was a prison chaplain.'

'Really?' Fred was interested despite himself. 'One of

life's more difficult jobs, I should imagine. I always thought that capital punishment should have been shunned by the clergy. Walking to the gallows alongside the hangman was very bad PR for God.'

'It was our duty to be there, Mr Carton. Not that I ever had to do it myself.'

'Your presence gave the event a dignity it shouldn't have had.' His seat, which was all wood, was as uncomfortable as any he had sat on. He leaned forward with his arms on his knees in search of a less painful position. The sheets of paper covered with words lay among open books. Borrowed thoughts tediously expressed, he thought. The Sunday morning ritual.

The vicar's hand rummaged suddenly beneath this litter to extract a desk diary.

'What we have to talk about is a date,' he said. 'I understand that we are looking for a weekend in January. It will be cold but perhaps a thicker wedding dress will disguise her condition. I hope, incidentally, that you appreciate the difference between a pretty, single girl and a young wife with a new baby?'

'What's that?'

'It's about the same as the difference between a spaniel puppy and a gorilla with a headache, but don't let me put you off.' His pious smile seemed particularly fraudulent.

'You won't do that,' Fred told him. His months of curiosity about the vicar of Arton had been almost satisfied now. It was time to blow him out of the water. 'I know you're in the persuasion business, but that would be too ambitious.'

The vicar focused his piercing eyes on Fred, sensing an insult, but his visitor was smiling back at him amiably enough. He found it hard to judge this man. He was obviously an agnostic, possibly, God forbid, an atheist, and at no time had he shown the respect which some might think would be appropriate. Never once had he said 'Sir' or even Mr Cattermole. He dressed in jeans, was an *habitué* of licensed premises and had no career. Only two things stopped him from wondering whether this wasn't the moment to ask this disastrously chosen son-in-law to leave the room. One, a *fait accompli* that tied his hands, was Kate's pregnancy; the other was the suspicion that he was appallingly wealthy. Alexander Cattermole despised money, but the church roof was in desperate need of it.

'Let's talk about dates,' he said.

'Let's not,' said Fred. 'Let's talk about shoulders.'

The vicar, unsettled by a distant memory, laid the diary on his desk.

'Shoulders?' he asked.

'And teeth marks.'

'I'm not following you, Mr Carton. What are we talking about here?'

Fred leaned across the desk and talked very quickly. 'You know very well what I am talking about, you lascivious old sod. We're talking about a night seven years ago when you went into Kate's bedroom and climbed into her bed. You ought to be in one of the prisons you used to work in. You need handcuffs, not a dog collar.'

The vicar stared expressionlessly at Fred and held his gaze.

'I have no idea what you are talking about,' he said finally. 'What on earth has Kate been telling you?'

'She told me which shoulder the scar is on. The left one.'

The vicar dropped his eyes at this and looked down at

his desk diary, which he moved a few inches to one side and then back again.

'Why have you come here?' he asked after a long silence.

'To rid you of the idea that you are going to officiate at Kate's wedding. That would be a laugh, wouldn't it? Another of your mistakes is thinking that we are going to get married in church. We are not.'

'And supposing I don't agree with any of this?'

'I haven't come here to consult you. I've come here to tell you. I want Mrs Cattermole to attend our wedding in a register office, so it's necessary that you don't oppose it.'

'I must. I'm a vicar.'

'In that case I will do what Kate should have done seven years ago and tell your wife what happened in that bedroom.'

'She won't believe you.'

The door opened at that moment and Mrs Cattermole came in with two cups of tea on a silver tray.

'Let's see, shall we?' said Fred.

'No, no,' the vicar replied, waving both hands.

'See what?' said Mrs Cattermole, placing both cups on the desk. 'What are you talking about?'

'The wedding,' said Fred.

'It's going to be beautiful,' said Mrs Cattermole. 'I just hope it's not snowing.' She left quickly, as if this bleak room was not territory in which she was encouraged to linger. Fred picked up his cup and drank it slowly, watching the vicar, who was ignoring his and waiting for the door to shut.

'I beg you to reconsider,' he said when it had. 'I'll be a laughing stock. A vicar's daughter gets married in a register office?'

'She's not your daughter,' Fred told him, replacing his cup. 'That's one of her attractions.'

This seemed to hurt the vicar more than anything else that Fred had said. He put both elbows on the desk and held his head in his hands.

'I've treated her like a daughter. I've brought her up. I've paid for her.'

'She was already fifteen when you married her mother. The hard work had already been done.'

Fred looked at his watch. Somewhere outside a taxi driver was waiting with his meter ticking, but Fred had still not got what he came for: an unambiguous undertaking that there would be no resistance to his wedding plans.

'It's time you got on with your sermon,' he said. 'I'm almost tempted to come and hear it.'

'I think my text had better come from Proverbs, Mr Carton. "He that repeateth a matter separateth very friends." Seventeen, nine.'

'If I was familiar with that book, I am sure that I could find something even more pertinent.'

'You would certainly find more charity in your heart.'

Fred remembered Mrs Fotheringay's comprehensive dismissal of all religions in the King's Head. 'I doubt that,' he said. 'The really fanatical Bible-bashers are the most hard-faced uncharitable bunch of bastards on earth, and that goes for any religion from Ireland to Iran.'

The vicar looked at him wearily. 'I think it's time you went.'

'I'm going just as soon as I have your promise that you won't create any arguments over our wedding in a register office.'

The vicar rubbed his eyes but did not look up.

'You have my word.'

Fred got up and left the room. The silence into which he might have dropped a goodbye seemed to echo.

In the hall outside Mrs Cattermole was hovering, looking pale.

'Is everything all right?' she asked.

'Everything is fine, Mrs Cattermole. I hope you will have a Christmas drink with us?'

Outside, the taxi driver said, 'I suppose you're getting married?'

'I am,' said Fred. 'How did you know?'

'That's why people go to see vicars.'

The year of accidents had not yet run its course. On the day that they were going to London thirty people were thought to have been killed, and thirty-five eventually died, in a three-train collision near Clapham Junction which had stopped the subsequent traffic.

Fred found a taxi and they crept up to the capital in a very old car that had not expected to embark on such a long journey. It dropped them in Knightsbridge, where they each had urgent business before the publishers' party. Kate was going on a Christmas shopping spree in Harrods; Fred was meeting Adrian Broatch.

They had arranged to meet in the bar of a small hotel in Basil Street, partly because the former MP was familiar with it and partly because it was near Harrods. He sat at a small table in the same suit, drinking a gin and tonic and clutching a black brief-case. He stood up as Fred approached.

'Mr Carton,' he said. 'Hallo.'

Fred imagined that Adrian Broatch saw him as a sort of

employer. He also sensed that despite his generosity there was a residue of resentment at the tax exile status he had chosen. He thought he would begin by chipping at that resentment.

'Hallo,' he said, sitting down. 'I see that the government is about to waste millions of tax payers' pounds on buying eggs that nobody wants because a member of the government told them that they were probably contaminated with salmonella, and another half million is going to be squandered on advertising eggs. We tax exiles notice things like that.'

'It's all very regrettable,' said Adrian Broatch.

'Regrettable? It's laughable. All that money that I should have paid in tax would have been wasted in sixty seconds.'

Fred ordered them both drinks, rather pleased with this pre-emptive strike. Adrian Broatch opened his briefcase and pulled out several sheets of paper.

'I have no money, Mr Carton. It's all gone.'

'That's the idea,' said Fred. 'Show me where.'

The accounts that were placed in front of him now were detailed to the last penny. The odd pennies figured in Adrian Broatch's expenses – train fares, meals, even bus fares – but nearly all the money had gone to old people in the north of England in amounts that ranged from £2,000 to £5,000. Names, addresses, and the signatures of not only the recipients but also a local government official were appended with each amount. Only £1,000 had so far been deducted by Adrian Broatch towards his salary.

'You've done a wonderful job,' Fred told him.

'It's been hard work, Mr Carton. I've travelled 1,000 miles and talked to almost as many people. What worries me is Christmas. That's when they need money for a turkey.'

'It's not a Christmas feast they need,' said Fred. 'It would probably make them ill if they've been living on a meagre diet. What they need is nourishment and warmth through January and February. Don't spoil them, save them. I've brought you a bank draft for £200,000 and will let you have the rest in January when I get back to my tax haven. I suggest you take your salary out first before you give it all away.'

Adrian Broatch looked at the bank draft. 'You're a remarkably generous man, Mr Carton. Why are you doing it?'

Fred looked at him and laughed. 'I've still got quite a lot left, you know, and it's growing all the time. I'm just glad I didn't stay in England and let the government waste this money on bloody eggs.'

'Even so . . .'

'I wanted to be a tax exile without guilt. People *do* die of hypothermia. An old woman *did* die after eating cardboard. It takes the edge off my pleasure.'

'It would be quite out of the question, I suppose, for me to recommend an appearance in an honours list?'

Fred's expression did not encourage the pursuit of this idea. 'It would be a gross violation of our agreement, Mr Broatch. The whole honours thing is a hangover from our public-school system where the good boy is made house captain. Other countries don't need it. They don't even understand it. It amazes me that your lot have anything to do with it. The trouble is they are always first in the queue.'

'I've got your message, Mr Carton. Perhaps you're the last real socialist left.'

'I'm not sure that's the compliment you presumably intend. Can I get you another drink?'

In Harrods Kate was laden with dark green bags covered in gold lettering.

'You've no idea how much money I've spent,' she said. 'Nearly £300.'

Fred didn't tell her how much he had just spent with the help of Adrian Broatch. Much as the idea might strike her in the abstract as praiseworthy, he was sure that she would think him slightly mad. Was he already withholding information from the woman in his life? How easily it happened.

She led him through the vast store and the Christmas shoppers who jammed it, past furniture and toys and clothes, until they came to the books department, where dozens of copies of the first Cockle the Emu book were piled prominently round a hardboard poster announcing the arrival of this exciting addition to the world of children's books.

'It's marvellous,' said Kate.

'It's wonderful,' said Fred. 'Let's get out of here. If somebody doesn't buy one in a minute you're going to get depressed.'

The publishers were far from depressed. They had their offices in a small house in Bloomsbury and Fred and Kate were escorted to a room on the second floor where guests were entertained on publication days with white wine. Kate introduced Fred as her fiancé, but it was to her that people wanted to talk.

'How are they coming along?' asked a young man who looked as if he had hardly had his first shave. 'We want the summer one within a month. Keep the conveyor belt going.'

'Your fiancée is a very clever girl,' murmured a man with a clipped moustache and a middle European accent, who seemed to be almost salivating at the prospect of huge sales. 'Very beautiful, too.'

The room was filling up with people but nobody was introduced. Around its edges were books on shelves, their bright new covers facing the wine drinkers who had gathered for this brief party. It was an eclectic publishing house. *Power: How to Seize, Keep and Wield It* sat oddly alongside Cockle the Emu. Fred picked up a new 600-page biography of a dead pop star.

'The names are the same,' said a man at his elbow. 'Only the facts have been changed to make it more interesting.'

The young man who had urged Kate to maintain her productivity approached Fred to refill his glass. 'There was a party like this once at Faber,' he said in the convivial manner of a well-trained host. 'T. S. Eliot used to be a director there, and one of the guests came back from the loo and said, "Was it Eliot's toilet I saw?" and another chap said, "That's a palindrome." They're like that at Faber.'

'A man, a plan, a canal – Panama!' said Fred.

The man looked at him. 'Sorry?'

'That's another palindrome,' said Fred. He picked from the shelf a book of a thousand facts and flicked through its pages. The world constipation record was 102 days.

The crowd had shifted now and seemed to be mostly around Kate. He realized that she was signing copies of her book. Was he about to marry a celebrity? She was wearing a yellow dress with a sort of collar that lay over both shoulders, and he knew that she would be the person who attracted attention even if she hadn't done a book.

He hovered on the periphery of this adulation until she came over.

'I think we ought to go soon,' she told him. 'I don't want to outstay my welcome.' But her eyes were gleaming at the compliments that she had received.

'It's your party and you can fly if you want to,' he said. They were interrupted by one of the secretaries whose presence had restored the sexual balance during this wine drinking.

'Miss Seymour, there's a phone call for you,' she said with a respect that Fred found fascinating.

'How can there be?' Kate asked, looking puzzled. 'Nobody knows I'm here.' She thought for a moment and then added, 'Except my mother.'

'It is your mother,' said the girl. 'I'm afraid she sounds upset.'

Fred was left on his own again and headed discreetly in the direction of the wine.

'Another glass?' said the young man who had spoken to him earlier. He filled Fred's glass and said, 'Straw? No, too stupid a fad. I put soot on warts. That's another palindrome.'

'I thought it might be,' said Fred.

'So you're marrying Kate Seymour. Some people have all the luck.'

'It's better than studying palindromes, I must admit.'

'She has a remarkable talent. Millions of people can draw but I've never seen anyone achieve her effect with line drawings. You want to keep her working. Don't let her slacken – it would be a criminal waste of her gifts.'

'I know what you mean, but I'm planning to be her husband, not her boss.'

'In the old days the husband was the boss,' said the young man, refilling his own glass.

'Those *were* the old days,' Fred told him.

Kate returned looking pale. 'It's the vicar,' she said so that only Fred could hear her.

'What about him?'

'He's been killed in the Clapham train crash.'

# NINETEEN

IN a lively Italian restaurant called the Verdi in Southampton Row Kate twisted green fettucini on to her fork and said, 'Apparently he was attending some church conference at Lambeth Palace.'

'I expect they'll manage,' said Fred. His inability to produce the conventional response to a death had left him feeling slightly numb. 'How did your mother seem?'

'Well, upset, naturally. What will happen to her? I suppose a vicarage is like a tied cottage and she'll be out in the street.'

It had been Kate's desire to rush home immediately but Fred had persuaded her to have a meal before the journey; they hadn't eaten all day and he had the idea that pregnant women should not go hungry.

'I promised to stay with her tonight,' Kate said. 'You'll have to use the hotel you're paying for.'

'Who is going to kiss me when I wake up in the morning?'

'That chambermaid with the moustache?'

Singing waiters whose laughter disguised their efficiency bustled round them as Fred thought how complicated life could become. Before they could have a wedding there would have to be a funeral. He wondered whether he would be expected to attend it.

'Has your mother got any money?' he asked.

The question seemed to depress Kate. 'I dread to think. I know Dad left her some, as he left me some, but I don't know how much. It's not something we talk about.'

'We can buy her a house if you want to, but it must be in your name.'

'We?'

'What's mine's thine, kid.'

She looked at him quizzically. 'Fred, tell me something. Have you got a lot of money? I've never understood this tax-exile business.'

'Quite a lot,' he told her. 'Enough to buy a few prams.'

'Tell me how much. Wives aren't kept in the dark any more. They've come out of the attic.'

'More than a million.'

She stopped eating and looked to see whether this was a joke. Her smile, on realizing that it wasn't, triumphantly combined dazed pleasure and shocked amazement, as if to possess so much money wasn't entirely reputable.

'I'm marrying a millionaire,' she said. 'I hadn't realized.'

'A very wise precaution these days, Kate. Of course if I don't hurry back to Monte Carlo after the wedding, there will be a lot less. I have to stay there until May and then we can return to England in June to have the baby and buy a house.'

'I shall have to turn your apartment into a studio.'

'I'll wait patiently in the King's Head so as not to disturb you.'

'I think,' she said, giving him a thoughtful frown, 'that we will have to find some work for you.'

'That's a task that has defied employment agencies for more than a decade,' he told her, and then he thought that he should tell her something else. He had been listening to Trader Ryan for long enough to be familiar with some of matrimony's hazards.

'Trying to change their husband is the mistake that every woman makes. I just thought I should tell you that.

If they didn't like him as he was, they shouldn't have married him in the first place.'

'I thought that you might get bored.'

'Only boring people get bored.'

'My, we are feeling confident these days.'

The rail chaos that had followed the crash meant that taxis were hard to find and, when they were, the drivers exhibited a traditional reluctance to venture far from the capital. But after some kerbside haggling, a fee was agreed and the two of them were cuddling in the back of an old cab, its floor covered with green bags from Harrods, as they chugged none too quickly through the falling dusk towards a part of the country where not all the ground was covered in cement.

Nestling in the crook of his arm, Kate said: 'I suppose it's solved one problem. Avoiding a church wedding.'

'He had already agreed,' Fred told her. 'I went to see him.'

'You went to see who?'

'The Reverend Alexander Cattermole.'

'I didn't know that. When was this?'

'A couple of days ago.'

'What did you think of him?'

'*De mortuis nil nisi bonum.*'

'That's right, he was a sod. What did he say?'

'He that repeateth a matter separateth very friends. He said it was from Proverbs.'

'He could find a quotation in that book to support genocide if he had to. So you told him you knew?'

'I sorted him out, Kate. I left him a chastened man. It's amazing what money does to you. I seem to be able to handle anybody these days. It's the confidence you mentioned just now.'

She kissed him. 'I want you to be confident. An insecure millionaire would be a bit of an oddity. I'm glad you went to see him. Was my mother there?'

'Not in the room. She thought we were discussing marriage arrangements.'

'Well,' she said, 'his God has punished him now.'

'Pity he had to kill thirty other people at the same time.'

When their taxi pulled up outside the vicarage Mrs Cattermole was already standing at the door. It was so peaceful here that she had probably heard their laboured approach when they were half a mile away. Fred gathered up the shopping bags while Kate rushed to hug her mother.

'Are you all right?' she kept asking. 'Are you all right?'

'I'm fine, darling,' said Mrs Cattermole with surprising cheerfulness. 'Good evening, Fred.' She offered her cheek and he kissed it.

Inside he was led to an old armchair beside the wood-burning stove and left to himself while Kate and her mother went to make some coffee. It was a dreary room that he could never have lived in. A surprisingly colourless painting of what looked like the Lake District hung on one wall and an old-fashioned bookcase at the end of the room was filled with identical brown books, presumably a set of encyclopedias. It was a house that, despite the stove, lacked warmth but even worse it was a home where the sound of laughter would somehow seem out of place.

Mrs Cattermole returned with a tray of coffee. Fred tried to see a vestige of Kate in her but the only similarity was that they both had pretty eyes.

'I don't want this to interfere with your wedding plans, Fred,' she said.

He thought it would be impolite to reassure her too

strenuously that her fears on this subject were quite unnecessary.

Kate came in and sat next to her mother on an old covered sofa. Her yellow dress was the brightest thing in the dull room. She linked her arm through her mother's, determined to rescue her from this fresh misfortune.

'I don't think Fred should come to the funeral,' she said.

Fred looked at her gratefully, but Mrs Cattermole had taken over. 'Of course not. There's no question of that.' She turned to her daughter, who seemed surprised by this immediate agreement. 'I know about it, Kate. I listened at the door.'

'Oh,' said Kate.

'Why didn't you tell me at the time?'

'I didn't want to upset you. I thought it might ruin your marriage.'

Mrs Cattermole shook her head. 'I couldn't believe what I was hearing in there. I had it out with him afterwards and he admitted everything and begged my forgiveness. It was awful.'

'It must have been,' said Fred.

'But in a way it has made it easier to bear today's news,' she said briskly. 'Except, of course, that I shall have nowhere to live.'

'I'm going to buy you a house,' Kate told her.

'*You* are?'

'Well, we. My husband and I.'

Fred sat on his hotel bed writing Christmas cards. The ones that he had bought were in aid of the British Retinitis Pigmentosa Society, and he wondered what it was.

Somewhere out in the country shocked parishioners had been saying goodbye to the vicar who had been taken from them so unexpectedly. Widow and step-daughter had stood expressionlessly at the graveside in the December gloom, wondering, no doubt, how actresses could produce tears to order when tears were what the occasion demanded.

Fred had used the opportunity to do his Christmas shopping: a compact-disc player for Trader Ryan, a portable TV for Mrs Cattermole. Kate's present was to be new clothes but he needed her to be there when he bought them.

He turned on the television with the remote control at his bedside. In the year of so many accidents the news should have come as no surprise but he still gaped incredulously at the screen. A Pan Am jumbo jet flying from London to New York had crashed in Lockerbie in the south of Scotland, killing more than 250 passengers and another dozen people on the ground. Television cameras had got there quickly but it was already dark; the full horror and damage would only be revealed at dawn. He stared at the murky floodlit scene wondering whether it was safe any longer to get out of bed, and then inferred from the staccato recital of horrifying facts that some of the victims on the ground were already in bed when death arrived.

Subdued, he went out and posted his Christmas cards – to Philip Hunt and Lena Ryan, Mrs Fotheringay and the Pringle brothers, and one to his mother's friend in Dover, Mrs Stroud.

Carol singers were gathered round a twenty-foot Christmas tree which had been erected near the site of Trader Ryan's stall. At its foot was a brightly lit crib. Fred wondered how painful to people like Alexander Cattermole was the irrefutable fact that Jesus had been born in a pub. The choir that had gathered to join this carol singing did not seem, from their lack of familiarity with the words, to be regular church-goers. The search here was for the Christmas spirit rather than salvation. Girls in jeans tucked into high-heeled, knee-length boots, which instead of producing the desired sexiness caused only an ungainly wobble, were accompanied by pale-faced young men in motor-cycle gear. Young parents with babies in prams, old folks with walking sticks, the lonely single and the entwined couples all stood smiling at the music that filled the street.

Through this festive crowd came a laconic, cheroot-chewing figure in a ten-gallon hat. It was Trader Ryan.

'You look ludicrous,' Fred told him.

'As good as that?'

Fred had wondered earlier what sort of Christmas Trader Ryan would have now that he lived alone, but then he remembered that the holiday had never posed a problem for him whether he had a wife or not. Many years ago he had disappeared into a public house on Christmas Eve with £150 in his pocket and emerged on New Year's Day without a penny.

'You're going to a fancy-dress party,' said Fred. 'Either that or you've got a slate loose.'

'I'm going as Clint Eastwood. What do you think?'

'He doesn't wear that sort of hat.'

Trader Ryan shrugged at the pettiness of this objection. 'Where is the future Mrs Carton?' he asked.

'She's been to the funeral and won't be out tonight.'

'Funerals, weddings, divorces.'

'Births,' said Fred.

'The tuning-fork of history. The social maelstrom.'

'I think we need a drink.'

'I think that as well. I know a place not a rod, pole or perch from here where you can exchange loot for hooch.'

'Show me this place.'

They walked along to the Cellar Bar. A man was playing carols on a xylophone outside the hotel.

'Scientists are struggling to discover intelligent life in space. I'm still trying to find any sign of it on earth,' said Trader Ryan, looking round the bar. He puffed on his cheroot and winked at Lorna the barmaid. 'Who are you going as tonight?'

'Nell Gwyn,' she said. 'I always go as Nell Gwyn.'

When they had their drinks, Fred asked, 'Have you had a Christmas card from Mrs Ryan?'

'As it happens, no. But I'm sending her an interesting little present that should keep her happy. A plastic motorized penis.'

'Philip Hunt will like that. He'll be able to get on with his book.'

Trader Ryan puffed vainly on his cheroot which had now gone out. He picked up some matches from the bar.

'I've had a new money-making idea,' he said. 'This one is mega. It's so big that you are going to be the poor friend.'

'Good. I'd feel easier in that role. It's what I'm used to.'

'I'm working on the idea with a little mechanical genius I know. In fact I shall have to take him on as a junior partner. His brains and my capital.'

'You don't have any capital. What you have is called a debt.'

'I'm coming to that. This idea is a device which you fix

to the carburettor on a car to halve the petrol consumption. Cars are going to do seventy or eighty miles to the gallon and I am going to be filthy rich.'

'You know what will happen? You'll be bought out by the petrol companies.'

'They'll need a lot of money.'

'I understand they have it.'

'In the meantime I need capital.'

Fred drank some lager. 'I catch your drift,' he said. 'As you repaid me so quickly last time, how can I refuse? How much do you need?'

'A bit more than last time, actually. Twenty-five grand would get the thing into production and then profits from sales would finance it.'

'Your Messianic visions are getting a bit pricey.'

'This is the big one, Fred. This is the one that puts me into a Roller. My bank manager is going to call me sir. In fact, if it comes off, the Queen will call me sir.'

'The apotheosis of Trader Ryan – Sir Dermot. For services to transport.'

'You realize the government will go bust from lack of revenue from the filling stations?'

'Perhaps we'll forget the knighthood then.'

Lorna came up. 'Clint Eastwood and Nell Gwyn! It doesn't sound quite right.'

'The love that spanned the centuries! It sounds fine.' He watched her retreating again down the bar and turned to Fred looking worried. 'What do you think then? Are you going to stake us to this idea?'

'What will this gadget cost to make?'

'About £3 each if we make a large enough quantity.'

'And what will it sell at?'

'Twenty. Or, just to be fashionable, £19.99.'

'I'll give you a cheque now.'

'Can you make it payable to T. R. Enterprises? I'm going to form a company. My own money isn't my own money any more.'

Fred got out his cheque book and wrote one out for £25,000.

Trader Ryan looked at it, kissed it, and put it in his wallet.

'I'll make you a director of the company,' he said. 'In the meantime which champagne do you prefer?'

# TWENTY

BY one of those curious tricks of fate that add piquancy to the drab routine of people's lives, Trader Ryan was divorced on the morning of Fred's wedding day.

He heard about it from a telephone call to the Cellar Bar at lunchtime. The grounds of divorce and the terms of the settlement had been agreed in principle by solicitors and because the divorce was not contested, there was no public hearing and neither Trader Ryan nor his wife was required to attend. An affidavit from Lena Ryan, attesting to the truth of the matters in her undefended petition, filed under a section of the Matrimonial Causes Act 1973 for unreasonable behaviour, had been sworn in Nice. With such trouble-free proceedings the Registrar could bring several marriages to a halt before lunch. Pronouncing a decree nisi, he awarded Lena Ryan £89,000, which was a half share in her former husband's declared assets and a half share of the value of their home. Her interest in the house was transferred to her husband and she was released from her covenants on the mortgage. In six weeks there would be a decree absolute.

'For one brief moment in time we are both bachelors,' he announced when he returned from the call from his solicitor.

'And you feel as if you've lost a leg.'

'A wooden leg.'

Sipping orange juice at the bar and feeling strangely apprehensive about the afternoon's formalities, Fred found it difficult to discuss divorce. It didn't seem either appropriate or real; but it was real enough to Trader Ryan.

'I have emerged into the sunlight from a long, dark tunnel,' he intoned. 'It's crazy. You start off spending a fortune to get a woman to lie beneath you, and end up spending even more to get her off your back.'

'This isn't exactly what I want to hear today, Dermot. In ninety minutes I'm going to be one of those bridegrooms.'

Trader Ryan stared glumly at the counter. The slogan on the beer mat in front of him said: 'Ownership of a dog is a twelve-year partnership.'

'You realize,' he said, pointing at it, 'that's longer than the average marriage? Dogs do as they're told and don't throw things at you, that's why. When you fall through the front door and collapse in the hall farting like a balloon, they don't say, "Where the hell do you think you've been?" They're delighted to see you. They lick your face. Why don't you get a Labrador?'

'It's too late now,' said Fred. 'I've made other arrangements.' He was wearing his second new suit of the year, a black and white wool and silk-slub creation from Ralph Lauren (chosen, with loving care and a fine disregard for the bill, by the bride-to-be), a white shirt and grey tie. Trader Ryan had rediscovered the suit he had worn to Monte Carlo and was attracting astonished glances from the Cellar Bar's regulars, who were accustomed to his more rumpled image.

The warmest Christmas for forty years had passed in a glow of family contentment at the vicarage. Fred, accommodated in a spare bedroom out of deference to Mrs Cattermole, had spent much of the time slumped in front of a brightly burning coal fire whose regular use had been discouraged by the vicar's stipend. The vicarage itself seemed liberated from those invisible religious constraints that had ruled the pattern of its austere life. Blowing up balloons and pinning up mistletoe, Fred felt as if he were engaged on a task of constructive vandalism, bringing joy where once there was gloom. As Christmas programmes slid by on the television and food appeared and disappeared, he was delighted to see the relationship between Kate and her mother become closer again, healed by death. Lovingly embraced himself in this cosy family Christmas, he recalled that the previous year Christmas dinner had been beans on toast alone in his flat, his mother having decided to spend the holiday with a friend in Scotland. This year it was turkey, cooked, he was encouraged to see, by Kate. Her mother helped him to drink the alcohol which Kate's condition prevented her from enjoying, and then tootled round the house singing carols with rather more fervour than she would be expected to show in church. Occasionally, when a visitor dropped in, Mrs Cattermole would grimace as if the caller represented a link with the Gothic church across the green that she would gladly see severed. Between the eating and the drinking and the television she insisted that they play cards, surprising Fred by naming poker as her favourite, a game that had been prohibited by her second husband. At some point in the muzzy stretches of time, while Fred was munching his way through a can of macadamia nuts, Mrs Cattermole asked that he call her Ruth, and talked about Kate's father who, forty when Kate was born in 1965, had managed to serve in the war while still in his teens. Long-hidden photographs were produced to Kate's joy and she commandeered the lot to have copies made, enlarged and framed. By the time that two hours of reminiscence had carried them along, the first husband had replaced his successor in the family's consciousness.

Now, on his wedding day, the sun had shone for a week. Perverse clouds that had hidden it from frustrated holiday-makers all summer had disappeared. The sky was a deep blue and rhododendrons, deceived by the odd climate, were blossoming all over the south of England.

At two o'clock a man in a chauffeur's uniform arrived at the hotel and there was a phone call from the reception desk to the bar. They finished their drinks and went out to find a shining grey Bentley in the car park.

'The condemned man drank a hearty orange juice,' said Trader Ryan. 'How do you feel?'

'Extremely strange.'

'We could divert him to Heathrow and leg it to the Côte d'Azur.'

'I'll be there this evening with my wife.'

'Why don't I take her and you stay here?'

'I'm beginning to wish that I'd had a few beers.'

'Get in the tumbril.'

The register office, picturesquely sited amid trees and fields, was in a manor house in the country. Wide steps led down from its main doors to a garden where a battle had been fought and lost against the confetti which lay in heaps at the edge of the flower beds. As they left the Bentley in a car park at the side a photographer hired by Mrs Cattermole appeared from nowhere and asked them to pose together. It seemed to take a long time. He was a busy little man with plenty of complicated equipment, and everything had to be just right before he could bring himself to take a picture – the pose, the angle, the light, the background.

He had taken four when another grey Bentley cruised into the car park. Kate climbed out in a dress of ivory silk, her dark hair up in the pony tail that she had been wearing when Fred first saw her. She was followed by her mother in a green suit, and two girls of around Kate's age who wore pink dresses and carried bouquets.

The photographer seemed to lose interest in Fred and Trader Ryan when he saw the new arrivals, and he scampered across the car park towards them, bent almost double under the weight of his equipment.

The two girls were introduced as Kate's cousins, Melanie and Susan, who had hurried up from Bristol, anxious not to miss this unexpected family occasion.

Fred put his arm round Kate and kissed her.

'You look absolutely ravishing,' he said.

She bowed demurely. 'You look pretty snazzy yourself, sir.'

Mrs Cattermole came over and started to rearrange Kate's dress.

'Good afternoon, Fred,' she said.

'Good afternoon, Ruth. I bet you thought I wouldn't show up.'

'With a bride like this? I never doubted it. Don't forget that we're going for champagne and a bite to eat at the Hotel in the Hills afterwards. There'll be plenty of time to catch your plane.'

'You must come and visit us,' he suggested.

'I may never want to come home.'

A few yards away Trader Ryan, mellowed by the appearance of nubility, had attached himself to either Melanie or Susan, one arm wrapped paternally around her shoulder, as if this was the wrong month for her to be out in so skimpy a dress.

'I'm the managing director of a small industrial company,' Fred could hear him say. 'As a matter of fact, the bridegroom is a colleague of mine on the board.'

Fred smiled and turned to Kate, who slid her arm round his waist. 'Come along, Mr Carton,' she said. 'We ought to be going in. Let me tell you all about the joys of feeding a baby at four o'clock in the morning.'

He looked down at the wind-blown confetti and up at the blue January sky and felt for a moment like a soldier in a bunker who could hear the distant order to advance. He was ready – ready for a prospect that looked as hopeful as any.

'Yes, tell me about that,' he said.

He took her hand and led her up sandstone steps into the future, convinced, like many fathers-to-be before him, that parenthood was something, at long last, that he would be good at.